ECHOES IN THE PINES

ECHOES
IN THE
PINES

Joe P. Snyder

ISBN: 979-8-218-91141-6
Hike Ninjas Press
Pensacola, FL

For my wife and my daughter, Elizabeth & Emma —
my heart, my home, my why.

For my Hike Ninjas, Steve & David —
my brothers who would show up with shovels in hand.
Asking no questions.

1

Five Nights of Quiet

The passenger door of the twenty-year-old F-150 groaned as I slammed it shut, rainwater still dripping from the roof in heavy drops. The old extended cab had been on more adventures across the U.S. than any of us could count, but it was well-maintained and reliable, the official trip truck. Roof racks up top, camper shell on the back—perfect for hauling packs, food, and gear. It had carried us to trailheads from Washington to Maine, Texas to Tennessee, and today it brought us here.

Rain hammered us the whole drive into the mountains with cold September sheets slapping the windshield, hissing under the tires, thunder pounding the ridges, lightning flashing just enough to keep you uneasy. Even now, with the storm easing, the ground seemed half-flooded, puddles gleaming under a stubborn gray sky. My boots sank with every step since leaving the truck. The air was wet, heavy, and smelled of pine and fresh earth.

The truck was parked in a rough gap off the gravel road. Not a proper parking spot. Just enough room to tuck it in and lose it behind a line of brush. Within eyesight was another truck, tailgate plastered with faded park stickers and a mud-caked cooler strapped down by a frayed bungee. No people in sight. Their boots already on the trail. A quiet reminder we weren't the only ones trying to step off the map for a while to trade headlines, deadlines, and glowing screens for something slower, older, quieter. The kind of quiet that doesn't just mute the noise outside but dials down the noise inside too.

The trail has a way of clearing everything else out. Out here, it's just us. No background noise. No half-distractions. No one fading behind a screen. We always show up for each other out here, fully. It's the only place where nothing's competing for our attention.

This is where the bond actually lives. In the miles. In the rain. In the silence between jokes and the grunt of the climb. We don't have to explain anything or keep up appearances. We just are.

These trips are the thread that holds everything together. When the weight of real life starts pulling at us—work, family, distance—this is where we reset. We live trip to trip, counting down to the next stretch of trail where it's just the three of us again—steady, solid, exactly where we're supposed to be.

We spotted it from across the gravel road, a single post stamped with "202," leaning like it had seen better days. No map. No trailhead sign. Just that number and forty miles of backcountry waiting.

Five nights of quiet. God, I needed that.

The trail has a way of stripping things down. Out here, what you carry matters, and names take on a life of their own. Real names fade. Trail names stick.

Steve became Chunk because of his size. At six-one and built like a linebacker, he was impossible to ignore. Short blond-gray hair. Cropped beard. The name started half in jest, but it fit, and now nobody calls him Steve on the trail. He's Chunk, the big man with the presence to match. A former marathoner and triathlete, ex–Air Force Cryptologic Linguist, he had stamina for days and the quiet authority that made him the natural leader and organizer of our trips.

David earned the trail name Zombie on a brutal hike years back. We were both out of shape on that trip, like normal, dragging ourselves up hills we had no business ascending. David's legs dragged as the intense fatigue set in, and Chunk laughed that he looked like the walking dead. Instead of being annoyed, David leaned into it, groaning and making zombie noises between breaths. By the end of the day, we had cemented the name. He's the shortest, but not short by any stretch, compact and stocky, with a frame built for power. He still conveys his Marine vibe through his steady posture, short goatee, and closely cropped blond hair. Zombie doesn't waste words, and when he speaks, you listen. Most of the time, his calm silence does the talking, until the trail gets tough enough that those old zombie groans make a comeback.

And then there's me, Joe. Trail name, U-Haul. Earned from my bad habit of carrying way too much gear. I'm lean and muscular, head shaved, beard long at the chin and laced with more gray than I'd like to admit. Tattoos cover both of my arms, stopping cleanly at the wrists so a long-sleeve shirt can hide them when necessary. My right sleeve tells the story I never stop chasing: a campfire flickering in the foreground, a mountain rising behind it, and a bluish-purple night sky burning with constellations. It's my love for the mountains etched permanently into my skin—a reminder of why I come out here, why I always will.

Over-packing is part of the problem. Too many clothes. An extra camp stool. Enough power banks to juice a small village, 100,000 mAh in total. I'd just upgraded from a 50-liter pack to a 70-liter, which only gave me an excuse to haul more. This trip, it tipped close to sixty pounds. Chunk and Zombie never let me live it down, and I can't blame them. But the banter always ends the same: one day, all this extra weight will save the day.

Trail names might start as jokes, but they grow into something heavier. They become shorthand for who we are, the bond you can't explain to anyone who hasn't put in the miles side by side. That's how it was with us: Steve, David, and Joe. But out here, we were Chunk, Zombie, and U-Haul—the Hike Ninjas.

Like clockwork, before I could even reach for it, Chunk grabbed my pack off the tailgate. His arms dipped under the weight.

"Jesus Christ," he muttered, shaking his head. "Every damn time."

Zombie reached over and hefted it with a grunt of his own.

"Unreal. Doesn't matter if it's one night or a week, it's always the same damn pack weight."

Zombie set it back down with a thud that rattled the tailgate. "Ridiculous."

I shrugged. "U-Haul gonna U-Haul."

They didn't laugh. They didn't need to. This was just part of it. Every trip. Every trail. No surprises.

Zombie shook his head and muttered something about me as he slung his own pack up. That's Zombie. Minimal words. Maximum meaning.

The sky stayed overcast as we stepped off the gravel road and onto the narrow ribbon of trail that cut into the trees. Pine needles dripped on our shoulders, the running of stormwater drowned the runoff hissing through the gullies, and the cicadas' chorus drifted down the ridges.

Civilization disappeared behind us with every step. No cars, no voices, no cell signals. Just the three of us and the steady rhythm of boots and trekking poles on soaked dirt.

Chunk took point, steady and confident. I settled into my usual spot in the middle. Zombie, as always, pulled up the rear, watching our six. It wasn't paranoia; it was habit. Years of being trained never to leave your back unguarded. Out here, it just made sense. I always joked we'd never get ambushed by a bear without warning.

The first stretch of trail wound through a cathedral of longleaf pines, their trunks dark and wet from the storm, the canopy dripping as the sky threatened more rain. The air was thick with the smell of damp soil and decaying needles, that deep, earthy perfume you only get in the woods after a hard late summer rain.

Less than an hour in, Chunk started bitching. Not new. Just the usual switch flipping the minute the trail tilted up.

"Goddamn," he barked over his shoulder. "Every hike it's the same damn thing. I swear to God, I should just hike alone and save myself the cardio hit from waiting on you two."

I adjusted my straps, already slick with sweat. Zombie didn't even answer. I turned around and gave him a look and a grin—the one we always shared when this part of the hike showed up.

Chunk kept going. "You know what's crazy? I slow down. Every. Fucking. Time. And somehow, you two still find a way to move slower."

Zombie's breath came heavy, but the grin slid onto his face. "Any minute now," he said between breaths, "Coach, don't make us run laps or do push-ups."

Zombie and I had started calling him Coach years ago when we were training for our Rim-to-Rim-to-Rim Grand Canyon hike. Any time Chunk slipped into complaint mode, the tone changed. Orders crept in. Standards. Expectations. The same voice he used when he was tired and didn't realize it.

That cracked me up, just like it always did. I laughed, head down, boots sucking at the mud. Chunk didn't say a word. He never did when Zombie pulled that line. He just kept stomping, grumbling under his breath like a pissed-off drill instructor.

We fell in behind him, still laughing, him still bitching. Same dance. Same rhythm. Every hike.

A couple of miles in, the trail narrowed and dipped into a shaded hollow where a swollen trickle cut across the path. The air felt cooler, heavier. The first real climb started on the other side, a steady grade that bit into your calves and made you question every ounce of your pack.

"Hauling all this gear, you'd figure I'd know better by now."

From up front, Chunk didn't even turn.

"You'd think." Zombie's voice floated up from the back, dry as sandpaper. "You'd think a lot of things. And you'd still be wrong."

I grinned despite the burn in my legs. Same banter, same rhythm. It felt good. Comfortable. Never offended.

By early evening, heavy clouds rolled in again,

muting the light and darkening the trees. The heat was gone, replaced by the damp cling of air before another storm. We pressed on, boots steady, straps creaking, the world narrowed to the next bend in the trail.

When the familiar curve of the creek appeared through the trees, we all breathed the same quiet sigh. The clearing looked the same as it had a few years ago, a sweep of smooth stones by the water, tall pines arching overhead, and just enough flat ground for three tents without feeling crowded.

Home, at least for the night.

I didn't know it then, but this was the only stretch of trail where life still made sense.

2

The Fire Between Us

Chunk and Zombie moved fast, like they always did. Packs down, tents up—practiced precision. They staked and squared their shelters in minutes, ensuring each corner was tight and every line was just right.

I wasn't as quick, but I was deliberate. I took my time getting the pitch correct, guy lines angled just so, seams pulled taut. It took longer, sure, but every trip I got faster, closer to matching their speed without giving up the details. By the time I stepped back to look at my tent, the three shelters sat neatly in a row, ready for the night.

With camp set, we fell into the next routine—gathering wood for the fire.

Chunk runs it like a mission. His rule? Dry wood only—nothing green, nothing soft, nothing thicker than your wrist. Normally, that's easy to find. But after a day of storms, the forest felt drowned. Every stick on the ground was waterlogged, more sponge than wood. Kicking through the underbrush only turned up soggy debris that wouldn't burn.

The best chance was in the branches already broken but still hanging in the air, caught on limbs where the rain hadn't fully soaked through. We combed the area for them—lifting our eyes, scanning the undersides of trees, yanking down anything that snapped clean instead of bending limp. It was slow work, frustrating work, but every dry crack was a little victory.

By the time we hauled back what we could, the pile looked small compared to the neat stacks we'd built on other trips. Just enough kindling and a handful of wrist-thick branches—barely a fire's worth. But out here, a small fire was far better than no fire.

Because nights without a fire never felt the same. The hanging out, the talking, the ritual of feeding flames—it was part of the routine, part of what made these trips matter. You could hike miles and climb mountains, but it was around the fire that it all settled in. That was the part I liked most.

We sank into our camp chairs; the fire throwing off just enough heat to dry the edges of damp clothes. I lit a cigar—my favorite one, a boxpresssed GTO Painkiller—and leaned back, letting the smoke curl into the darkness. Sobriety had sharpened these moments. The fire seemed brighter and more peaceful. Bourbon once kept me warm on the trail and most nights back home, but years of sobriety have shown me there's a quieter kind of fire in a good cigar. I didn't miss the bourbon, not anymore. Cigars were enough. No missing hours of my life. No hangovers. No watching everything I loved slide out the door because I couldn't hold it together. I came close to losing everything, closer than I'll ever admit out loud.

Chunk and Zombie each carried Jack Daniel's, portioned carefully to stretch across five nights. Not enough to get drunk on any night, but enough to pour into tin cups, clink them together, and loosen the talk that always followed. It was their ritual as much as mine was the cigar—a measured indulgence that fit the rhythm of the fire.

The fire cracked and threw sparks into the dark. They sipped their shares, and the bond found its way back—the kind that only exists out here. It wasn't just a fire. It was the fire between us, the quiet place where friendship burned steady and sure, stronger than any storm waiting outside the circle.

The talk rolled the way it always did. Jokes, stories, and eventually the dream, winning the lottery. Chunk leaned forward, elbows on his knees, firelight flickering across his face.

"The first thing I'd do is take care of my family. Make sure they're set. No debt, no stress, just freedom. And then my boys," he looked at each of us, "I'd wipe your slates clean. We'd quit tomorrow. Because what's the point of being rich if I can't take my boys anywhere I want?"

I puffed the cigar slowly and let the smoke drift skyward. "You know damn well I'd be out. No notice, nothing."

Chunk laughed deep. "That's the spirit, U-Haul. And Zombie? Maybe you'd finally relax for once."

Zombie gave the faintest grin, voice dry as ever. "Not likely."

The fire popped, sparks floating up into the pines. For a while we just let the silence settle in, the kind that only happens when you've shared enough miles that words aren't always necessary.

After a while, the silence thinned and habit took over. No speeches. No plan. Just the three of us reaching for our stoves and getting on with what came next. We set up for dinner the same way we always did—three Jetboils hissing in the dirt like a chorus of angry kettles. Our meals were already repacked into quart-sized Ziplocs, cutting out the bulk of those oversized freeze-dried pouches we never wanted to carry back out. Once the water hit a rolling boil, we poured it straight into the bags, each one tucked inside an insulated sleeve to keep the heat locked in. Every few minutes, we gave them a stir in the firelight. Steam rolled off our hands as the food thickened, softening just enough to eat without torching our tongues. It wasn't gourmet, but it was hot, fast, and it worked—always did.

Eventually, the ritual started. No one had to say a word. Packs opened, anything with a hint of scent—food bags, trash, even toothpaste—went into the bear bags. Zombie tied the knots with Marine precision while Chunk and I scouted branches tall and sturdy enough to keep critters out.

This was bear country. Not the grizzly kind you see tearing up salmon runs on TV, but black bears—real ones, close enough to make your gut tighten if you've ever stood too near to one. They roamed these woods, big, quiet, and always looking for an easy meal. Human food was easy.

But it wasn't just the bears. The raccoons and rats out here were little bastards, mean as they were clever, and they'd rip through a pack like it owed them money. We'd learned that lesson the hard way once. Nobody left their food out anymore.

"Chunk, can you hang your boots up there?" I asked as we hoisted the first bag. "Might keep the funk from killing me in my sleep."

"Wouldn't help," Chunk said, giving the rope one last tug. "Pretty sure whatever's living in my boots is sentient by now."

"Those socks are gross. Pretty sure that's how the next pandemic starts," I shot back.

Zombie smirked, just barely. "God help whatever smells your shoes tonight."

By the time we were done, the fire was nothing but coals, soft heat breathing in the night. The chairs sat empty, shadows stretched by the embers, and we peeled off to our tents one by one. We always dumped water on the fire before heading off to bed. Chunk and Zombie saw to it.

Chunk was always the first to fall asleep—he could unzip, crawl in, and be out before the zipper closed. Zombie followed not long after, his steady snore rising low and even. And then there was me. I was the type who needed background noise to stay sane. Podcasts, stories, anything but my own thoughts.

About an hour from the trailhead, I'd realized my mistake: I hadn't downloaded enough podcasts before service faded. What would've been nothing back at home turned into a problem as the bars dropped off one by one.

All I had were two episodes: one Ancient Aliens story about recovering the Ark of the Covenant and a Why Files compilation on moon mysteries. Not much variety for five nights, but it would have to do.

By midnight, the symphony was in full swing— Chunk's thunderous snores, Zombie's steady rumble, and my phone whispering conspiracies into the dark. Three men in their forties, dead to the world, cocooned in nylon, while the woods carried on around us.

Despite that, despite the racket, there was comfort in it. That strange, steady rhythm of being out here together.

Tomorrow would bring another long day, another long hike. But for now, it was enough to let the woods hold us, the fire between us still glowing in memory as we drifted, one by one, into sleep.

3

Miles To Burn

I woke to the sound of rain hammering my tent. Not a sprinkle—a full-on downpour, the kind that pounds the nylon so hard you feel it through your sleeping bag. Gray light seeped through the fabric, just enough to remind us morning had arrived whether we wanted it or not.

Chunk, of course, was already up. He was always up first. Somehow, while Zombie and I lie there listening to the rain, he'd rigged a community tarp between two pines. By the time we crawled out, there was at least one dry spot big enough to huddle under and cook.

Breakfast was quiet, just the hiss of the stoves and the steady splash of rain off the tarp's edges. Puddles pooled beneath us, rippling with every drop. Setting up camp in a storm is miserable, but breaking it down knowing there are more nights ahead in the wet is worse.

We lingered as long as we could, stretching out coffee and oatmeal, watching the rain ease from sheets to steady drops to a half-hearted drizzle. As soon as it broke to a trickle, we hauled ass. Tents unzipped, sleeping bags and pads yanked free before they could soak through. You can survive in a damp tent, but a wet sleeping bag is a death sentence when the nights turn cool and raw. I almost paid for that mistake a few years ago. Came closer than I like to remember.

We shook the rainflies hard, trying to guess if the water dripping down was from the trees or the sky. It didn't matter—wet was wet. Not ideal, but better than the monsoon we'd woken to. If the storm hadn't broken, we'd have been stuck making a choice: pack it up in a downpour, or gamble on waiting out weather with no clue how long it might last. Out here, no cell service meant no radar. Just patience, luck, and the sky overhead.

When the site finally looked clean, stripped back to its untouched state, we shouldered our packs. The storm had wrung out the forest, and it smelled sharp and fresh, like pine needles and wet earth. Chunk gave a satisfied nod. We walked the clearing one last time, scanning for anything out of place—a forgotten stake, a scrap of wrapper, even a boot print pressed too deep in the mud. That was part of the ritual too: leave no trace, no sign we'd ever been there. Only when we were sure the spot looked as untouched as when we'd found it did we pull the last straps tight on our packs.

Chunk gave a satisfied nod, drained the last sip from his mug, and grinned.

"Boys, let's go," he said, voice light but sharp. "We've got miles to burn."

We fell into our usual formation and stepped back into the mountain wilderness. The morning air was heavy and damp, washed clean by the storm, carrying the sharp scent of wet timber and turned earth. Droplets clung to every branch and leaf, falling in soft ticks as we passed beneath. The trail glistened dark and slick, winding ahead through mist still rising off the ground like smoke.

As the trail carried us deeper into the mountains, the talk turned easy—just guys being guys. We swapped stupid jokes, the kind only dads would laugh at, and traded old stories about girlfriends and breakups from years ago, the kind you can laugh at now but couldn't then. The laughter cut through the stillness of the woods, carrying just far enough to feel like the trail was listening in.

Then, like someone flipping a switch, the forest went silent. The birds stopped. The bugs stopped. Even the breeze seemed to hold its breath. Zombie slowed, scanning the trees like he'd caught something we hadn't. None of us said anything, and after a moment, the sounds returned—first a distant chirp, then the low hum of the forest waking back up. Chunk didn't notice. Zombie didn't say a word, but his eyes stayed on the ridges a little longer.

Later, we came across an old, cracked water bottle half-buried in the dirt, the plastic bleached white by sun and time. It wasn't unusual to see forgotten trash out here, but it caught my eye anyway—the way it sat untouched in the shade like it had been there forever. Zombie glanced at it, then at me, and gave a small shrug, but his hand hovered near his pack strap, just out of habit.

By mid-morning, the trail climbed, switchbacks carving through dense rhododendrons and thick patches of fern. The air warmed; the sweet dampness was replaced by the clean scent of sun-baked pine. Sweat dampened the straps of our packs, and our breaths fell into sync with our boots. No one said much then, but every so often, I'd catch Zombie's eyes sweeping the tree line, quiet and sharp, like he knew something we didn't. But that was his normal routine.

The miles dragged as we chased the halfway point for the day. Every rise felt like it had to be the last before the flat stretch; every bend had us hoping for the glint of water through the trees. By the time the sound of rushing water finally reached us, we were more than ready.

The stream was perfect—wide, clear, and cold enough to push the humidity back. Cool air spilled off the water, sharp against the heat. Without a word, packs were dropped and camp chairs unfolded. Chunk handled his stove while Zombie filtered water through his Sawyer filter, quietly topping off bottles beside him. The only sounds were the rush of water and the quiet clatter of gear.

Lunch was better than usual—maybe because we'd earned it. We sat in the shade, eating and talking in low tones. Chunk started in on a story about an old Air Force buddy and a god-awful weekend in Biloxi, which had Zombie laughing so hard he nearly choked on his food. For a few minutes, it felt light again, and not just from dropping my pack.

Then Zombie, ever the quiet one, pointed out something across the stream—fresh boot prints in the soft mud of the opposite bank. They were sharp, recent, not softened by time or weather. Nobody said much. Chunk glanced at them, then back to his stove, and went back to stirring his food. Zombie stared a little longer, then turned back to his bottle, filling it in silence.

I leaned back in my chair, pulled my hat low over my face, and let myself drift. The murmur of their voices faded into the background, mixing with the sound of the stream. I didn't mean to fall asleep, but thirty minutes later, a sharp voice snapped me awake.

"Pack it up," Chunk said, his tone cutting through the haze of my nap. "Fill your bottles, take a leak, and let's hit the second half. Six more tough miles before we can call it a day."

I rubbed my eyes, folded up my chair, and started packing up gear alongside Zombie. The clearing was quiet except for the low rush of the stream and the soft zip and snap of bags being cinched shut. Chunk stood and motioned toward the ridge.

"Gonna take a leak," he said, heading up the slope toward a stand of pines just beyond the trail.

Zombie and I kept working, stuffing chairs into packs and making sure every strap was tight, the simple rhythm of the routine settling back in. A couple of minutes passed. Then five. The quiet felt heavier, the woods pressing in with that stillness we'd felt earlier on the trail.

I glanced at Zombie. He was already fixed on the ridge, his expression hardened, pack half-zipped.

"You think we should—" I started, but stopped when I saw movement through the trees.

Chunk came down the slope, moving slow and steady, his face unsettled, caught somewhere between confusion and disbelief. He didn't say a word as he tightened his straps and heaved on his pack, but one look was enough. Whatever he'd seen up there, we knew something wasn't quite right.

4

Blue Tarps

Zombie finally broke the silence. "What is it?" His voice was low, but sharper than usual.

Chunk hesitated, eyes flicking toward the ridge he'd just come from. "I don't even know how to explain it. Thought I was just walking far enough to take a leak in peace. But up there—" He paused, shaking his head. "There's something. A corner of a wall, maybe concrete, maybe stone. Square edges. Too clean to be natural. Didn't want to get too close without you guys."

I felt the weight of his words settle in my gut. Out here, many miles from civilization, there wasn't supposed to be anything man-made. Not like what Chunk described.

"Show us," I said, already dropping my pack beside the stream.

Zombie followed suit, unshouldering his gear and setting it down slow, his eyes never leaving Chunk. He gave the faintest nod. "Lead the way."

Chunk glanced at both of us, then turned back up the ridge. "Alright. But when you see it, you'll understand why I came back down first."

We left our packs behind, boots crunching softly on pine needles as we followed him up the hill, the woods tightening around us with every step. The slope was steady but not brutal, just enough to get your lungs working. About halfway up, through the brush, something caught my eye on the left.

At first, it looked like nothing more than another shadow in the trees. But as we pushed closer, I saw it clearly—a small pump house, half-swallowed by brush and vines. Its paint was peeling in long strips, weather-beaten to gray. A thick electrical line ran from its side, stretching off through the woods in a direction that felt wrong, like it didn't belong here. Nature itself camouflaged the place so well that if you weren't looking, you'd walk right past it.

We followed the line, pushing through branches and undergrowth until the trees opened just enough to show what Chunk had seen. A concrete block structure sat in a shallow dip of the ridge. Perfectly square, maybe fifteen feet by fifteen feet, not large—but definitely out of place. It looked old. The foundation had settled unevenly, cracks splitting through the mortar and running in jagged lines up several of the blocks. Weeds and thick brush choked the perimeter, nature pressing hard against the walls like it wanted to reclaim the whole thing.

It was obvious no one maintained it. No paths. No clearings. Just this stubborn little square of concrete, tucked away where it shouldn't exist.

Then Zombie's voice cut the quiet. "There." He pointed to the ground. At first, I didn't see it, but when I looked closer, it was clear—a narrow path, just wide enough for a couple of people, worn through the undergrowth. It led straight from where we stood to the front door of the building. Not a trail meant for hikers, but the faint track left by footsteps over time.

We followed it slowly. The front of the structure came into view—a metal door, weathered and streaked with rust, a heavy deadbolt lock set deep into the frame. On top of that, a rusted steel hasp had been bolted to the door, holding an industrial-grade padlock, the kind you'd see on storage units. Whatever was inside, someone clearly didn't want it found.

On each side of the door, there were two windows. No curtains, no signs of care. Just moss, grime, and the dirt that built up over decades. No bottle of Windex had ever touched that glass.

Chunk stepped to one window, Zombie to the other, each wiping away just enough of the filth to make a hand-sized hole to see through. I stayed back at first, watching their shoulders stiffen. Even without words, I could tell. We'd been friends for over twenty years, and I knew when something wasn't right. Their body language screamed it.

"What the fuck?" Chunk muttered, his tone low and confused, not loud but heavy with disbelief. Zombie didn't say a word. He just kept staring through the glass, frozen.

My chest tightened. I stepped forward, wiped a circular patch of grime from the nearest window, and leaned in. The dim daylight revealed the inside, and what I saw made my pulse kick hard in my ears.

Four bunk beds, one in each corner of the room, their frames plain and metal. Someone had neatly made each bed, tucking the top sheets perfectly at the corners and placing a thin pillow at the head. And covering half of each bunk was a neatly folded blue tarp, identical in size, all placed with military precision. Four bunks. Four tarps. All the same.

In the middle of the room sat five chairs—four wooden, worn and scarred, and one metal, its paint chipped down to the steel. They didn't seem to be arranged neatly; it was as if someone had left them after standing up in a hurry. The scuff marks on the floor indicated they had been moved often.

The air inside appeared stale, but not dusty, as if someone had sealed the place tightly and only opened it occasionally. Bootprints marked the concrete floor where people had clearly stood. Empty water jugs leaned against one wall, and someone had piled a few flattened ration boxes neatly in another corner. A single bulb dangled from the ceiling on a thin wire, not the heavy line we'd seen feeding out of the pump house, but close enough in style to make the connection clear. It wasn't on, but its presence sent a chill down my spine.

Above the bunks, a length of metal ducting snaked toward the ceiling—rough, homemade, like someone had punched a hole through the roof and rigged a fan to push air out. Around the base of the duct, someone had slathered spray foam into the gaps, the kind that hardened into a lumpy, yellow crust. A quick, dirty seal to keep the fumes from leaking back in. A vent that didn't belong in the middle of nowhere. Whatever happened inside needed to breathe, or it would choke itself, and others out.

Two closed interior doors broke the side wall, their paint flaking, but the handles polished from use. Whatever was behind them saw traffic. More than the rest of the room.

And then there was the smell—faint but sharp, like

bleach or some other cleaning agent. It clung to the air in a way that didn't belong this deep in the woods. Sterile. Controlled.

It was confusing, unsettling, and in a way I couldn't explain, deeply wrong. My heart thudded harder, and the unease that had been whispering at us all morning suddenly had a voice.

Both Chunk and Zombie pulled back from the windows almost at the same time, each blurting out some version of the same thought: "Let's get the fuck outta here." Though their voices were not raised, the urgency was undeniable.

I didn't argue. We turned and moved fast, retracing our steps down the narrow path Zombie had spotted earlier, the pump house now on our right as we pushed downhill. The three of us tried to be quick but quiet, every snapped twig sounding like a gunshot in the silence.

It was obvious we'd stumbled onto something that wasn't abandoned—something still in use, something never meant to be discovered out here in the middle of nowhere.

At the bottom of the slope, the stream came back into view, our packs waiting where we'd left them. Zombie spoke in a clipped and direct tone. "Load up your packs quickly. Let's hit the trail fast and put distance between us and whatever the fuck that was."

I had never seen him like this. Never seen Chunk like this either. Both of them carried themselves with instincts sharpened by years in the service and decades on the trail. If anything spooked them, it was serious. That realization sank into my gut like a stone.

We packed fast, with no wasted motion, shouldered

our loads, and without a word fell back into our formation. Boots hit dirt, and we booked it down the trail, our pace quicker than usual, every sound behind us making my head turn.

The forest swallowed us again, but the silence clung to me, heavy and wrong. We pushed harder. The deeper we went, the stronger the feeling grew—that building wasn't finished with us yet.

And no matter how fast we hiked, I couldn't shake the thought that someone, or something, was already on our tail.

5

Decision For Them

We hustled down the trail, boots hammering dirt, packs shifting with every stride. None of us said a word at first. We didn't deviate from the mapped course— just stuck to the trail we'd planned, eyes forward, like leaving it would somehow make us more vulnerable. The only goal was distance. Distance between us and that building.

After a couple of miles, the silence cracked, not with laughter but with the banter that felt forced. Zombie tossed out a dry one-liner about how Chunk should've just pissed closer to where we were, and Chunk shot back that maybe he'd start peeing on Zombie's pack. Usually, we would have joined in and kept going until someone was laughing uncontrollably. This time it faded quickly, leaving a weight behind.

I tried to play along, throwing in a weak joke about how I'd probably stumble on the next "secret government outhouse," but even as the words left my mouth I could hear the edge in my voice. None of us were really into it.

The trail didn't make things easier. Days of heavy rain had turned every dip into a mud trap. Shallow streams cut across the path, brown with runoff, and we danced around them at first, trying to keep our boots dry. But it didn't take long to realize it was pointless. Every rock was slick, every edge soft. One slip and the water seeped in anyway. Eventually, we stopped trying. As Chunk liked to say, "Embrace the suck."

We only paused to hydrate, check our watches, and confirm we were still on course. No long breaks. No wasted minutes. Chunk's pace was quicker than the day before, and it showed. Zombie and I traded looks, both of us smirking at the same thought—we really needed to train more before these trips. Following Chunk was like following a man with Sasquatch-sized lungs and a heart to match. He ate up the miles while we tried to keep up.

When we reached a weathered wooden post with 202 burned into the sign, relief washed through me. Trail markers usually meant we were getting close to dispersed campsites, maybe one with a firepit. I was ready to call it a day. More than ready. Still, the further we got from that concrete building, the better I felt. Distance was its own kind of comfort.

Another half mile carried us into a sharp right bend, our watches flashing that we'd be crossing a large water source soon. Not a stream, not a tiny trickle. More like a wide creek—something big enough to notice but nothing to fear. At least, that's what we thought.

When we broke through the trees and reached the bank, all three of us stopped cold.

It wasn't a creek at all. It was a river—swollen from the storms, churning hard and fast. The normal bridge was gone, swallowed beneath a rolling, mud-brown surge that moved like it had a grudge. It ran deep too, far past wading depth, the kind of water that could sweep a grown man off his feet before he even had time to swear. The fall air hung in the low 60s, the river colder still—probably in the high 40s, maybe low 50s. That kind of cold didn't just bite—it stole the breath right out of you.

Chunk and I both used to be avid whitewater kayakers. We knew this kind of river, knew exactly what it could do. Most deaths in whitewater don't come from big drops or wild rapids—they come from foot entrapment. One wrong step in fast water, your foot wedges between rocks, and the current does the rest. With heavy packs and the flow ripping the way it was, that risk wasn't abstract, it was waiting. And in water that cold, you don't get second chances. Hypothermia would hit fast, sapping strength in minutes. Surviving a swim in that current wasn't likely. Not for long.

Chunk and Zombie went straight into problem solving mode, eyes scanning the riverbanks, voices low but steady as they weighed options. Chunk pointed upstream, the bank narrowed there. Zombie countered, shaking his head, pointing at the way the current funneled harder to the right and how slick the rocks would be.

The silence that followed said the rest.

Chunk gave a small, humorless laugh. "Yeah... one of us goes in, the other gets to explain it to their wife. Not exactly a fun conversation."

Zombie's face went hard. "Yeah. 'Hey, sorry your husband died doing something stupid in the woods.'"

Neither of them said anything else. The river had made the decision for us.

6

River Roared Louder

I never brought much to the table when it came to navigation or trail strategy. Never have. I was the guy who showed up with too much gear and enough "just in case" supplies to outfit a scout troop—then fell in line behind Chunk like his compass was carved on stone tablets.

At my age, I've stopped pretending otherwise. My sense of direction is trash. Not just out here in the woods, either. I've lived in the same city for over twenty-five years and still use my truck's GPS to get to places I've been a hundred times. That's just how it is. I follow. I carry. I trust the guy who doesn't get lost.

So once the call was made, there wasn't much left to discuss. We adjusted straps, shifted weight, and turned our backs on the river. It roared behind us, a reminder of where the line had been drawn. The air felt cooler in the shade of the trees, the kind of damp that clings to you, and the trail ahead sloped gently upward, just enough to make every step a little heavier.

Chunk and Zombie moved in that quiet, practiced way they had—scanning for landmarks, rerouting in their heads without needing to say much. I just kept pace, boots crunching against the packed earth, watching their backs and the trail they carved.

That's the thing about trips like this: the trail doesn't care if your plan gets washed out. It keeps going. So do you.

Still, we pushed forward, scanning the woods for anything that might work. Every dip was too wet, every ridge too sloped, every clearing too small. The sun had started its slow dive, and the shadows stretched long across the trail. My shoulders ached with the weight of the pack, my legs burned with each climb, and the only thought circling my head was the same as theirs: we need to find camp soon.

We'd put about a mile between us and the first crossing when a huge "Fuck!" echoed back through the trees. Chunk was a good hundred feet ahead—his trail lungs putting him on a whole other level. By the time Zombie and I caught up, we already knew it wasn't good.

When we broke through the brush and saw what he was staring at, the reason for his outburst was obvious. Another crossing. Same swollen water, same angry current, only this time it was wider, nearly cresting its banks.

The shitty part? The trail ended right there. No switchback, no side route, no way around. It was cross or turn back.

And just to twist the knife, on the far side of the water sat what had to be one of the best campsites in the mountains. Elevated high enough off the banks that the river could crest and we would be in no danger. The ground was flat, space for many tents, and a perfect fire ring already waiting. I could almost see the glow of an imaginary fire, smell the smoke, hear the crackle. It was the kind of site you dream about on a long hike.

The three of us stood on the bank, staring at the perfect campsite we couldn't reach. Taunting us from the far side of the flood.

The longer I looked at it, the worse the feeling grew. It wasn't just frustration anymore. It felt like the woods were pushing back, keeping us penned in, herding us away from where we wanted to be.

Behind us, the trail we'd come down had already faded into shadow, the canopy pressing low and heavy. The river roared louder than it should have, like it wanted to drown out any thought of crossing. Every option looked worse than the last—backtrack, bushwhack, or risk being swallowed by the current.

For the first time all day, it hit me in my gut: this wasn't just bad luck. The forest wasn't going to let us have what we wanted. And standing there in the fading light, I couldn't shake the feeling it didn't want us to leave at all.

7

The Hiker

Backtracking is always a gut punch, but the river wasn't giving us a choice. We turned around, boots dragging in the mud. Nobody said much. The mood was heavy, the silence where even breathing felt too loud. Every step away from that perfect campsite on the far bank felt like defeat.

The trail wound narrow and slick, the runoff from the storms turning every low spot into an ankle high puddle. My calves burned, my pack tugged at my shoulders, and I caught myself counting steps just to push forward. We'd gone maybe half a mile when Chunk, still out front, slowed down. His hand went up—a subtle stop sign.

And then he appeared.

A thin man came up the trail toward us. At first glance, maybe just another hiker. But then the details landed one by one. All black clothing. A small daypack—way too small for backcountry nights. A radio clipped to his hip. Black military style boots that looked spotless, almost shiny. That's when I noticed the pistol on his chest. A .45. Full-sized. Heavy. That's not a trail gun. That's a gun you carry when you're expecting trouble.

We all carried, but not like that. Chunk had a .380 tucked into his hip belt. Zombie's Keltec 9mm was small, clean, practical. Mine—a single stack S&W .40. It usually gave me peace of mind out here. Not now.

And most unsettling of all, a black face covering pulled up ninja style, with only his eyes showing.

He looked like a Hike Ninja, just not one of us.

We stopped. So did he.

The sound of the river filled the silence between us, steady and low, like it was waiting to see what came next.

Chunk raised a hand and motioned for him to pull the mask down. The guy didn't move at first. Just stared. Then, with a sharp tug, he lowered the fabric to his chin like it cost him something. His fingers lingered near it, ready to pull it back up at a moment's notice.

"River too deep to cross?" he asked, voice flat.

Chunk kept his tone even. "Yeah. Bridge is under. Banks are cresting downstream. We looked for another way, nothing."

The man nodded slowly, his eyes flicking over us like he was taking inventory. "How far down'd you check?"

"Half a mile or so," Chunk said.

"You camped out here long?" he asked.

Zombie shifted. "Not long."

The guy tilted his head. "Got anyone else out here with you? Back up the trail?"

"No," Chunk said, flat.

He let that hang for a beat. Then: "How many nights you planning to stay out?"

"Couple more," Chunk answered. "We already did one last night."

That was it. Just enough to sound normal. Nothing more.

His gaze moved between us again—slow, deliberate. It didn't feel like small talk. It felt like he was counting something in his head.

"I'm gonna forge ahead," he said finally. "Might try fording it."

The words landed heavy against the river's roar. The way he was dressed didn't match what he was saying. No dry bags. No waterproof gear. No rope. Not even trekking poles. Nothing. That river wasn't just a bad idea—it was suicide. Which meant this wasn't really about the river.

The hiker gave a faint nod, then stepped past us. He moved quiet and smooth, like someone who'd done this before, not bothering to look back.

We watched him until the trees swallowed him and the river drowned out the sound of his boots. None of us said a word, but the air between us felt different now.

Thicker. Charged.

The woods weren't empty anymore.

Once we were certain he was out of earshot, Chunk let out a sharp breath.

"That was fuckin' weird," he muttered. "Way out of place."

Zombie's eyes stayed locked on the trail behind us. "Boots. Did you see his boots? Shiny. Clean. Military style. You don't hike in boots like that. Not on this trail. Not in this mud."

I nodded, uneasy. "And that little pack? What's he carrying, a sandwich and a poncho?"

Chunk's expression sharpened. "Radio on his hip.

Out here? In these ridges? You don't bring a radio unless you're talking to somebody. If he was hiking alone, why would he need a radio?"

Zombie finally glanced at me, then at Chunk. "And the way he asked if we had more people…" His voice dropped lower. "That wasn't curiosity. That was a head count."

Chunk's mouth flattened into a line. "Yeah. He wasn't just making conversation."

We walked on, but the weight of it clung to me. My boots were caked with brown, my shirt plastered with sweat, my gear dulled by miles. He hadn't looked like us. Not even close.

Zombie broke the silence again, voice flat and certain. "That guy wasn't here to hike."

I was about to give my two cents when it came—a sharp burst of radio static, quick and ugly, tearing through the quiet like someone had keyed a mic and let it squawk before cutting off.

We all froze.

The noise didn't come from the direction he'd gone—not from the river. It came from in front of us. From the trees we'd walked through to get to the river before turning around.

For a few long seconds, the forest held its breath, and so did we. No birds, no bugs, not even the sound of wind. Just the echo of that static buzzing in my head.

Chunk's whole body shifted—not panicked, not sloppy, but precise. He dropped his hand to the strap where his .380 rode, his eyes scanning the ridgeline above us. Zombie slowed his pace, his breathing controlled, shoulders loose, eyes flicking tree to tree like he was back on patrol. No words. No wasted motion. Just instinct.

And me? My mouth went dry. My pulse thudded in my ears. I felt the weight of my .40 in my pack, but it didn't comfort me the way it usually did. If they were acting like this, if they thought this was serious enough to go back into that old training mode, then it was bad. Worse than I wanted to admit.

We stood there a moment longer, three men listening to nothing, waiting for another crackle that never came.

Then, without a word, Chunk started walking again. I followed, with Zombie following behind me, but every step felt heavier, the weight of the forest pressing in from all sides.

The static had lasted less than two seconds. But it was enough to change everything.

He'd counted us.

And somewhere out there, at least one more was watching.

8

Second Skin

We stopped only because we had to. The sun was bleeding out behind the ridges, and we were still a good fifteen miles from the truck. No way we were going to push many more miles into the dark, not on this mud-soaked trail.

A few miles back we'd passed three perfect clearings with fire rings, flat pads, and good tree cover. Normally, that's where we'd have dropped our packs and called it a night. But not tonight.

Chunk and Zombie didn't want us anywhere near the beaten path. They pushed us a hundred yards off the trail into a patch of uneven ground crowded with brush and low limbs. Less comfortable, sure. Harder to pitch a tent on, yeah. But it gave us what we wanted most: seclusion. Sacrifice comfort to stay unseen.

Still, I tried to make it make sense. A lone hiker on a trail like this wasn't strange. To a novice, hearing a radio out here might not raise an eyebrow. But to anyone who's spent time this far off-grid, it doesn't make sense. I told myself there were explanations— hunters, rangers, weather chatter, whatever. But the more I turned it over, the less it fit.

I couldn't square why he had a radio. And I couldn't

explain why we'd heard another one squawk back.

I kept trying to convince myself it was normal.

I couldn't.

That thought lingered as we set up. We moved differently this time—quicker, tighter, sharper. Every motion had an intention. Normally I'd sprawl my gear out like a yard sale—socks on branches, food bags dropped until later, chair unfolded before tents. But not tonight. Tonight it was all close and controlled, packs stacked, gear sorted just enough to be useful, everything ready to throw back together if we had to bug out fast.

Chunk and Zombie never stopped moving, but somehow they never stopped scanning either. Their heads tracked the ridgelines, their eyes cut through the trees, their ears tuned to sounds I couldn't even pick up. Despite that, with all that vigilance, their tents went up with military precision—stakes driven, guylines taut, rainflies snapped into place like they were on a timer. I did not know how they did it. It was like they had an extra set of eyes and ears, one for the camp and one for the woods.

I felt more locked in than ever. The normal rhythm, that simple comfort of setting up camp with my Hike Ninjas, was gone. No laughter, no lazy chatter, no shared bitching about sore legs or wet boots. Just silence and motion.

And I hated it. I was pissed, honestly. The best part of our trips had always been the fire at night—sitting around the flames, bullshitting with my best friends, recharging our batteries after miles of grind. That's what made the pain worth it. But not tonight. Tonight, the fire stayed cold, and so did we.

Dinner was quick, forgettable—boil water, dump in the pouch, wait, shovel it down. Nobody lingered over it. The hiss of the stoves was the loudest sound in camp, and even that seemed too sharp, like it carried farther than it should. We kept our voices low, not by decision, just instinct.

For a while, nobody said much. Just the scrape of spoons and the rustle of gear. Normally, this was when the jokes started, when Chunk would rip into me about carrying too much, or Zombie would deadpan some one-liner that had us wheezing. Not tonight.

They only sipped their whiskey that night. No clinking cups, no half-drunk jokes. Just slow pulls from the plastic bags with screw tops they carried it in. Chunk sat with the bag pressed to his knee, drinking it straight, his eyes fixed somewhere beyond us.

I still lit a stogie. Part habit, part nerves. The truth was, I needed it—the familiar ritual, the steady burn, the way it kept my hands busy. Normally I'd end up relighting a few times over a long smoke, either puffing too fast or letting it go out. But not tonight. Tonight, I was completely focused, and the cigar burned evenly and perfectly with every draw.

I kept the cherry low, cupped between my knees, hiding the ember so it wouldn't glow too bright. A fire might've comforted us, but a cigar could give us away all the same. Out here, every little thing felt like it mattered.

We sat in a circle like we always did, only without the fire. Just three men in chairs facing each other, though our eyes were mostly on the dark. It was impossible not to bring up the hiker.

"Too clean," Zombie said. "Boots shiny. Didn't even look winded."

Chunk took another sip, nodded. "And that pack? Kid wasn't carrying enough to stay out here half a night. But he's got a gun and a radio?"

I tapped ash into the dirt, keeping my voice low. "He felt…wrong. Out of place. Like he wasn't just passing through. Like he was trying to figure us out."

Chunk's brow tightened. "Yeah. The way he asked about how many of us there were? How long we've been out here?"

Zombie leaned forward, elbows on his knees. "That was him building a picture of us. Inventory."

The night around us felt heavier then, like the trees were listening.

We tried to throw out other explanations, tried to make it sound less sinister. Park ranger undercover. Off-grid loner. Some idiot who thought a mountain hike was cosplay. But none of it landed. The unease stayed, hanging between us with the smoke.

Then the theories started.

Chunk leaned forward, voice low. "It's got all the signs of a serious setup. Pump house for water. Power line for lights. Bunkhouse for bodies. Radios for coordination. You don't build something like that out here unless you want to keep it quiet. Remote ridge like this? Perfect place to run something off the radar without drawing heat."

Zombie shook his head. "That's the thing—it wasn't just quiet, it was squared away. Too squared away. Everything lined up. No trash. No slop. That wasn't some off-grid group trying to stay hidden. That was structured. Disciplined. Militia, maybe paramilitary.

These mountains are full of them if you know where to look. A place like that isn't a hideout. It's a base."

I leaned back and tried to blow a few smoke rings, something I usually had down to an art. But the wind shredded them before they could take shape, leaving nothing but twisted curls drifting wherever the night carried them. "You know," I said, "I don't think either of you's wrong. You're just saying the same thing in different ways. Whether it's some off the grid setup or something more structured, it's organized. Purpose-built. Someone put time and planning into it."

I watched the ember glow at the end of my cigar. "Doesn't really matter what name you give it—militia, off book project. The point's the same. Someone's out here, and they're serious about staying hidden."

Looking up to watch the smoke I noticed the sky had cleared, though only a few stars managed to slip through the dense canopy overhead. The branches formed a lid that sealed us in, blotting out the night. That made it worse somehow. Knowing the stars were shining above us, just out of reach, made the darkness feel heavier—like we were cut off from the rest of the world, staring into the black, wondering if something out there was staring back.

Adding to the tension was every little noise from the woods—a snap of a branch, a rustle in the leaves— cut the conversation short. Zombie or Chunk would raise a hand, signaling silence, scanning into the black. Usually, that kind of alertness only followed a really loud crack in the distance, or a very close owl call, as if it were perched in camp. Tonight, it was every sound, no matter how small.

Then came something different. A whistle—sharp,

clipped, three short bursts—then silence. Too clean to be the wind, too deliberate to be chance. We froze, ears straining for another note, but none came.

The night pressed in on all sides, a wall of black that swallowed distance. We couldn't see far, couldn't tell what was watching from the dark, only that something might be. With the canopy cutting us off from the stars, it felt like the world had shrunk to the circle of our camp, small and exposed.

That's when the plan came together. Not a military shift rotation, but something close.

"No conspiracy podcasts for you tonight," Chunk said, looking at me. His voice wasn't harsh, just firm. "Ears open. All night."

Zombie nodded. "Any noise, we're up. No questions."

The routines came next. Toothbrushes flicked clean, food tied up in the throw bags and hung high, knots tight. But it wasn't about bears or mice this time. It was about discipline. About being ready.

Chunk pulled a waterproof bag from his kit. "Essentials only," he said. "If we've gotta move, this is what we grab." One by one we copied him—pistols, wallets, fire starters, protein bars, snacks, headlamps, phones—packed tight into small bags we could snatch on the run. He said it was worth the risk to have some food by our tents just in case.

Normally, the boots would've lined the tent flaps, angled for a quick grab-and-go. But this time, Chunk and Zombie both said the same thing—boots stayed on. No one liked the thought of tracking mud inside, but the idea of fumbling for them in the dark was worse. If something went sideways, we'd need to move fast.

No jokes. No ribbing. Just quiet men preparing for something we couldn't quite name.

When I finally slid into my tent, waterproof bag tucked by my side, bottle lined up, pistol close, the silence hit harder than it ever had. Normally the fire faded into coals, and we faded into laughter. Tonight, the dark pressed down like a second skin.

And for the first time on a trip, I wasn't sure if I wanted to sleep at all.

9

Not Alone Out Here

The woods had gone dead quiet. Not the gentle calm of a forest night, but a silence so thick it pressed on our ears. It felt wrong—manufactured, like someone had flipped a switch and shut the woods off. No bugs. No owls. Not even the faintest stir of leaves.

Inside the tent, the quiet was unbearable. Every breath I took sounded too loud, every shift of fabric like a gunshot. My own breathing echoed so hard it made me think I heard footsteps and whispers that weren't there.

Zombie and I had been down this road before—long talks about conspiracies, alternate history, things hidden in plain sight. But tonight, none of it felt like idle talk. It felt like the woods were proving us right.

Then it started.

First came a faint metallic echo—a sharp clang like steel on steel, deep in the trees. It rang once, then died. Not natural. Not even close.

"Tell me you heard that," Zombie muttered from his tent.

Chunk didn't hesitate. "Get up, grab your pistols."

We moved fast, pistols in hand, safeties off. I clicked the light on my .40 with my right pointer finger—the beam cutting through the dark like a blade. Chunk and Zombie already had theirs out, moving like guys who'd done this a hundred times before.

That was the thing with them—they weren't casual owners. They were gun guys to the core, with collections that spanned every caliber imaginable. Around the campfire, in the truck, even in our text thread, they'd slip into these long back-and-forths about ammo weights, barrel lengths, optics, and which platform outperformed the other. To me, it always sounded like another language—one I'd heard a hundred times but never bothered to learn. But they lived for it. Constantly tinkering and testing. I never caught every word, but I caught enough to know one thing: if something went down out here, they'd know exactly what to do.

That's when the hum came—a low vibration, faint but steady, more felt than heard. It buzzed in my chest and teeth, then vanished the second I focused on it.

Zombie broke the silence. "What the fuck?"

Before Chunk could respond, a flash of white light pulsed across the ridge. Quick. Gone. Not lightning, not fire. Just one blinding pop.

We froze, pistol beams crisscrossing in frantic sweeps. The forest stayed still. Following Chunk's lead, Zombie and I cut our lights off as soon as we could reach the buttons.

Minutes passed before the thud came. Heavy. Final. Like something massive had dropped onto the earth. No follow-up. No movement.

Zombie whispered, "Dogman. Or Bigfoot. Heavy steps. Purposeful."

I shook my head. "Underground testing. Black-budget. This is exactly how people describe it."

Chunk finally cut us both off. "You two sound like idiots."

We didn't have our headlamps on. Far off through the trees, thin beams of light swept across the dark. Not close, but close enough to tell they weren't just wandering—they were looking for something. Or someone.

Then Chunk broke it. "This is stupid. Spread out like this? We might as well hang a sign that says pick us off one at a time."

Zombie grunted, already yanking at his tent stakes. "Should've thought of that earlier."

They were both pissed they hadn't. After they spoke about the idea, it was obvious, and it no longer seemed like paranoia but necessity. Headlamps on and set to red, we worked fast, dragging and pivoting nylon, and hammered stakes into the ground until we could reshape our camp into as perfect a triangle as the terrain allowed. All three tents sat tight, each door facing outward, giving us as much of a 360 view as possible. A little fortress of thin fabric—laughable against whatever was really out there, but better than the way we'd had it before.

We crawled back inside reluctantly, not because we were afraid of being tired for tomorrow's hike, but because the bigger concern was making it to that hike at all.

Just before I ducked fully in, Zombie muttered: "We're not alone out here."

No one argued. And in that moment, with the headlamps flicking off one by one, it was impossible not to feel it—something was out there, watching, patient, waiting.

10

Sending a Message—Deke

Deke crouched by the pines, the stolen bags stacked neatly beside him. He spat tobacco into the dirt and grinned.

They hadn't stirred. Three grown men, tough enough to haul packs through storm mud, snored like babies while he cut them clean out of their food. He didn't even need to hurry. Years of training had made his hands quiet as shadows.

Normally, he wouldn't bother with hikers. Let them sweat through their vacation miles, take a few pictures, limp back to their trucks, and brag about surviving the wilderness. They never knew how close they came to death already. But these three weren't normal. They'd wandered too far, found something they shouldn't have—the original bunkhouse on the ridge. That place wasn't meant for outsiders.

The ridge wasn't just turf to him—it was the only place that had ever felt like it belonged to him. After Afghanistan, when the VA visits dried up and every town felt too loud, too bright, too judgmental, these woods were the only thing that didn't look at him like he was broken. He'd slept under its pines before he'd ever slept in a real bed again. The ridge had kept him alive when nothing else did.

Territorial control wasn't about money—money just kept the lights running. This was about order. Silence. Claiming one piece of the world where no one told him what he was allowed to be. Outsiders threatened that balance, threatened to drag the ridge into someone else's hands, someone else's rules. And Deke would burn the whole mountain down before he let that happen.

This ridge had been the first place that asked nothing of him but silence. No orders. No explosions. No brothers bleeding out in his hands. Just trees. Just wind.

He'd carved a life out of this place long before the money came—a life nobody was going to take from him again. So when outsiders stumbled in like they owned the ground, it wasn't business. It was personal. The ridge was his because he'd earned it.

Who were these three, really? Weekend warriors with more grit than sense? Or something else? They moved like they knew what they were doing. Military shoulders. Steady steps. Body language never lied. How the hell had they sniffed out the bunkhouse when half the county walked these woods without anyone ever seeing it?

Deke spat again, wiped his mouth, and checked the pistol snug in his waist holster. The weight was comfort—like a seatbelt. He shifted the radio on his hip until the static hiss smoothed into silence. His boys on the far ridge were already watching, keeping track of where the strangers moved. Nobody came through here without being seen. Not anymore.

This wasn't about the hiker not eating—this was about sending a message. Outsiders didn't get to walk through his ridge like it was a public trail. Not without permission. Not without payment.

And the message was simple: turn around. The only way out was back the way they'd come. Too close to other hikers to make things any dirtier, too messy to solve in the middle of the woods. Not yet. They'd better get the hint before he had to push harder.

He leaned back against a pine, letting the needles press into his jacket, and let himself drift for a moment. He thought about the first time he'd set foot on this ridge after Afghanistan—lost, broke, nothing to his name but a rucksack, a rifle, and a bad habit of looking over his shoulder. The woods had been empty then—truly empty. Just trees, rocks, and silence. But silence lied. These hills carried echoes, and if you knew how to listen, the echoes told you everything.

Deke tapped a finger against the stolen bags, feeling the weight of the hikers' food inside. A simple thing, but powerful. The strangers would wake hungry, rattled, knowing someone had walked straight into their camp without them ever knowing. That was the lesson. Not to kill them, not yet. Just to remind them the woods weren't theirs.

He pushed himself to his feet, slung the bags over one shoulder, and gave a low whistle—faint, clipped, three notes carried through the trees. A moment later, the radio on his hip crackled—a reply from the far ridge. Eyes were on the hikers. They weren't going anywhere he didn't want them to.

If they were smart, they'd turn around.

If they weren't—well, the forest had ways of swallowing men whole.

11

Eviction by Starvation

"What the fuck! Get up now!"

Chunk's voice ripped through the morning, panic and anger fused into one. I lurched upright, half tangled in my bag, heart hammering like I'd already missed something important. The inside of the tent was a mess—mud smeared across the floor and the walls, boots kicked crooked from where I'd slept in them.

We'd all agreed to keep them on in case we had to bail fast, but that didn't make waking up in a swampy nylon box any less miserable. Everything felt damp, gritty, and wrong.

Zombie was cursing under his breath, fighting with his zipper, mud streaked up the side of his bag like a bad joke.

Chunk stood at the edge of camp, pointing to the trees where we'd hung the food. "They're gone! All of it! Food bags, ropes—like they were never there."

I blinked into the early light, my brain scrambling for explanations that didn't exist. The ropes we'd tied off the night before were gone. Not cut, not shredded, not chewed through. Gone. No bags on the ground. No scraps. No drag marks. Just empty branches swaying gently in the morning breeze.

In an instant, we all knew. This wasn't an animal. There was no debate, no half-hearted guesses about bears or raccoons. We didn't even consider it.

This was people.

And the message was clear: you don't belong here.

The realization hit like a stone in the gut.

Whoever had been out there in the silence with us hadn't just taken food. They'd erased it—clean, deliberate, and without waking a single one of us. And by doing that, they hadn't just left us hungry. They'd given us a deadline. No food meant no staying. No lingering. If we wanted to keep moving, we'd have to leave.

It was eviction by starvation we had been served. A push out of the woods. A warning we couldn't ignore.

Chunk balled his fists so tight his knuckles whitened. Zombie stood rigid, eyes darting into the treeline as if the thieves were still watching us. I just stared at the space where our supplies had hung, stomach sinking lower with every second.

Whoever it was, they wanted us gone. And they'd made sure it would happen fast.

12

Into the Trees

Morning hit harder than the night. No food, no coffee means no jolt of caffeine to clear the fog. Just the hollow weight in our stomachs and the echo of Chunk's voice still hanging in the air: "they're gone."

We didn't pack the way we usually do. Normally, Chunk had us squared away like clockwork—gear rolled tight, food balanced, tents broken down in a rhythm we'd built over dozens of trips. This morning, none of that mattered.

It wasn't haphazard, but it wasn't methodical either. It was urgent. Focused. Every move was about one thing: getting out of that site. Tents collapsed and stuffed down fast, bags shoved in without thought for order, stakes and lines bundled instead of coiled. The neat little camp we'd built last night was gone in minutes, erased like it had never been there—just like our food.

As the three of us tightened straps and shouldered packs, Chunk cursed under his breath. "Son of a bitch... we've only got one bottle each."

Zombie stopped too, realization hitting him like a punch. Both of them had stashed their filters in their bear bags—now gone along with the food. For a second, nobody moved.

No food was bad. No food meant weakness, hunger, maybe a miserable hike out. But no water? That meant death. Or a slow crawl toward it, getting desperate and drinking straight from a creek, gambling on parasites that would cripple us with sickness and dehydrate us faster.

Then I pulled out my pack. "Got mine."

Chunk turned, saw the filter clipped inside, and for once he didn't have a comeback. Zombie just shook his head.

They didn't argue. They didn't need to say it out loud—we all knew. Food we could live without for a while. Water was different.

Chunk wanted to keep pushing toward the trailhead, fast and direct. Zombie argued for veering off, taking a slower line that was less predictable. We stood there in the early light, packs on, mud still clinging to our boots, going back and forth in low voices. No one liked either option. One felt reckless. The other felt like a trap waiting to happen.

In the end, we chose the slower route—off the main line, through the trees. Less predictable, maybe harder to follow. It wouldn't be easy, but it felt like the only move that didn't play straight into someone else's plan.

Then we moved straight into the trees.

Our boots pressed against damp pine needles as we moved out, our packs lighter than normal but heavier with the knowledge of what had been taken. The forest was alive again—birds chirping, insects buzzing, shafts of light cutting through the canopy—but it all felt staged. Too perfect. Too loud after last night's silence.

By midmorning, sweat was dripping into my eyes, my shoulders already sore from the uneven pack job. Hunger soon followed, and it whispered reminders of the deadline that someone had given us.

Chunk moved a half-step ahead, fast and tense, his whole frame coiled like it wanted to run. Zombie lagged behind, slower than usual, stopping every few minutes to check the trees. The staggered pace rubbed them both raw.

"Pick it up," Chunk snapped over his shoulder.

"I am picking it up," Zombie fired back. "Maybe if you'd slow down half a step, we wouldn't look like idiots stumbling into a trap."

Chunk stopped dead, spun on him. "Trap? We are not even on a trail. You walk. That's it. The faster we're out, the better."

Zombie laughed, dry and bitter. "Yeah, keep thinking like that. You're doing exactly what they want. Predictable. Straight line into nowhere."

Their voices carried sharply through the trees, every word bouncing around like an invitation. My gut twisted. "Enough," I hissed. "Keep it down. We're already loud enough."

The silence afterward felt heavier, but the damage was done. The forest swallowed our words, and for the first time it felt like it might hand them back to someone else.

Not long after, Chunk's hand shot up, signaling stop.

We all froze.

There, on the trunk of a pine was a streak of paint—faded but deliberate, a rough slash of red too straight to be natural. It was not your normal trail blaze, not a trail blaze at all. Below it, a small stack of stones sat balanced just off the trail, five high, each one flat and perfect.

Chunk's voice was low, steady, like he was holding back rage. "Territorial markers. No question."
Zombie shook his head slowly. "Or military. I've read about this—coded waypoints, trails marked for drones or ground teams. Same look. Same style."

I said nothing. My throat felt dry, tighter than it should. Because either way, the truth was the same: this wasn't just wilderness anymore. This was a perimeter.

We weren't lost hikers. We were trespassers.

13

Running Out of Options

The markers changed everything. Once we passed them, every step felt like trespassing.

We each had one liter of water and no idea how far it would carry us. My tongue stuck to the roof of my mouth, and the fog in my head only thickened without caffeine. I kept catching sounds in the trees—a footstep? A whisper? Or just my brain firing blanks from lack of calories?

We weren't on our charted trail anymore. No true blazes on the trees, no markers to reassure us we were still inside the lines. The detour we'd taken the night before, camping off-trail, had bled into something longer. Now we were somewhere else entirely. The woods felt bigger because of it. Wilder. Owned.

Chunk and Zombie both had watches linked to their phones. More than once, we stopped so they could pull them up, squinting at the topo maps. The blue GPS dot kept pulsing steadily with every step, showing exactly where we were. We weren't lost. That was almost the worst part.

The more we progressed, the more that dot pulled us away from the truck. Not because we wanted to, but because the terrain forced it. Between us and the trailhead sat a maze of ridgelines, flooded rivers, and ravines too steep to scramble without burning half a day or risking serious injury. The truck was less than ten miles away as the crow flies, but we don't have wings.

Backtracking wasn't much better. Going back meant retracing into whoever had taken our food. If they wanted us gone, the last thing they'd allow was us slipping out the way we came.

Calories and water dictated everything now. Bushwhacking cross country would chew through both. Backtracking uphill would drain us faster. The path we were on wasn't the right one, but it was the only one we could still walk.

By late morning, the heat closed in, and our bottles were already half gone. When the trail cut down into a shaded hollow, we heard it before we saw it—running water, faint but real. Not a creek worth naming, just a finger of cold stream trickling over rocks. Moving water, not stagnant. Safe enough.

We stopped in the shade and crouched around the flow. I pulled the filter from my pack. The squeeze bag filled slowly, the filter hissed low, and for a moment it felt like every sound in the forest had gone silent to listen.

Chunk squatted with his pistol laid across his knees, eyes on the slope. Zombie scanned the opposite ridge, chewing his lip, fingers tapping the grip of his pistol. I squeezed water into bottles, one by one, my shoulders tight. We all knew that our exposure was too great here.

When I filled and passed around the bottles, nobody said it, but we all thought the same thing—water wasn't enough. We needed calories. Still, once the bottles were full, we drank more than we really wanted to, long greedy gulps that felt too good to stop. Then we topped them off again, like that extra half bottle might buy us time.

I dug into my waterproof bag. Between the three of us, we pooled the scraps: a few strips of beef jerky, fistfuls of trail mix, a protein bar each. Pathetic, but it was something.

Chunk chewed his jerky like it had personally offended him. Zombie savored every almond like it might be the last thing he'd ever taste. Most of the time, protein bars are a chore—dense, chalky bricks you choke down out of necessity. But right then, that same bar tasted like something plated at a four-star restaurant.

It wasn't much, but within minutes I felt a faint charge in my arms, a lift behind my eyes. We'd bought ourselves more miles.

Not long after we left the stream and started climbing again, we stumbled on a clearing scarred by a makeshift fire ring. When I leaned closer, I swore I felt heat lingering just beneath the gray crust, and the stones were still blackened with ash mounded in the center.

Whoever camped here hadn't been gone for long. Multiple tent prints overlapped in the pine duff, scattered boot marks trampled the edge of the ring. Four, maybe five sets of feet. Chunk gave a low whistle. "Not long gone."

The trail climbed again, unblazed, narrowing between close-packed trees. Every sound pressed harder—the flap of a bird's wings, the crack of a branch, the sigh of wind through needles. I couldn't tell anymore what was real and what was a hallucination.

Then, as we angled east trying to work closer to the main trail, the woods opened to another problem. The ground dropped away into a river that was nothing like the crossings before—water bunched and slammed over slick rock, the current a white, snarling wall that ate sound and left a low, hungry roar. I wouldn't take my kayak down this, even in my younger years.

We stood on the bank, staring at it. The water moved fast, fast enough to drag a body under before it even knew which way was up. Just looking at it made my stomach tighten. Crossing wasn't a risk—it was guaranteed death.

Chunk shook his head, shoulders tight. "This just keeps getting better," he muttered.

Zombie didn't answer. He didn't have to. I could see it in both their faces—the concern that had been simmering since the night before was starting to take shape. Obstacle after obstacle, the woods kept pushing back. It wasn't panic yet, but it was getting close.

We stood on the bank, staring at the water tearing past, knowing we weren't going forward here. And behind us? Just miles of mud, no trail, and the same silence waiting to swallow us up again.

The truth sat between us, unspoken but loud—we were running out of options, and worse, we didn't have a plan that didn't feel like wandering blind.

My stomach knotted hard. Hunger, fear, frustration—all braided together until they felt like the same thing.

The roar of the water followed us as we backed off

the bank, steady and relentless. It didn't sound like a river anymore. It sounded like a countdown.

14

Don't Let Them Get Far

Once backed away from the edge, the roar fading step by step until it was gone. The air felt thinner away from the water, hotter too. We rechecked bottles—and fell into a pace that wasn't quite fast, wasn't quite cautious, a compromise none of us liked.

The trail stitched along a sidehill of loose dirt and roots. Every foot placement asked for attention I didn't have. My calves fluttered. Hunger pulsed behind my eyes in bright, stupid little stars. The watch came out in short bursts, Chunk and Zombie taking turns tilting screens into shade. The blue dot blinked with cold patience, leading us along a contour rib that slanted away from the truck like something already decided.

We slid down onto softer ground where the trail dipped between firs. That's when we saw it: half a dozen cigarette butts pressed into the duff, filters browned, fleck of ash still clinging. None of us smoked, cigarettes at least.

We stopped and stared at it longer than we should have, like it might explain itself. Chunk crouched, arms resting on his knees, head cocked. Zombie circled it twice, scanning the ground for prints that weren't there. I just kept my eyes on it, waiting for it to twitch.

"Fresh," Chunk muttered. "Rain didn't hit it. Edges clean."

"Who the hell smokes out here?" Zombie asked. His voice was too loud, like he'd forgotten how sound carries.

The cigarettes didn't answer, and none of us touched them. But our pace slowed after that. Not just because of the butts—though it haunted every step— but because the lack of calories was finally grinding us down.

My legs felt lead-wrapped, my stomach cramped and hollow, and my head buzzed with static every time I bent or turned.

It was midday, and on any other trip we'd be scanning for a spot to sit, unpack lunch, fire up the stoves for a little afternoon pick-me-up coffee. I would've traded anything for a cup of strong coffee and one of those dehydrated trail meals I always cursed under my breath. I'd promised myself I'd never choke down another bag of trail mush on the next trip, but right then I would've eaten anything—anything with calories to feed muscles that were already threatening to seize into constant cramps.

Instead, we had no trail, no food, and no clue what was waiting around the next bend. Just fresh cigarette butts and a creeping certainty that it meant we weren't alone, and someone was close.

We walked slower after that, every step heavier. Calories gone, patience gone. The trail, if it even deserved the name, shouldered around the ridge, forcing us to single-file on a shelf of dirt.

That's when the forest gave us something new.

At first, it was a cough of noise, faint and

mechanical, drifting through the folds of land. Then it came again—longer this time, unmistakable. An engine. Small. Throaty. Close enough that we all froze at once.

Zombie's lips barely moved. "ATV."

Chunk's face had gone stone. "Too close."

We ducked low, pressing into the brush off-trail, branches scratching our arms. The engine revved once, then cut off, leaving a silence worse than its growl. My heart thudded so loud I was sure it carried farther than the sound had.

For a minute, maybe two, the woods went silent. No wind. No sound. Just us, crouched and sweating, eyes fixed on a ridgeline we couldn't see past.

Then a voice floated down. Male. Sharp syllables tossed into the air, carried on just enough breeze to make them words without meaning. Another voice answered, lower, steadier. Then both went quiet.

We stayed pinned in place, not daring to move. Every muscle cramped, screaming for relief, but nobody shifted an inch.

Finally, after what felt like an hour but couldn't have been more than a handful of minutes, Chunk eased his pistol higher and whispered, "They're not looking for deer."

The words had barely left his mouth when the voices carried again, clearer this time. A bark of laughter. Then one sentence, flat and certain, aimed into the woods like a rifle round:

"Don't let them get far."

My stomach dropped. They weren't talking about deer.

They were talking about us.

15

Might Be Those Hikers

The engine noise came low and rough, like a throat clearing. Small motor. ATV, I thought. Then it cut off fast, leaving silence that presses against my ears.

We dropped into the brush, collapsing our trekking poles and tucking them in tight. Knees burned, lungs shallow. Chunk's hand rose, palm flat. Wait. Zombie tilted his head, brim shading his eyes, watching with that stillness that feels louder than motion. Sap and dirt carried in the air—and under it, the sharp bite of ammonia and reeking of cat pee.

A bird ticked twice, metronome regular. Further away, wood snapped. Could've been a squirrel. Could've been a boot. The ammonia smell thickened, then thinned with a breeze you couldn't feel, only taste.

We eased under a fallen oak, dirt cold on our stomachs. Ants used our arms like roads. Voices floated down, breaking on ridges—two men.

"...damn hose kinks every time..."

"...don't lay it right, that's on you..."

Chunk's face went rigid. Zombie shot me a look. Then the voices faded out, and all that remained was the roar of my own breath.

We eased back up, angling away from the trail. That's where we found the first hose. Black poly line, thin as a finger, half-buried. A cut in it wept water like a wound that wouldn't close.

Zombie tapped it. "Drip line."

Chunk's voice was stone. "Move."

We climbed. Oak roots twisted underfoot, slick with moss. Rhododendrons tore at our sleeves. The sour, animal tang of ammonia stalked us—close, then gone, then back again. My stomach cramped hard, sharp and mean, like the fumes weren't just in my nose but sliding down my throat. Every breath felt like swallowing something I couldn't spit back out.

Then came the drums. Blue plastic, fifty-five gallon, lids cinched with steel. Around them, nothing lived— moss browned, leaves curled. Hoses ran in and out, pulsing like veins.

Two more drums ahead. One patched with duct tape, peeling and wet, bleeding a chemical sweetness into the air. The ground was scuffed with boot marks. Fresh.

Chunk whispered, "Cut around."

Zombie's voice was flat. "Whoever set this up is close."

"Doesn't change what we do," Chunk said.

We shrugged out of our packs and hauled them across first, passing each one hand to hand. Then we crawled over the slick, moss rock, elbows digging in for grip, scrambling up the other side one at a time. The hose kept reappearing—bridged across gullies with sticks, hidden under leaf litter, shadowing a thicker, insulated line.

Zombie muttered, "That pump's pushing more than

water."

Chunk said, "Quiet."

At the rise, the trees opened. Through two oaks we saw it—tarps stretched low, blue and green sheets weighed with rocks. Under them, rows of plants in black pots, leaves jagged and dark, heavy with buds. A grow patch.

Beyond it, a shed leaned crooked, tin roof rusted through in patches. The ammonia stung stronger here, flooding my gut with cramps. It felt like I was drinking it every time I swallowed, my stomach gnawing at itself.

A small engine sputtered, caught, stuttered, then hummed steadily.

The sound froze me. Same cough, same cut. The "ATV."

Zombie breathed, "That's it. That's our four-wheeler."

Chunk didn't blink. "And it hasn't moved."

Two men worked below, masks strapped hard across their faces. One stood with a shovel, shirt pasted to his back. The other crouched by a pallet, rubbing at the raw skin beneath his respirator. Their voices carried—filtered, clipped, sharp.

"Told you not to leave the lid off—now the coons got in it."

"That weren't me, that was your dumb ass."

"Yeah, well, boss ain't gonna like it either way."

This wasn't some ATV camp gone quiet—the engine we'd heard wasn't from a four-wheeler at all. A small generator sat on a plywood platform beside a stump, the kind of beat up contractor model you'd see on a job site. Its paint was scratched raw, a smear of oil staining the base, exhaust puffing in short, uneven bursts. Propane tanks sat locked in a rusted cage, tubing looping across a worktable like veins, feeding something deeper in the trees. A half-peeled laundry jug perched on the stump, crust hardened around its mouth.

Nothing about it belonged out here. Not this far off the grid.

Chunk's palm pressed my shoulder, pushing me down. His meaning was clear: Back.

We moved slow. Every leaf felt like a tripwire. Boots scuffed dirt above.

"This shovel's bent again. Told you not to leave it in the damn truck bed."

"It ain't the shovel, it's you don't know how to use it."

"Keep talkin', I'll let you haul the next barrel up this hill by yourself."

We froze under oak limbs. The generator coughed once, then steadied. Boots scraped again. The echoes in the pines gathered tight around us. Then the footsteps pivoted, fading the other way.

Chunk's whisper brushed my sleeve. "When it coughs again, we move."

We waited. Thirty seconds stretched like thin wire. The machine stuttered twice. That was the signal. We slid, brush clawing at skin, ducking to the hose line again.

Just below the slope, a trickle of groundwater leaked from the earth, feeding into an old metal livestock trough. The water inside was black and stagnant, a thin layer of sludge coating the top. A small pump sat inside the tank, humming steadily as it pushed the water through a ribbed hose that disappeared into a clearing up ahead. We swung wide, keeping the tree trunks between us and the shed, slipping deeper into the treeline. The hose stretched ahead like a dark vein, half-buried in mud and leaves, pulling us farther from the generator's low hum. Each step bled the sound thinner, until it was just a faint vibration under the forest noise.

Then my boot slid on a loose rock, pitching me forward. I slammed into the ground with a heavy thud, the impact knocking the breath out of me. "Shit!" The word ripped out before I could stop it, cutting through the fog like a flare.

Chunk and Zombie spun around, eyes wide—half checking to see if I was okay, half pissed I'd just announced our position to anyone with ears. Neither of them said a word, but the look they gave me was loud enough.

Chunk grabbed my arm and yanked me upright while Zombie swept the tree line, tension etched across his face. No lectures, no jokes—just a pull, a nod, and we were moving again.

We pressed on, faster now, the adrenaline buzzing under our skin. Every footfall felt heavier but quieter, each of us hyperaware of every branch, every loose stone, every breath. The silence around us seemed sharper.

We'd barely started moving when it hit us—voices, low and rough, drifting up through the fog from somewhere down the slope. I couldn't make out everything, just broken pieces carried on the wet air.

"...what the fuck was that..."

"...might be those hikers..."

"...let's go..."

The rest blurred as we pushed deeper into the trees. But it was enough. They weren't sitting still anymore. They were moving.

It was a hundred percent clear now—whatever was happening out here wasn't meant for us to find. Whoever they were, they either wanted us gone or found. No doubt in my mind they were the ones who cut our food bags down.

As we progressed my head flushed hot, the way it does when nerves spike and your body hasn't caught up yet. Every sound seemed crisper, closer. It wasn't just unease anymore. It was the kind of feeling that tells you you've already crossed a line you can't step back over.

Zombie and Chunk both turned to me, faces tight, no words needed. This wasn't some unlucky run-in. Someone had already put our number out.

When the voices didn't pick back up, we moved— slow, deliberate, but fast as we could without giving ourselves away. No more arcing the shed. We needed distance now, space between us and whoever was down there.

We ducked under oak limbs, belly flat. Two sets of steps above us. Long pause. Then the men shifted, drifting off sideways.

Chunk crouched, lifting his wrist to check our position before moving. He tapped the face of his watch. Nothing. He tapped again. Still black.

"Shit," he muttered. "Watch is dead."

None of us had charged our phones or watches since leaving the trailhead. Normally we'd top everything off—phones, watches, headlamps—while we sat around the fire, then toss the power banks into the bear bag before turning in. If it didn't help us sleep, it didn't stay in the tent.

So when they took the bags, they took the power banks too. No bags meant no charging.

Chunk pulled his phone out first, squinting against the sunlight bleeding through the trees in thin, sharp bands. "Fifty-two," he muttered.

"Sixty-one," Zombie said, checking his own.

Mine lit up weak and pale against the daylight. "Seventy-two."

Chunk slid his phone back into his pocket, his expression tightening with purpose. "Turn 'em off," he said. "No reason to burn battery unless we've got something to work with."

He kept his on long enough to open the hiking map app, finger flicking across the screen. The GPS pin spun uselessly for a few seconds before settling on nothing. "No signal," he said. "Nothing cached either. We're blind out here."

I slipped my phone out one last time—no bars, no surprise. My phone still showed SOS across the top, a quiet reminder that even if the world was out there, it wasn't reaching us. Not here. Not now.

I shut mine down completely with no hesitation. Besides the filter I carried, it was the one piece of gear that might still mean the difference between escaping and not. But even with a charge left, I couldn't help thinking the same thing: maps or no maps, it wouldn't matter. I wouldn't be the one leading us out.

Once they were all shutdown we kept the slow crawl into the unknown. All I did, like normal, was follow in Chunk's footsteps.

A hose hissed faintly in the quiet, the last trace of what we'd walked through. No generator. No voices. Just the woods settling back into themselves.

The sun was already slipping behind the ridge, and the light changed fast—one minute it was golden, the next fading into long shadows that stretched through the trees. The oaks blurred into dark shapes, the air warming even as the light thinned.

My heart thudded hard—not just from nerves, but from the slow drain of calories and the burn of miles. The first drop of sweat slid straight down the center of my back, that slow, cold crawl everyone knows. And once it started, it didn't stop—the trickle widened into a steady stream, soaking through my shirt like someone had opened a valve.

We moved deeper, careful but steady, putting distance between us and whatever was left behind.

16

Leaving Only the Dark

We were well off the trail by the time night swallowed the woods. No blazes, no markers, just dense forest from every direction. The storm clouds smothered any hint of moonlight, leaving us blind without help. Out here, every step felt like it could pitch us into a hole, or right into someone's camp.

Headlamps were the only option, but light was a double-edged sword. In country like this, it drew eyes as quick as it cleared a path. Another concern was batteries—if we drained them too soon, we would be stranded in the dark for good. So only Chunk wore his, flipped to the red beam. It gave us just enough to move, smearing the ground in bloody shadows, but it kept us hidden and saved our night vision.

I stayed tight on his heels, boots whispering over damp needles, and Zombie ghosted behind me, silent as ever. The forest closed in heavy, carrying only the soft groan of trees rubbing against each other in the wet.

Every other sound was ours—a strap creaking, a pack shifting, the faint whistle of breath.

We moved in silence, the fog swallowing every sound.

Then it flashed—a single white light, thin and cold, cutting through the trees. It vanished as quickly as it appeared, leaving only the dark. A beat of silence, then it came again—only now it had company.

Two…then three.

White beams flickered through the fog, weaving in and out of the tree line in a jagged, erratic pattern. Wrong color and too small to be fire. Too scattered to be anything natural.

Chunk froze mid-step, eyes locked on the glow. His thumb slid over his headlamp and the red light vanished instantly. Zombie didn't say a word, but I felt him go still beside me—shoulders tightening, breath catching for half a beat.

Whoever was up there wasn't just standing around. The beams swept, stopped, then jerked on again.

They were moving. Searching.

We sank lower without talking, letting the dark take us while we waited to see if the lights angled our way again.

At first I heard nothing, just the blood in my ears. Then faint—maybe a voice. Or wind pushing across the ridgeline. A low murmur that rose, dipped, and then cut off.

We held still, not daring to shift. After a long minute, Chunk slowly eased his hand away, the faint red glow blooming back onto the ground. He didn't say a word, just moved us forward again.

A cough carried on the damp air. Once, laughter— or something close enough to it—drifted from the black. Each time, Chunk killed the light, and we froze, hearts hammering, waiting to decide if what we heard was real or our own nerves playing tricks.

The woods never gave us answers, only silence. But the silence was worse, because it always left the possibility that someone was out there, listening too.

We were thirty yards further when the forest seemed to lurch awake. A low hum built beneath our boots, then roared alive. The generator. Close. Too close.

We were hiking in circles. Its rattle rolled softly through the ground, but pounding in my head.

Chunk's hand cut the red beam again, plunging us into black. None of us spoke. None of us breathed.

Because this time, over the machine's hum, came something unmistakable: the crunch of boots on gravel. Not one set. Several. Moving steadily, deliberately, just beyond the treeline.

Gravel didn't belong out here. It wasn't something nature left behind—it was something trucked in. Laid down for delivery trucks, generators, propane tanks, maybe even water tanks. Out here, that meant infrastructure.

We hadn't stumbled into their territory.

We were already surrounded by it.

17

Cowboy Camping

The night settled heavier after the generator's hum faded. None of us wanted to say it, but we couldn't keep moving like this—bushwhacking blind, straining to hear every sound, stopping every time a branch snapped.

The dark belonged to whoever was out here. We were just stumbling through it.

Then the sound shifted. The crunch of boots on gravel started to drift, not closer, but away—slow at first, then fading deeper into the fog. Through the trees, the headlamp beams swung with them, no longer facing our direction but sweeping out into the black.

We didn't relax. Not even close. They hadn't disappeared. They were just moving.

And now we didn't know where.

We argued in whispers, crouched low in the brush, voices sharp from hunger and exhaustion. Every option felt like a trap. Push forward in the dark and risk stumbling straight into whoever was out there, or stop and risk being found while we slept. Neither choice sat right, but standing in the middle of the woods arguing about it wasn't a good option either.

Chunk finally made the call. "Off trail. Far enough to disappear. We'll make do."

Zombie gave one quick nod. That was all it took.

We started moving again, slow and deliberate, scanning for anything that could give us cover. The further we got from the gravel, the easier it was to breathe, though the weight of their presence clung to us like fog.

We weren't just trying to vanish—we were looking for a place to hole up for the night. Somewhere far enough off the path that a flashlight sweep wouldn't catch us. Somewhere they wouldn't stumble into by accident.

Eventually we found it: a massive slab of rock jutting out of the ground, slick with rain but broad enough to block the wind and break the line of sight from the trail. Not perfect. But better than nothing.

We circled it in silence, scanning the tree line, listening for anything that didn't belong. This wasn't about comfort anymore—it was about not being found. If they swept the woods, this was as close to invisible as we were going to get.

Tents weren't an option tonight. Too noisy, too obvious, and too slow to tear out of if we had to fight or run. Instead, we rigged our rainflies low with trekking poles, angled on a slight slope to shed water if the skies opened again.

Chunk and Zombie set theirs up with the speed of muscle memory, poles driven into the ground, guy lines pulled taut, edges staked tight. I stood over mine a little too long, rainfly stretched out like a puzzle I'd never solve. Normally, they'd give me hell for not learning this skill years ago, but tonight there were no jokes. Chunk just shook his head, moved over, and had mine standing in minutes while Zombie secured the lines. Whether it was because I'd been lazy before or just because they knew time mattered more than pride, they didn't say.

Packs slid under the edges to double as makeshift pillows and to keep our gear close at hand. It wasn't comfort. It was survival. Cowboy camping.

The last time I'd tried to rush setting up or breaking down gear in the rain, I'd paid for it. One trip—just a few years back—I'd stuffed my sleeping bag straight into my pack without a dry bag while breaking camp in a morning storm. By the time we made camp that night, it was soaked through, heavy and useless. The temperature was going to dip into the 40s that night, and there was no chance of drying anything in that wet air. I hated it. Hated knowing I'd made the kind of mistake that could put my life at risk.

Chunk and Zombie never said a word. Not once. We broke camp and hiked out a day early. It sucked, but it stuck.

Instead of using our sleeping bags, we layered up— base layers, fleece, jackets—then pulled our rain gear over it all. The shells didn't breathe, sticky and clammy against skin, but they guaranteed one thing: our warm layers stayed dry. Out here, if your last dry clothes were gone, so were you.

Boots stayed on and laced tight. Pistols sat within arm's reach, chambers checked. We wanted rest, but being ready to move mattered more.

We split the night into shifts. Two down, one awake. The one on watch didn't just listen to the woods—he listened to us too, ready to shake one of us quiet if a snore rumbled. Out here, even sleep could give us away.

But sleep never came easy. When it was supposed to be my turn to rest, my eyes refused to close. My mind would fixate on every sound in the brush—a snapping twig, the wind echoing through the pines, my own heartbeat thudding in my ears. It's like the quiet wouldn't let me off guard. I'd lie there wide awake, knowing I should be recharging, and instead just burn through the hours.

Then, like clockwork, the second it was my turn to keep watch, the weight hit me. Heavy. A hammer to the skull. My head sagged, eyelids dragging like they'd been waiting all night to betray me. I'd fight it minute by minute, clawing to stay present, reminding myself one slip wasn't just on me—it could cost all three of us.

It's backwards like that out here. When you have the time to rest, your mind won't let you. And when you need to be sharp, your body tries to shut down. The forest doesn't care which one wins.

Then the night cracked open. A single gunshot—deep, heavy, large caliber—tore through the fog. It was far off, but not far enough. We all jerked upright at once, the reverb rolling through the woods like distant thunder. No one said a word at first. We didn't have to. In the silence that followed, the forest felt thinner.

Zombie exhaled slow. "That wasn't a .22."

Chunk's voice was low but certain. "Nope. That was a big bastard. .308, maybe .30-06."

The sound sat in my chest, heavy and familiar.

Late-night gunshots had a way of peeling back years.

One of our early trips came flooding back—the night we got plastered around a fire, young and stupid, feeling invincible. Someone—I honestly couldn't even remember who—drew their gun and, with the kind of confidence only bourbon can give, fired straight into the campfire. The flame exploded up, sparks showering over us like shrapnel. We all hit the dirt at once. Then, through ringing ears and drunken wheezing, came the slurred victory cry: "Break yo'self fool!"

And that wasn't even all of it. That same night, I'd managed to waste an entire can of bear mace—sprayed it all over the wood pile like an idiot, convinced it would "keep critters away." Hours later, Zombie grabbed a few logs to feed the fire, completely unaware. The second the smoke hit, he started coughing, clawing at his face like he was fighting a swarm of hornets. His eyes watered, snot poured, and then—cherry on top— his nose started bleeding profusely.

He stumbled back toward us, eyes red and leaking, and croaked, "Do I look alright?"

Chunk, way too drunk to help, just burst out laughing and pointed. "Your nose, man!"

To be young and dumb. We were so lucky we didn't end up dead or maimed that night. A mix of bad decisions and blind luck had carried us through, and somehow, that stupid chaos turned into one of those stories we never fully told right.

I blinked the memory away, pulling myself back to the now—to the wind still bleeding through the trees.

I tried to steady my breathing, but my heart was hammering.

Chunk tilted his head, still listening. "That's a hunting rifle, not some plinker. Big round. Carries clean through the air."

Zombie shifted, pulling his jacket tighter.

We sat in the dark, straining for another shot, but the woods went still again. No second shot. No voices. Just the kind of silence that settles over a place after something sharp cuts through it.

Chunk finally spoke, barely above a whisper. "That distance… whoever fired that ain't too far. A mile, maybe less."

Nobody answered. We all understood what that meant. Someone out there was awake, armed, and close enough to matter.

We all wanted morning, because morning meant we were alive. But none of us wanted to see what the next day had in store.

18

Make Today Count

It started with faint taps, almost nothing—drops ticking against nylon. At first, I thought it was just the trees shaking loose what yesterday's storm had left behind. But then it grew steadier, louder, until it was clear the clouds had opened up again.

The steady rain quickly turned into a soaking sheet that drummed against our rainflies. Thunder grumbled far off, rolling through the ridges. It never felt dangerous, but it reminded us we were exposed.

This wasn't a storm meant to break trees—it was meant to grind you down, soaking everything, turning dirt to mud and air to soup.

Our rainflies held, angled just right with trekking poles and pitched on a slope to drain the water away. The rock at our backs shielded us from the worst of the sideways gusts, and that probably saved us. Our boots and socks were soaked through, and the damp crept into us like an unwelcome guest. The sleeping bags had stayed stuffed deep in their waterproof sacks—dry, safe, untouched. Keeping them that way could be the deciding factor when it matters most.

The storm finally tapered before dawn, the pounding easing into a steady drizzle. First light crept in slow and pale, bleeding through the trees in thin streaks. The forest hung heavy and dripping, the air thick with the sour smell of rot and wet leaves. Fog clung low, curling around the trunks, swallowing the distance and softening the edges of everything.

We were wearing our rain gear, so our bodies stayed dry, but every step today would squish and be loud from the material rubbing against itself. Still, it was far better than being caught without the rain gear—if our warm layers had gotten wet, they'd never dry under this humid canopy.

We sat up slowly, boots still laced, pistols still close, rainflies sagging with water. Although none of us spoke, it was written all over our faces. The kind of exhaustion that doesn't just live in your eyes—it settles into your bones.

We looked wrecked, every one of us. Mud-streaked, hollow-eyed, shoulders slumped from a night that didn't give us an inch. We hadn't slept. We'd endured. And that was the difference between looking tired and looking like survivors. The question now was whether the day waiting for us was going to let us make it through again.

Huddled in the ashen light, our feet were cold and wet, muscles stiff, and exhaustion etched into every movement. With little debate, the decision was made: it was time to eat the few calories we had left. There was no sense in saving them now. If this were the day we were getting out, we'd need every ounce of strength. If it wasn't—then we were already in trouble.

The food wasn't much—scraps, really—but even those bites hit like fire in a dying engine. For a moment it gave the illusion of energy, but I knew better. It was borrowed time, nothing more. The push that might carry us through one more climb, maybe one more ridge, before the tank went empty for good.

The food went down quick, more fuel than flavor, each bite scraped down with sips of air temperature water. It wasn't enough to satisfy, but it dulled the edge just enough to move.

Chunk finally broke the silence, voice low and rough. "We can't do another night like that. Not out here."

Zombie nodded, his breath fogging in the damp air. "We've got maybe a day's worth of calories left to burn. Less if we get turned around again."

Chunk stared out into the fog, the muscles in his face tightening. "Then we make today count. We push as far as we can. Higher ground, better line of sight. If we can get even a hint of where we are—ridge, old logging road, anything—we follow it out."

"And if we don't find anything?" I asked.

"Then we keep moving until we do," he said. "We stop again, we might not get back up."

The weight of it settled between us. No map. No signal. Just three exhausted men gambling on instinct and whatever luck was still out there waiting.

We pulled our trekking poles out of the ground and shook the rainflies until the water came off in sheets, then stuffed everything into the outer pockets of our packs. No sense putting anything wet inside if we could avoid it.

I cinched the straps on my pack, the nylon stiff from the moisture. Either we walked out today, or the woods would decide how the story ended.

Boots squelched with every step, socks already

soaked through but laced tight. Pistols were checked, magazines seated, chambers verified.

There was no talking, no wasted words. Just the quiet understanding that whatever waited for us out there, we had no choice but to meet it head-on.

Even the trekking poles, normally a lifeline, turned against me. My arms shook the way my legs did, trembling from fatigue, wet and cold, every plant of the pole sending a shiver up my shoulders. I wasn't walking so much as scuffing forward, feet sliding more than stepping, poles clattering in rhythm. It felt like I was shuffling across the forest, dragging myself inch by inch instead of hiking.

Chunk kept pushing, steady as ever, but even he moved differently—shoulders hunched, like the weight of his pack had finally gotten through the armor. Zombie stayed quiet at the rear, but his breathing told its own story: shallow, controlled, each exhale just a little sharper than it had been the day before.

We stopped at a small runoff where the rain had carved a thin channel down the ridge. The flow was just enough to fill the bottles. My arms trembled as I pressed the dirty water through the filter, every press slower than the last. My hands were cold and stiff, the kind of cold that crawls into your fingers and stays there. Each squeeze bled out a little more strength, the chill turning my grip weak and clumsy, fingers starting to feel numb. When the first bottle came clear, I drank deep—more than I wanted, more than was comfortable—because I knew I had to. Then I refilled it, leaving with it full, the same as the others.

We filled in silence, the sound of water trickling louder than our breathing. Packs creaked as we stowed them away, heavier now with the slosh of fresh water.

That's when Chunk froze. He didn't say a word—just pointed with the tip of his pole at the mud a few feet off the trail.

Footprints, multiple sets.

They weren't ours. Too many, too clean. Fresh enough that rain hadn't blurred the edges, still sharp against the slick earth. It faced the same direction we were heading.

For a long moment, none of us moved. My throat tightened, and not from thirst. Somebody was ahead of us. Not last week, not yesterday. This morning.

Zombie crouched low, eyes narrowing. He touched the edge with two fingers, he swore they were from combat boots.

We shouldered our packs again, no one saying what we all thought: footprints meant people. And people meant risk. One way or another, this ended today.

The fog pressed closer, the woods muffled, and suddenly the weight of every tree felt different. We weren't just hiking anymore. We were following. Or being led. And whatever waited ahead already knew we were coming.

19

Waiting for its Actors

The trees eventually opened just enough for us to see the shape of the place—small, unnatural, a pocket of cleared ground that didn't match the wild around it. The brush was beaten flat, branches bent back the way they get when people pass through the same spot over and over.

Then we saw them: two metal folding chairs, not knocked over or abandoned, but set out deliberately, facing the same direction like they were meant for someone to sit and watch the treeline. One held a bag on its seat, perched too neatly to be trash or something blown there by wind. Nothing out here arranged itself like that.

We froze. Out here, a setup like this meant someone wasn't passing through. They'd built this spot. Used it. Planned to come back. The two metal chairs made it worse—angled toward the trees, turned outward as if whoever sat there was meant to keep an eye on the woods.

Then Chunk leaned forward, squinting through the fog. "Zombie... tell me that is your bag."

Zombie whispered, "It sure as shit is."

Even through the fog, the bag on the chair hit us

with a punch of color—bright yellow, bold as a warning sign. The cartoon zombie graphic on the side sealed it. It was Zombie's food bag. No question. We didn't need to get closer to know.

We scanned the clearing in absolute silence—the brush, the trees, every shadow deep enough to hide someone. The whole setup felt too deliberate, too placed, and the bag sitting there made the coincidence feel impossible. Someone had gone into our camp, taken Zombie's food bag, and positioned it here like a breadcrumb, or a warning.

"Could be a set up," I muttered. "Like we're supposed to find it."

A trap wasn't out of the question.

Chunk kept his voice low. "Zombie—go slow. We've got you."

Zombie nodded once and moved forward under our cover, each footfall measured. He reached the chair, grabbed the dry bag in a single quick motion, then backed out the same careful path.

Only when he reached us did we breathe again.

He knelt and opened it, sifting through the contents. His face told the story before he spoke.

"Power banks are gone," he whispered. "Energy blocks too. Beef jerky's gone."

He held up one of the dehydrated meals. "But these are untouched."

Someone had taken exactly what they wanted—electronics, quick calories—and left the rest, all in a place where we'd be guaranteed to see it.

Not scavenging.

Not random.

Intentional.
Like a stage waiting for its actors.

20

Heat in My Hands

Zombie rolled the top of his food bag down tight, the plastic crackling as he sealed it. Five meals left. Nothing else. Whoever tore through it had taken everything that would've kept us moving days ago.

We didn't stand around debating it.

We turned uphill and put distance between us and that clearing, trekking poles clicking softly as we threaded through rock and roots. None of us said the word 'trap', but it sat there in the air anyway. Maybe someone had watched Zombie take the bag. Maybe they were still watching, pacing us through the trees.

Every gust sounded like footsteps. Every birdcall felt rehearsed. We moved fast but careful, breathing shallow, ears hunting anything that didn't belong.

When Chunk finally slowed, he didn't raise a hand for silence—just gave a small nod that meant here's far enough for now.

We stepped off the faint trail into a tangle of mountain laurel, their waxy leaves forming a low, tight canopy overhead. The fog pooled under it, softening the light until everything felt distant.

Zombie dropped his pack and pulled out the meals—three repacked pouches, each one folded into neat plastic squares the way he always did it. He handed Chunk the first.

Chunk grinned like he couldn't help himself. "Pad Thai. Hell yes!"

Zombie passed me mine. Spaghetti with meatballs. He kept the chicken and rice for himself.

We didn't reach for spoons. They were gone with the bear bags, and no one bothered to comment. Calories mattered more than how we got them.

We didn't talk after that. No one needed to.

The stoves came out—metal legs clicking into place, pots settling on top. We poured water straight from our bottles, flames flickering low under the laurel canopy. Steam curled upward, disappearing into the fog almost as fast as it formed.

The smell hit me first—a warm, salty tang that made my throat tighten. Days of running, hiding, starving…and now hot food. After mashing the hot bag with my hands to be sure it stayed stirred, I tipped the pouch and ate straight from it, the heat soaking through the plastic into my fingers as I took the first bite. It felt good to finally have some heat in my hands.

Chunk let out a quiet sigh. "Man…this is so good."

Zombie nodded, chewing slow, conserving every calorie like it mattered.

For a few minutes, the forest wasn't hunting us. It was just quiet. Just a place where three tired men sat with warm food and tried to remember what it felt like not to be chased.

When we finished, Zombie tucked the empty plastic into a small pile. Normally we'd pack out everything— we weren't the type to leave trash buried in the woods. But this wasn't a normal trip, and none of us wanted to walk around smelling like a buffet for every bear on the mountain.

We dug a shallow hole with our poles and boots, dropped the empty bags in, and covered them with heavy, wet earth. No trace. No scent. No temptation for anything bigger than us.

Warm food inside us.

Cold fear behind us.

And ahead—just more forest waiting to decide what we were worth.

21

Ghosts Too Long

Zombie exhaled through his teeth, the sound tight, controlled. "We've been ghosts too long. If we're getting out tonight, we need eyes before the light's gone."

I sat up, rubbing grit from my eyes. The air felt heavier now—charged. "We get higher ground. A ridge. A bald. Somewhere we can actually see."

Chunk nodded, already scanning the tree line. "Elevation gives us line of sight. If they're moving, I want to know before they do."

Zombie leaned forward, elbows on his knees. "And maybe..." He hesitated, then gave a short nod. "If we're lucky, we catch a bar. Even one. That's all we need to get a heading and call for help."

"Exactly," I said. "No more drifting in the dark. We find high ground now, set our line, and when night hits—we move."

I pushed to my feet, shoulders aching from the hours on the ground.

For the first time all day, the silence wasn't heavy. It was focused.

We had food in our bellies. We had some daylight left. And now, finally, a direction.

That's when it came—distant at first, carried thin through the fog. A howl.

Not the sharp bark of a stray, but the long, rising cry of dogs. It rolled through the trees, stretched and frayed, bending with the wind. One howl became two. Then more. A slow, uneven chorus that climbed the ridgeline and bled down into the hollow where we crouched.

We froze. Nobody spoke. The sound slid through the fog, bouncing between the trunks, making it impossible to pin down where it started. It was far...but not far enough.

Another howl broke through—closer this time, cutting through the stillness. Not frantic. Controlled.

The forest went silent after that. No birds. No rustling. Just the weight of the barks pressing in around us.

The shit wasn't hitting the fan yet, but the blades were spinning, and we all knew it.

22

Dogs Don't Lose Trails

The howls subsided, swallowed by the fog, leaving a silence that felt heavy. None of us spoke. None of us moved. The air was damp against my face, thick enough to taste. My pulse thudded in my ears louder than the sound had been.

Then came something worse. Voices.

Low at first, carried through the trees, but clear enough once the wind shifted. Two men. Sharp, clipped. Not wandering hikers. Not hunters. These were men with purpose.

"...they said three of 'em. Saw the lights last night."

"...boss don't care how tired you are. We flush 'em out tonight."

"...don't matter where they run. Woods'll hold 'em till we find 'em."

My stomach dropped. Three. They knew.

Chunk's hand came up, palm open: freeze. We crouched lower, backs pressed to slick rock, the mist beading on our jackets.

The voices grew louder, closer, rolling with the fog like they were everywhere at once.

"...check the ridge. Saw movement up there."

The fog had thickened into a soft wall, muting everything around us. Dusk bled through the trees in streaks of bruised gold and gray, just enough light to blur shapes and twist shadows. Every movement felt too loud, too exposed.

Somewhere up the ridge, branches cracked—sharp and clean. Then another. Not wind. Not animals. A rhythm. Measured. Human.

We didn't move. Not a word between us. The forest seemed to lean in, holding its breath.

A third crack followed, closer this time, rolling down through the fog like a warning we couldn't ignore.

They weren't rushing. They didn't need to. Whoever was up there was moving slow, confident, like they knew the terrain.

Zombie's whisper barely stirred the air. "They're hunting us."

The sound grew softer, like footsteps cresting the ridge, then fading just enough to leave us wondering how close they really were. The silence after was worse than the noise. It always was. At least with voices we knew where they were.

Chunk's eyes met mine, hard and certain. His lips shaped the word I didn't want to hear: move.

We slid downhill, inch by inch, packs scraping bark, boots sinking into mud. Every step felt loud, like the forest would sell us out. Somewhere above, a rock turned under a boot, and one voice barked sharp, close enough that I could picture the man's head snapping in our direction. They were just above us on the ridge.

Couldn't be more than thirty feet at most.

"…you hear that?"

"…yeah. They're moving."

My throat dried. They weren't guessing anymore. They knew we were right below them.

We froze in a thicket, brush closing around us, branches clawing at our sleeves as we sank low. The voices grew louder—not frantic, but confident. Taunting. They cut through the fog in sharp bursts, the kind that carried easy through trees.

"…push down. Drive 'em into the hollow."

"…don't let 'em circle back. Boss said three—I want three."

A third voice joined in, deeper, rougher, the kind that made orders stick.

"…dogs are close. Keep it tight."

The sound followed almost at once—a faint, high bark, stretched thin by the mist. Then another.

They weren't close yet. But they were coming.

The forest swallowed us whole, but no matter how deep we pressed into the brush, I knew the truth: dogs don't lose trails.

23

The Fight Was Near

The dogs and voices drifted the other way, thinning into the fog until they were just whispers, ghosts smothered by the trees. For the first time all day, it felt like we could breathe. Relief, but thin, brittle. None of us said it out loud, but we all knew what it was: a false calm.

Chunk motioned with two fingers, and we slipped out of the thicket, keeping low, moving fast and quiet. The climb started gradual, but the ground tilted steeper with every step, pine needles giving way to loose rock and slick patches of mud. Our breathing stayed tight, controlled, every footfall placed like it mattered—because it did.

The ridge looked closer than it was. It always does. The trees thinned just enough to tease us with a sense of height, but when we finally pushed through the last stand of brush, it wasn't the peak we'd hoped for. Just a sliver of spine on the mountain—a false summit. The trees here were still taller than we were, their crowns blotting out what little was left of the dusk. No sight lines. No advantage. Just more forest.

Zombie spat into the dirt, a quiet, frustrated sound.

Chunk didn't say a word. We all knew it—the climb hadn't bought us anything.

So we turned to the last tool we had. One by one, we pulled out our phones. The screens glowed dim and cold in the gathering dark, little islands of light in the fog. No signal bars on mine. None on Zombie's either. But Chunk lingered, thumb swiping over his screen.

"Hold up," he muttered. "Got something."

Not a connection. Not really. But his map app scraped together just enough from the GPS to pull up a blurry topo overlay—jagged lines, elevation bands, the faint outline of where we were wedged in the ridgeline. It wasn't much, but it was a dot on a map. A place. A direction.

Then came the soft, unmistakable click of a screenshot—the kind of sound you could pick out even in a storm. He didn't need to explain; the shutter said enough. We had a sliver of information, something to hold on to. It wasn't a way out yet.

But it was a start.

The glow from our screens faded as we shut them down again, but the world around us had already changed. What little light had been bleeding through the trees was vanishing fast. Dusk wasn't sliding in—it was dropping, sudden and heavy, like someone had thrown a tarp over the ridge. The fog thickened with it, swallowing the shapes of the trees until even a few feet away felt like a mile.

Chunk glanced up through the breaks in the canopy, his expression flattening. "It's going quick," he said.

Zombie shifted his pack higher on his shoulders. "We push now, maybe we find the trail before it's pitch black. Sit too long, and we're blind again."

"Yeah," I said quietly. "But moving blind gets us lost faster than anything. We screw up here, we don't just waste time—we burn our energy."

The three of us stood there, boots sinking into the damp earth, the last light bleeding out behind the ridge. No one wanted to say it out loud, but it was written all over our faces: we were out of easy options.

"Two plays," Chunk said finally. "We move now and risk walking into their laps, or we hole up, let it get good and dark, and slip out when they can't see a thing."

Zombie let out a long breath through his nose. "We've made it this far by not doing stupid shit in the open."

Silence stretched, broken only by the distant drip of rain off the pines. The night was closing in too fast.

"Dark's our best chance," I said. "We wait it out. Then we move. Wait until the late night when they are sleeping or less alert because of the hour."

Chunk gave a single nod. Decision made. The ridge wasn't where we wanted to be—but for now, it would have to be enough.

We didn't risk tents. Nobody even mentioned it. The idea alone felt too loud. Instead, we moved along the ridge in a loose line, hands scraping the rock and low brush, headlamps kept dark. The fog was thick enough to catch and reflect any glow, so light was a luxury we couldn't afford.

The mountain was full of rock faces—we'd passed plenty over the last few days—but luck had never dropped us anything useful when we actually needed it. Tonight, we needed cover. Something that could break the skyline, block a flashlight beam, and keep the rain off if the clouds opened again.

So we pushed on, hugging the contour of the slope, scanning every dark shelf and shadowed cut in the hillside. Most were too shallow to hide a dog, let alone three grown men. But fifty yards later, Chunk slowed, lifted a hand.

"I've got something."

At first it looked like just another rock seam, but as we angled up toward it, the shape resolved—deeper, darker, the ceiling pushed far enough back to swallow us whole. An overhang. A real one. The kind that didn't happen often and never when you needed it most.

We checked it quickly—no scat, no fresh prints, nothing living inside but cold air and silence. Good enough.

Under the overhang, we worked without words. Gear got cinched. Water staged. Everything else stayed exactly where it was on our backs. We moved with the kind of practiced quiet that comes from too many nights like this.

Chunk checked the wind, Zombie studied the slope below, and I kept an ear turned to the hollow behind us. This wasn't a spot we'd stay if things went bad— just somewhere we could vanish for a few hours, wait for the darkest stretch of the night, then make the push.

We didn't expect comfort. We expected to disappear. And this little scar in the mountain was as good as we were going to get.

The voices and barks still floated below the ridge, but fainter now, blurred by distance. At first, it sounded like they were pushing east, sweeping hollow after hollow, always moving further from us. My shoulders eased, just a fraction. Even Zombie's eyes softened, tracking the tree line less, breathing a little deeper.

And for a brief second, it felt like maybe—just maybe—we'd managed to slip through and bide our time.

Then the night split open. Not one shot—several. Sharp, heavy cracks echoed through the trees in quick succession, rolling over the ridge like a warning. It wasn't wild or panicked. It was measured. Controlled.

Nobody said a word. We didn't have to. Every shot landed like it carried a message, bouncing off the trunks, threading through the fog until it wrapped around us.

They weren't just shooting.

They were letting us know they could, sending a very clear message.

The forest consumed the last echo, but the weight of it hung in the air long after the sound was gone.

None of us moved. None of us spoke. My pulse kicked so hard it felt like it shook the stone at my back.

Chunk broke first. Not with words, but with motion. His head tilted, eyes narrowed, every line of him calculating. He wasn't rattled—he was measuring. Sound, distance, angle—all running through that sharp, methodical filter that made him our leader.

Zombie's hand eased toward his pistol, unhurried and steady. His expression settled into something cold, eyes going flat as if something inside him snapped into place. I knew that look—straight Marine, all business. He didn't have to speak. The fight was near, too near, and he was already locked in.

Me? My hands shook. Not much, but enough to feel it. The gun at my side was loaded, chambered, and close. But I hated how alive it suddenly felt, how heavy, like I wasn't ready to pull it even though I knew I might have to.

No more shots. No voices. Just the echoes fading into nothing.

Then, from the ridge—clear and deliberate—came three sharp whistles, each one spaced, each one rising higher.

Signals.

And then the dogs barked again. Louder this time. Closer.

For the first time since we'd started, I realized the question wasn't if they'd find us. It was when.

24

First Blood

The laughter came first. Not strained voices lost in the fog, not distant echoes—but close. Casual. The kind of sound men make when they're comfortable enough to forget where they are.

We stayed still beneath the rock shelf, pressed into the shallow protection it offered, listening. The sound carried oddly through the trees, close enough to feel wrong, close enough that staying put suddenly felt like the bigger risk.

Laughter meant people. People meant answers—or trouble—and either way, we couldn't afford to ignore it.

So we moved.

We eased out from under the shelf and pushed through a tangle of brush, sinking to one knee as the ground leveled out. Bodies low and balanced, we used the undergrowth to break our outlines. The ridge flattened here—a narrow shelf just below the crest, hidden enough to keep us low, but not far enough to feel safe.

Through the gaps in the brush, we saw them. Three men. Standing in the open like they owned the woods.

Assault rifles slung lazy over their shoulders. Each carried their own bottle of whiskey, the kind that needed a chaser. Every few sentences they'd lift it, take a long pull, and let the fog swallow their laughter. It wasn't the kind of drinking you did for fun. It was the kind that settled in your bones.

Their voices rolled through the mist, loud and easy, like they didn't need to hide.

They weren't hunting right now. They were taking a break.

"…three boys running scared…," one of them yelled.

The others barked out laughter. Not mocking. Confident. Like they weren't guessing. Like they knew exactly where we were.

We were too close—close enough to hear wet leaves drag beneath their steps and low branches scrape as they pushed through.

And then one of them broke off.

We saw it before we heard him—the white glow of his headlamp peeling away from the group, cutting through the fog like a blade. It wasn't wandering. It was coming straight for us, steady and unhurried.

A half-empty bottle swung from one hand, glass clinking softly against his belt. His boots dragged through the brush, each step too measured to be random. Ten steps. Maybe less from us.

He stopped, unzipped, and the sound of liquid hitting wet ground sliced through the dark. The brush around us felt paper thin, the night suddenly too quiet.

Then he turned, and the headlamp swung with him. The beam drifted lazily at first, bouncing across tree trunks, catching the fog and spreading it like smoke.

And then it found us—just a flash. A buckle. A slick

edge of nylon.

The beam locked in place.

No movement. No hesitation.

He wasn't just close anymore. He'd walked straight into us.

His breath hitched—one sharp inhale—and his hand dropped instantly, not to his zipper but to the AR across his chest. He grabbed the pistol grip and yanked, the muzzle already rising, cutting through the fog toward us.

"Shit—" I started, but the barrel was already level, aiming right at us. His headlamp blinding me.

A single crack ripped the air, my chest vibrating with the shock and my ears instantly ringing.

He staggered once, then crumpled hard, rifle clattering against stone.

Zombie still had his pistol raised, smoke curling from the barrel, his face carved from stone. No hesitation. No warning. Square in the chest.

The laughter from the truck cut off sharply.

Then Chunk moved. Instinct, clean and fast. He broke cover, boots chewing dirt, and was on the body before the others could react. With one hard yank and the rifle strap tore free, the dead man rolling with the force. The only sound was the man gurgling what I assume was blood.

That's when Chunk saw it—clipped to the vest, a radio.

He ripped it loose, killed the static with a twist, and spun back toward us. His eyes were wide but steady.

"Run!"

The first blood was spilled, but it wasn't ours.

25

They're Executing

We tore through the woods like hunted animals, red headlamps cutting faint tunnels through the black. No more stealth. No more slow steps. All three lights burned, jerking with every stride. Branches clawed at our arms and faces, thorns tore fabric, but adrenaline made it weightless.

Chunk barked directions between breaths, angling us through gullies and thickets, never in a straight line. My legs burned, lungs on fire, but the sound behind us kept me moving.

Then—voices. Too close. Yelling. Not random shouts—frantic, desperate, calling out to their buddy we'd just dropped.

We dove into the brush, chests heaving, hands clamped over our lamps to choke the glow. The woods pulsed with noise. Shouts carried through the trees, raw and ragged.

"Reed's down! Those fuckers, I'm gonna kill them!"

My stomach dropped.

The radio cracked, spitting static, then a harsh voice cut through.

"Reed's 86, rifle and radio gone. Copy."

Another, more controlled voice snapped back a beat later.

"All units, initiate Sierra-Five. Shift comms to Hotel-Nine. Confirm: Sierra-Five, Hotel-Nine."

A third voice echoed the order, rushed, shaky.

"Copy Sierra-Five, Hotel-Nine. Moving now."

Zombie's whisper cut the air. "They're switching. We lost 'em."

Chunk shook his head, already twisting the dial, movements tight and deliberate. "No. That's garbage code. I've seen cleaner work from amateurs overseas. They want to sound official, but it's lazy phonetics. Just give me—"

The static bent, then cleared, voices threading through again.

"…Red team sweep the ridge. Blue hold east. Dogs cut south. Three targets confirmed. Armed."

The words made my ribs feel like they'd been cinched with a strap. Three targets. Not hikers. Not strangers. Us.

Silence for a beat. Then a third voice, cold and certain, cut through like a blade.

"Deke says no more games. Shoot to kill."

No one moved. The forest seemed to pause with us, waiting for the weight of those words to sink in.

Zombie's breath hissed out. "They're not chasing us out anymore. They're executing."

The red glow caught Chunk's eyes—steady, but hard. My pulse thundered in my ears. This wasn't paranoia anymore. No shadows, no guesses. They knew who we were, where we were, and what we carried.

We needed a plan, and fast.

The silence was stopped when Zombie snapped his

fingers, just once, sharp enough to pull our eyes to him. Zombie kept his voice low, steady. "I'll pull them east with boot prints. Big and dumb. You two keep north and stay light."

We'd done this kind of thing before—not with men hunting us, but lost on trails, separated by storms or fog.

Back then, we'd built our own signals. Yelling was obvious, but not always smart. So we'd made a quieter option: two short whistles. If one of us couldn't risk shouting, that was the call—short, sharp, unmistakable.

"Meet up point?" mumbled Zombie.

Chunk's mouth tightened. "The rock—the one we crashed at last night. We meet back there. We'll circle back after setting a path."

Chunk nodded once, already adjusting his pack. "If they bite on your trail, we'll be there within an hour," he said.

Zombie gave a half grin that didn't touch his eyes. "Yeah. If they bite."

Both Chunk and Zombie said they could find it blindfolded—the ridge had earned itself into their heads.

"One hour," Zombie added. "Meet at the rock in one hour. We move on my signal."

The plan snapped into focus: rendezvous at the same slab where we'd sheltered before, run the route from there, and push hard enough to be gone before sunrise. If we didn't make it out by then, everything changed—no more timing, just survival.

Then he faded into the trees, measured and quiet, boots landing where they wouldn't speak.

For a moment the woods swallowed him whole, and the night grew heavier around us. We didn't say it out loud, but it was there, sitting between the breaths we didn't take: he wasn't just laying a false trail. He was walking into their path.

26

Trail's Hot

Chunk and I angled north, just like Zombie had said. We moved in looping, messy lines, doubling back and cutting across the slope to muddy the picture. Every footprint was calculated—enough to give a story, not a straight line.

After about thirty minutes we cut off the path entirely, sticking to wet leaves that wouldn't hold a clean print. No tracks, no clear trail for anyone to read.

We threaded back to the rock where we'd crashed the night before and dropped down behind the slab, breath quiet, packs still on. Chunk pulled his phone out only long enough to check the time. Fifty-eight minutes. Close. We settled in, tucked into the stone, listening.

Minutes folded into more minutes. An hour was long gone. Chunk checked the ridge again, something unreadable settling over his face. "He should've been back by now," he murmured.

Then the silence snapped. The radio—the one Chunk had taken off the body—hissed and popped, then cut through the dark with a voice that sounded like commands.

"Status. Reports."

The voice carried the weight of authority—calm, cold, and absolute. The kind that didn't ask. It expected.

A static-torn reply came back quick, clipped.

"Team one—eastbound prints, following. Looks fresh."

Another voice answered immediately after, flat and professional.

"Copy. Same. Trail heading east. We're on it."

Chunk's hand went cold on the rock. The net was closing, and Zombie was late. We didn't need to say it aloud.

"Team two. Update."

Static hissed, then a reply came, low but clear. "Trail's hot. Real fresh."

Another voice followed, sharper, clipped. "Visual... might have—"

The rest dissolved into static, but it was enough. Too much.

Chunk's eyes snapped to mine. Neither of us spoke.

The air felt thinner, like the fog was pulling tight against my chest. My stomach dropped out from under me, the cold settling bone-deep.

They weren't just on the trail anymore.

They were close.

Maybe right on top of him.

27

Fire Set for Two

Nothing but dead air now. Whatever had been said, whoever had spoken, it was done. The silence that followed wasn't static—it was deliberate. Controlled.

My chest felt hollow, like the air had been stripped from it. Chunk crouched low, his features going blank and intent, eyes fixed on the treeline as though the fog might whisper the truth.

"Somebody killed that feed," he muttered. "That wasn't an accident. Somebody didn't want us hearing the rest."

The quiet stretched, thick and heavy. I glanced at him, and he already knew what I was thinking.

We could go after Zombie. Follow nothing but the dark.

No trail. No signal. No idea what we were walking into.

But moving blind out here wasn't a plan. It was a death wish.

So we stayed where we were, hearts hammering, listening to a forest that suddenly felt like it was listening back.

The thought twisted my stomach.

That's when the smell hit. Acrid. Bitter. Smoke.

Not campfire, not the damp burn of wet wood. This was chemical, sharp, riding the night breeze with the weight of plastic and fuel. We both turned, almost in unison, eyes tracking the faint orange shimmer bleeding through the fog. Flames.

It wasn't big—not yet—but the glow flickered high enough to show itself through the trees. Something man-made was burning out there. And maybe someone had lit it for a reason.

Chunk's face shifted, just slightly. Not hope. Not fear. Both tangled tight. He spoke low, as if he didn't want the words leaving the air between us.

"Zombie."

His name sat heavy between us. It could be him—lighting a blaze to let us know he was alive, signaling in the only way he could. Maybe he'd gotten turned around, separated too long, and this was his way of pulling us back together.

But there was another side, darker. The flames hadn't come long after the radios went dead—too close to shrug off as chance. And there was no explaining a fire out here. Not now. Not with everything soaking wet.

Zombie would never break. Not to them. Not to anyone. If he was still breathing, he was fighting. Which only made the fire worse—because it meant it wasn't him.

That kind of blaze in the dead of night wasn't comfort. It was a signal. Or a trap. Something meant to draw us in. One last pull on the hook.

We didn't know. Couldn't know. But we couldn't ignore it either.

"Careful," Chunk said, adjusting his strap, his

entire frame coiled tight. "We don't go charging in. We slow roll. Eyes wide. Intel first, always."

So we angled toward the glow. Step by step. Boots soft in the leaves, heads low. Every flicker of orange through the fog pulled us closer, every curl of bitter smoke feeding the same thought neither of us wanted to say out loud.

If it was Zombie, he was alive. If it wasn't—then we were walking into a fire set for two.

28

Shadows Of Ourselves

The fire was too far to sting our eyes or choke our lungs, but the smell carried—bitter smoke, thick and chemical, riding in the breeze. Orange pulsed faintly through the fog, not natural.

Chunk slowed us at a ridge, eyes cutting the dark.

"We stash the weight," he said. "Packs'll drag us down. If we need to move quickly, we move lean."

We found a rock face with a lip just deep enough to hide under. Packs slid into the cavity, covered with branches, leaves, and dirt until they blended into the ground. Still, it wasn't enough for Chunk. "If they stumble on this, it's done. Mud 'em up!"

We smeared handfuls of damp earth across the fabric, dulling straps and buckles until they looked less like gear and more like debris. By the time we finished, our hands were black, nails caked, and the smell of wet soil clung to our skin.

Then Chunk looked at me. "Not just the packs. Us."

The reference hit immediately—Predator. Arnold in the jungle, vanishing into mud and shadows. It was the same playbook now. We stripped branches, crushed leaves, ground mud into fabric until the lighter tones of our jackets dulled to gray-green. Every bit that could catch a stray beam of light had to go.

By the time we finished, we weren't invisible, but we appeared blurred. Shadows of ourselves, harder to spot in the woods that wrapped us tight.

"Better." Chunk muttered.

We started toward the glow, slow and careful, every step measured, every branch bent instead of snapped. The fire's light flared brighter, licking against the fog. It wasn't wild—it was controlled, or at least contained. Not a forest fire. Not lightning-struck brush.

The closer we got, the clearer it became. Barrels. Metal drums. Some stacked, some toppled, flames clawing out of the mouths. They burned too hot, too clean, like whatever was inside wasn't just wood or trash.

Voices barked through the mist, carrying through the smoke. Shapes moved in and out of the glow—men with hoses, another shaking a fire extinguisher, white spray hissing against orange flame.

Then the radio came alive.

"They torched some of our barrels—metal ones. Whatever's inside, it's burning hot. Get water on it, get the extinguishers now!"

Another voice cut in, harder, angrier. "Contain it. Now!"

Static chewed the rest into nothing.

I froze. My chest went hollow.

Chunk turned his head just enough for me to see his face in the faint glow. He didn't say a word, didn't have to. The thought hit both of us at once.

We hadn't set it. And if they hadn't set it...

Then who the hell did?

29

Ƶ

We stayed buried in the brush, bellies damp, faces streaked with mud, watching the chaos below in broken flashes. We crawled closer, inch by inch. Stopping to see what we could without risking getting seen. No steady light—just the shake of headlamps slashing through smoke and fog. A beam raked across metal, then whipped away—another jittered over a pair of hands, a cheek, the edge of a lid. We stitched the scene together like a strobe, one harsh glimpse at a time.

One man wrestled a hose that coughed more air than water, the stream hissing uselessly against a barrel's lip. Another shook a different fire extinguisher, cursed, pulled the pin, and got a sad sputter of white before the nozzle choked dry.

"Lids! Get the damn lids!" someone shouted.

A figure sprinted to a shed, yanked two circular tops out of the dark, and came back swinging. His headlamp swung wildly as he slammed the first lid down.

Crooked, loose—but enough to choke the flame, smoke bleeding in gray ropes from the edges.

He went for the second and got sloppy. Heat licked

his arm. He yelped, jerked back, dropped the lid. It clanged off the rim, bounced once, and skittered into the mud.

"Son of a—"

He snatched it with a rag and jammed it down hard. This one sat better. The barrel coughed, then sulked, fire pinched to a smolder.

One left. The hose hissed. Foam fizzed. Men cursed. The white beams shook with every muttered argument, every shove, every near miss. The final flame didn't extinguish due to competence—instead, it died because it ran out of fuel. Black smoke still poured up, a dirty tether tying the ground to the night.

The radio cracked.

"Status," a firm voice said. No greeting. No soft edges. Just the word, flat and hammer-hard.

One man keyed up too fast. "Deke, two capped, one out."

The reply snapped back like a whip. "Stop using my name! You slip again, I'll put you in the ground myself. Copy?"

A pause. Then the voice again, smaller: "Copy."

Whoever Deke was, his voice cut through the static—hard, cold, absolute. "If this problem is not fully resolved by morning, it's your asses on the line. You'll be in the hole with them. Square it up. Now."

The radio went dead, leaving only the crackle of the fire below.

Then it came again—not from the radio this time, but from the clearing.

Headlamps jerked, boots scrambled. The loose chatter that had filled the air seconds before vanished.

Even in the haze, it was obvious. The way they

moved, the way they listened.

Deke wasn't just another man in the woods.

Deke was in charge.

The air shifted with that truth—heavier, tighter.

Every order he barked snapped the others into motion like a well-worn drill. This wasn't chaos anymore—it was a system, rehearsed and dangerous.

My eyes locked onto the barrels whenever the headlamps cut across them. Soot and scratches, dents and drip lines—noise. Then one beam steadied long enough to catch something else.

At first, it looked like random scuffs. Then the lines became a letter. A "Z." Big. Cut quickly with a knife. A hard slash through the middle, the same way Zombie always drew it.

"Chunk," I whispered, stabbing the air. "There. Look."

He spotted it on the second sweep—brief as a spark, then gone. Something flickered across his face. "Jesus."

Zombie.

Not painted. Not burned. Scratched. Fast, on purpose. A message only someone looking would see.

The men below kept at it, but their voices carried sharp, nervous edges.

"Smoke's a goddamn beacon."

"Bossman ain't happy, he's pissed."

"Shut your mouth."

Deke's voice snapped back on the line, harder and flatter than before. "Smoke showing up on my end. I'm on the way." Beneath his words came a low mechanical rumble—an ATV coming up through the static—and it made the message worse than the words alone.

"If I roll up and see slack, you're done," he growled, no patience left in the syllables.

Chunk kept the radio clamped to his palm, the set buzzing faintly against his skin as the engine thumped through the feed. The sound under Deke's voice was a promise: he could see it, he was coming, and he was not happy.

The headlamps dipped lower, beams chasing mud, dragging tarps, hiding footprints. One lamp steadied too long on another barrel with the scratched "Z." The man froze, staring like he was trying to make sense of it.

"Hold up," he said, voice low. "I think—"

The radio hissed over him. Somewhere beyond the ridge, an engine coughed. A stick snapped under a boot.

We went flat, hearts pounding, every muscle wired.

In another breath we'd know: Deke in the open, Zombie in the dark, or a noose tightening from both sides.

The forest was dark and endless. Zombie might've been twenty yards away or twenty miles.

My chest tightened around his name.

Zombie didn't carve things unless he had to. He wasn't theatrical. He wasn't careless. If he cut that mark, it meant time was short, light was bad, and whatever he'd seen or learned mattered enough to risk leaving himself behind. It meant he wanted us to know he'd been here—and that something here belonged to him now.

A mark like that wasn't just a breadcrumb.

It was a flag.

It said I was here.

It said I'm still moving, come find me.

Hope told me he was right there in the fog. Reality asked the harder question: how do we find him without signing our own death warrants?

30

Promise of Someone Worse

Chunk cupped his hands and whistled—two quick bursts, sharp and clean, the signal we'd always used when separated in the woods.

We waited.

Nothing.

A couple of minutes dragged by, the silence heavier with every second.

He tried again. Same pattern. Still nothing.

We crouched close, whispering through options.

Do we fall back to the bags and hope Zombie shows? Push deeper and risk bumping into Deke's boys? Stay put until morning? Nothing felt safe.

Then, faint as smoke, it came. Two short whistles in reply.

We froze.

Two minutes later, it came again. Louder now. The same pattern.

Chunk answered fast, blasting our call into the dark.

The response came back crisp, closer this time.

Then came footsteps. Slow. Careful. Deliberate.

Crunching through needles and snapping the smallest twigs. Not hurried, not clumsy. Someone who knew how to move quietly.

Both pistols came up, muzzles fixed on the dark. I slid my left hand onto Chunk's right shoulder—the way he'd drilled me earlier in the day. Shoulder contact kept us aligned, no risk of me swinging across his lane. He shifted forward, slow and controlled, and I matched him.

We dropped lower, keeping tight. My heartbeat thundered in my ears, but my breathing stayed steady—slow in, slow out. Chunk's weight shifted with each step, a silent signal I mirrored.

A shadow moved between the trees, blurred and wrong. For a moment I was certain it was Deke. Or one of his hillbilly scouts easing in for a closer look.

The footsteps drew closer, steady as a metronome.

Then he appeared.

Zombie stepped out from behind a pine, face streaked with dirt, eyes wired open. Relief surged through me so fast I almost sagged. Instead, I squeezed Chunk's shoulder once—the signal for all clear—before lowering my pistol.

Chunk surged forward first, clapping Zombie hard on the shoulder, muttering half relief, half curse. Zombie gave the faintest smile, but his eyes never stopped scanning the trees.

We didn't waste time. The three of us moved in file, spacing tight but disciplined, back toward the rock.

Zombie's pack was dead weight—he shrugged it off as soon as we hit the hollow, and we dropped it with the others.

Only then, in whispers thin as wind, did he start.

"Not what we thought," he said. "Bigger. Organized. Smelled it before I saw it. Not one... more."

His eyes darted between us, making sure we understood without him saying too much.

"Concrete. Vents. Power lines." A pause. "Not just a hillbilly operation."

That was all he gave before the night shifted again.

A low growl cut through the trees, faint at first, then building. Tires on dirt. Engine whining high.

Deke.

It was still distant, but closing fast—chewing up ground like a predator on the hunt. The sound bounced off the ridges, impossible to pin down, first left, then right, then directly ahead.

We crouched low, hands locked on our pistols, eyes cutting through the black timber. Headlamps flashed between trunks, white beams carving erratic streaks through the pines. Then came the roar—closer, sharper—as the machine broke into a sprint. Branches snapped. Headlights flared. The ATV wasn't just passing through. It was coming straight for us.

Before we could move, the radio in Chunk's hand crackled again. Deke's voice—still sharp, still pissed, but now carrying something else underneath. Nerves.

"Look," he said, "I'm gonna have to call the sheriff. Give him a heads-up before this turns into a bigger mess. He ain't gonna like it."

That line hit like a punch to the ribs. Not the promise of help—just the promise of someone worse.

"We're tightening the perimeter now," Deke went on. "When he gets the call, he'll expect it handled."

Chunk didn't say a word.

He didn't have to.

The look he shot me said everything—handled meant eliminated.

The engine's roar swelled again, drowning the rest of the night. Any stray hope we'd had withered and died right there.

The sheriff wasn't coming to save us.

He was the one they feared disappointing.

And once Deke made that call—the sheriff would be awake.

He'd be coming.

31

Ridge Ain't Quiet—Sheriff

The phone's buzz yanked the sheriff out of sleep like a
bucket of ice water. Middle of the night—the kind of
hour where nothing good ever called. He lay there for
half a breath, staring at the ceiling fan, hoping it would
stop. It didn't.

The name on the screen made his stomach knot.
Deke.

He thumbed the phone alive before it could wake
his wife. Deke's voice came raw and ragged, like he'd
been chewing gravel.

"We got movement. Ridge ain't quiet anymore."

Then the line went dead.

The sheriff sat on the edge of the bed, hands over
his face. This was the deal, wasn't it? Years ago, back
when he thought earning that badge would scrape the
rust off his family name. Back when running for sheriff
felt like a way to make something clean out of
something broken.

Then Deke walked into his office.

Not a delegation. Not some shadowy crew from
down south. Just Deke—boots muddy, knuckles raw,
confidence thick as diesel fumes. He had closed the
door behind him and laid it out plain.

"You want to win this election? I'll make it happen. Signs. Ads. Donations. Votes. All of it. You just keep your patrols away from my ridge."

The sheriff hadn't said yes. He hadn't said no.

Turned out he didn't need to. Silence had been close enough to a signature for Deke.

And when the election dust settled, the badge was his—because Deke had handed it to him. He told himself he could balance it. Keep the town safe on the surface while Deke and his boys treated that ridge like a kingdom. As long as things stayed quiet—as long as nothing spilled into town—he could pretend the deal hadn't carved a piece out of him.

But nights like this—nights when outsiders poked the wrong nest and Deke's call dragged him out of bed—this was the bill coming due.

They'd told him earlier there were three hikers stirring things up out there. Not tourists. Not locals. Just unlucky enough to walk straight into something they shouldn't have. He figured Deke would already have them scared back to the trailhead. He always did. Quiet. Clean.

But tonight?

Deke's voice hadn't been the one he knew. There had been an edge under it—tight, thin, the kind a man gets when he's losing control and knows it.

Something was wrong on that ridge.

And if Deke couldn't fix it—he expected the sheriff to.

The sheriff pulled on the same uniform he'd worn yesterday, the one that had stopped representing "law" the moment he shook Deke's hand. His duty belt felt heavier when he buckled it. The pistol on his hip felt less like a weapon and more like a reminder.

The drive out was silent—just the county truck humming and thunder muttering somewhere far off. By the time he rolled the ATV from the shed and kicked it to life, his jaw ached from clenching.

He didn't want to go up there.

He didn't want the ridge.

But Deke didn't care what the sheriff wanted.

The engine snarled to life and carried him up the slope. With every yard deeper into the trees, he felt like he was sinking, in more ways than one.

32

Skin in the Game

The ATV roared closer, chewing up ground. Headlamps flickered between the trees, beams slashing the dark until they locked onto a patch of clearing ahead. The engine whined high, then braked hard, spraying dirt and rocks.

The rider swung into view. Heavyset. White. Uniform shirt stretched tight across his gut. Must be the sheriff.

He slid off the machine with a grunt, one hand on the seat, the other gripping a steel flashlight nearly as long as his forearm. When he thumbed it on, the beam cut through the timber like a blade, white and blinding.

"Deke!" he barked, his voice booming against the ridge. "Where the hell are you?"

Footsteps hurried out of the dark. Deke appeared, his shadow jumping in the flood of light. Even from where we crouched, his posture gave him away— shoulders hunched, arms moving sharply. Defensive.

"Bout time you showed," Deke muttered, trying to mask it as a jab but carrying just enough edge to test.

The sheriff stood taller, anger rolling off his dominating presence. "You think I enjoy getting dragged out here in the middle of the night? My job is keeping the county clean. Your job is keeping this ridge quiet. You screwed your half, and now I'm standing in the mud cleaning up."

Deke squared his shoulders, voice low but hard.

"My half? Sheriff, your whole seat's built on this ridge. Don't pretend you're cleaner than I am."

The sheriff jabbed a finger into Deke's chest, light jerking with the motion. "Don't you ever forget who signs the warrants in this county. Who makes sure state troopers never drive this road? You and your boys act like moonshine cartel cowboys, but if the Feds step foot here, you'll be in shackles before the sun's up. You need me."

For a moment, the two men stood locked, silence like a wire stretched between them. Then the sheriff's voice dropped almost too low to carry. "...rotate crews by sunrise... same as always... keep the trailheads clear..."

The sheriff's head twitched. He spun around, mounted the ATV, and kicked it back to life. The headlamps swung wide once, then the machine tore off the way it had come, its growl fading into the ridges.

We stayed frozen until the last echo was gone.

Then we slipped back through the brush, moving fast and low, not speaking until the rock hollow rose in front of us.

Only then did Zombie finally open up.

"Three cook labs. Three grow houses. Three bunkhouses. Two general purpose buildings. A storage shed stacked with pallets. All tied to the ridge. Orientation's clean. It's mapped like a grid. Whoever built this planned it with intent—irrigation, power lines, venting. Professional. Not backwoods."

He crouched in the dirt, dragging lines and boxes with his finger. "I could see enough because they were sloppy. Red headlamps bobbed around, and lazy patrols barely looked up, but they were armed. Lights bleed out of every structure—glows through walls, bare bulbs strung outside. The grows lit the treetops, the labs pulsed with their fans. They weren't trying to hide. Out here in the middle of nowhere, they don't think anyone's watching."

Zombie leaned back, voice steady. "Compared to overseas, this was simple. Basic. I've mapped villages under blackout conditions with nothing but shadows to go by. This was lit up like a Christmas tree. The layout's clean enough—staggered buildings along the ridge, cover where they needed it, vents and power lines placed with purpose. Easy to read. Too easy. The system's sharp, but the people running it aren't."

Listening to him, I realized I'd always known Zombie was a Marine, but I never thought it would matter on one of our hikes. Now, hearing the specifics he carried in his head—spacing, orientation, blind spots—it hit me how much of that training was still alive in him.

That's when I remembered the small trail notebook buried in my pack. Waterproofed in a Ziploc, usually just scraps of gear notes or ideas for future trips. Nothing important—until now. If it had stayed dry, it could be more than scribbles. It could be a map.

I leaned close and whispered, "Once we're back at the packs, I'll check my notebook. If it's good, You can jot this stuff down."

Zombie gave the faintest nod, eyes still on the dirt

sketch.

Chunk spat into the dirt. "Systems break. Somebody screws up. That's our chance—if we're alive to see it."

His eyes cut to me. "Adrenaline's about to burn off. Calories are gone."

"The bunkhouses are close," Zombie said quietly. "If that's where they stay, then there's a way in and a way out. They wouldn't haul gear through the woods every time."

No one argued. It wasn't about what we wanted anymore—it was survival. And survival meant pushing closer to the center, not backing away. If there was a trail leading out from where they lived, we could find it too.

We'd done plenty of great trips before. The kind where the worst thing waiting was bad weather or bad knees. A few years back we'd hiked Pikes Peak, our first 14'er together. That trip felt big at the time—hard climbs, long miles, something to brag about afterward.

This wasn't that kind of trip. This was supposed to be easy. No satellite beacons. No backup plan. Just a few guys with packs, boots, and too much faith that we could handle whatever came our way. And now, that decision felt like it might bury us.

We all had skin in the game. Chunk and I had kids waiting at home. Zombie was barely a year into his marriage. Different lives, same weight pressing down. The question chewing at all of us was the same: if we made it out, would this be the last time?

The big hikes—the bucket list stuff—those came with pictures, group texts, check-ins every night. These smaller ones? They were built on trust. Dates, vague details, no real trail of breadcrumbs. That trust would only stretch so far back home.

With the last cell bars gone long before the trailhead, no one was coming for us. No text to send. No GPS ping to trace. If the truck was still waiting up top, it would tell anyone looking that we were somewhere out here. If it wasn't—then someone else had already moved the pieces of this game.

Either way, there was no cavalry. No search party. No easy way out.

It was us, and us alone.

33

Now We Move

The forest was black, heavy, and endless. The kind of night that pressed on your eyes and made every step feel blind.

Before we pushed closer to the bunkhouses, we slipped back to the hollow and dug out our packs.

Mine was a mess. I'd stuffed it in a hurry, gear crammed at odd angles, nothing where it should've been. To find the notebook, I had to dump everything—tent, spare clothes, stove, odds and ends—all of it sliding into a heap on the pine needles. Even that small rustle felt too loud, like the gear was relaying our coordinates.

Finally, I found it—a Ziploc tucked deeper than I remembered. Inside, the little trail notebook, corners damp but still good, and a short pencil like the kind you'd use to keep score at a golf course. Usable.

I shook out the last scraps from the pack, and that's when I heard the crinkle. Buried at the bottom was a half-forgotten pack of beef jerky. Relief hit me hard, a sudden jolt like I'd struck gold.

We split it three ways, chewing slowly, trying to trick our bodies into thinking it was more than it was. Salty, tough, barely a mouthful—but it steadied us.

Reminded us we weren't completely empty.

Water was worse. Bottles light. Just a few swallows left. Refilling wasn't optional. It was survival. But it meant noise, movement, exposure.

Zombie clicked on his red light, the narrow beam spilling just enough to work. He pulled the Ziploc open, set the notebook across his knee, and with that short golf pencil began sketching the ridge, the buildings, the way the system sprawled across the terrain. Watching him, I thought again about how much of his Marine training lived under the surface. To him, this wasn't wilderness anymore. It was a map. And he was already dismantling it in his head.

When he was done, he clicked off the light, slid the notebook and pencil back into the bag, sealed it tight, and whispered: "Now we move."

We packed fast, straps biting tight, and set off in a wide arc. Zombie took the lead—not Chunk. Nobody said a word. When Zombie moved like that, you didn't ask why. You just followed. He trusted his instincts. We trusted him. Straight lines got you killed. Arcs showed you the edges without stepping into the middle.

Ten minutes in, the brush thinned and Zombie froze, hand up. At first I thought patrol, but then I saw it—a black hose snaking through the needles, thick as my wrist, dew glistening on its surface. It cut across the path and vanished deeper into the trees, faintly hissing where water leaked at a coupling.

Relief surged. I dropped to one knee, pulled my fill bag from my pocket, and started fishing for my filter. Before I could uncap it, Chunk's hand closed on my wrist. His shake of the head was sharp.

"Not here," he whispered. "Filters knock out

bacteria, protozoa—the normal stuff in the woods. They don't filter chemicals. We don't know what's running through that line. Could kill us faster than any hillbilly out here."

The weight of it sank fast. He was right. Whatever flowed through that hose might carry pesticides, fertilizer, solvents. Things a filter couldn't touch.

I put the fill bag back and we pushed deeper, keeping the arc, widening our circle to steer clear of the hose lines. Another ten minutes, we found what we needed—a narrow stream cutting across the ridge. Cold, moving quick, out of sight of pumps and hoses. We dropped to our knees and filled in silence, drinking just enough to take the edge off before topping bottles.

Relief came quietly. Not full, not safe—but better than empty.

Zombie stayed on point, eyes cutting through the dark. I kept in the middle. Chunk guarded the rear, head always on a swivel. The formation was simple, but it worked.

We kept circling, tightening the loop toward the faint glow ahead. The bunkhouses. Light bled weakly through the trees. Red headlamps bobbed in the distance, lazy, drifting, rifles slung low.

That was close enough for me.

Zombie breathed it out first, barely a whisper. "Within range, just not in reach."

Chunk's voice stayed low, all gravel and edge. "Pick the wrong cover, and we're done before we even figure out what's happening."

The glow from the bunkhouses shined through the trees in slow, flickering pulses, each one whispering for us to stay back. We moved low and careful, searching for a pocket of shadow that gave us a clean line of sight without putting us in theirs.

The night settled around me. The bugs fell quiet. The wind dropped out, as if it didn't dare speak.

And through that dead air, the low, grinding rumble rolled in—distant but too familiar. The ATV. Again. Like it was circling, waiting for us to make a wrong move.

34

Ten Years of Quiet

The rumble of the engine drifted down slope, angling straight toward the bunkhouses.

Chunk leaned in close, his voice barely above the wind. "We need to move up. Sitting here ain't gonna tell us shit."

Zombie squinted toward the glow ahead. "Not just see what they're doing," he muttered. "We need to hear what they say. Numbers. Who's out there."

He wasn't wrong. The main objective hadn't changed—find the road and get the hell out. But it was too damn dark to see where the ATV had come in from. Too many folds in the terrain, too many blind angles.

"Closer," I whispered, "but not too close. We wait for a clean window, then we figure out where that road cuts through."

Chunk let out a slow breath. "Let's find that damn road… and get the fuck outta here."

We shoved our packs under a thick snarl of brush. The fabric was already streaked with mud and forest muck, disappearing into the shadows without a trace. Then we dropped flat, pressing into the cold ground as we crawled forward. Wet leaves clung to our sleeves. The light flickered in the woods, rhythmic and alive.

The ATV rolled into view, its headlight slicing through the mist. Deke. No sheriff this time. He killed the engine and swung off fast—not cocky, not casual. A man moving like he knew the clock was ticking. A man trying to save his own skin.

Deke's voice rolled up the ridge, rough and sharp, carving through the black like a blade. "Wake the fuck up, all of you!"

That's when we saw the movement.

The yard outside the bunkhouses filled fast, boots on gravel, voices bleeding over each other in nervous bursts. Some men carried rifles. Most of them still looked half asleep, shirts inside out, one dragging a cigarette like he'd woken up in the middle of a dream. They weren't soldiers, not even close—just bodies Deke had shaped into something resembling order.

"Out of the bunkhouses, now!" Deke barked again, and the muttering died. He let the silence stretch until every eye was on him.

"Reed's dead!" He let the name hang there. "That's blood on this ridge, and it didn't come from a bear. Three men did that. Outsiders. They're not tourists, and they're not lost. They knew where to go. They found the original bunkhouse as if they had a map in their pocket. I should've killed them in their tents."

A kid in the back shouted, "So let's go take 'em, Deke!" A few others grumbled in agreement.

Deke spat in the dirt. "You don't get it. This ain't about flexin' or chasing deer through the woods. This is about ten years of quiet. For ten years this ridge has kept us fed with money in our pockets. Before that? I was one more ghost drifting these woods, sleeping under deadfall and talking to the dark like it was an old friend. This ridge gave me purpose. Order. A place to bury the things I couldn't leave overseas. You break that quiet, you break everything. Sheriff don't cover noise. He covers silence. That's the deal."

He scanned the circle of half-awake men, eyes sharp.

"If this gets loud, we are all fucked. You want deputies sniffing up here? The sheriff cannot keep his men from doing their jobs. His job is to keep them from coming here. You want news cameras on my lawn? Then keep stumbling around like drunks. Otherwise, you listen."

Deke paced slowly in front of them.

"Orders are simple. Patrols doubled. Radios hot at all times. North ridge, east slope, creek crossing—eyes everywhere. If they head back, you get 'em before they reach 202. But if they come forward again, if they step too close to what's ours." His voice dropped until they all leaned in. "Then they don't walk out. We put them in those barrels."

The silence that followed wasn't discipline. It was fear. That was what he counted on. They weren't trained—most probably couldn't hit a damn thing past thirty yards, and half were more likely to shoot a tree than a man—but numbers and noise could still crush three hungry strangers in the woods. And that was enough.

"Back to posts," Deke said.

One of the older men gave a stiff nod. "You got it, Boss."

"Sheriff wants quiet. I want quiet. You give me that, and we keep this ridge another ten years. You don't, and Reed's just the first body." His gaze swept their uneasy faces. "And these men might not be just lost hikers. They're too stealthy."

They broke apart, muttering, boots kicking gravel as they scattered back into the bunkhouses to get dressed and gear up. Ill-trained, sloppy, probably drunk most days—but they were his. And for now, that had to be enough.

We waited for them to all pile out of the bunkhouses and go in separate directions. Most headed north and east, while a few headed in other directions. We counted five ATV's heading out across the ridge. You could almost tell the ones that were still tired and drunk, slightly stumbling as they wandered off.

The forest went still after the ATV noise bled out down the ridge. Just the kind of quiet that makes you second guess. That's when Chunk spotted them.

Two ATV's parked in front of the bunkhouses, the only ones not taken out with the patrols.

He leaned in close. "If one of those has a key in it, we're gone," he whispered. "No wandering. No guessing. Just straight off this damn ridge."

Zombie nodded. "Worth a look."

Chunk didn't wait for a vote. He moved low across the ground, keeping to the shadows until he was crouched beside the first ATV. We watched him run his hands along the ignition, the frame, the little compartment under the seat.

He looked back at us and shook his head.

Nothing.

Zombie motioned to the second ATV, but Chunk had already checked—another quick search, another shake of the head.

No keys on either.

He jogged back to us, breathing hard but quiet.

"They definitely didn't take all the spare keys with them," he whispered. "Nobody does. They'd keep a set close. Inside."

Zombie stared at the dark outline of the bunkhouse.

"That's the only place they'd be."

I felt the weight of it settle. We weren't going in for supplies, or maps, or anything extra. Just one thing— the keys that should've been in those ignitions.

Without them, we were slow, exposed, and guessing our way down a mountain full of armed men.

Chunk wiped his hands on his pants, nerves disguised as impatience.

"Thirty seconds. I crack the door, look for a pegboard, a hook, a damn drawer. If they're not right inside, I bail. But if they are..."

He didn't have to finish.

A working ATV meant the difference between running blind in the dark—and escaping before the next patrol looped back.

"Regroup?" Chunk asked.

"Back here," Zombie said, tapping the dirt with a finger. "No detours. You hear something, you run."

Chunk gave a single nod, then dropped to one knee beside his pack. He didn't bother picking through it— just stripped it off and let it fall. The less he carried, the faster he could move. The quieter, too.

The pack slumped against the dirt, a dead weight he couldn't afford to drag with him. If he came back, it'd be waiting—and hopefully he'd bring the keys that meant we wouldn't have to spend another night out here.

If he didn't make it, the pack would sit right here,

silent and useless, like a gravestone without a name.

He stood, pistol in hand and started the trek towards danger. His figure blurred against the ridge, just another shadow among many, trekking down toward the bunkhouses.

We stayed frozen, watching him go. For a moment, the timing felt perfect—Deke pulling every man all over the ridges and trails, the bunkhouses open, the window wide.

Out of nowhere, a red headlamp flickered to life in the dark—moving back toward the bunkhouses. My gut tightened. We were banking on Chunk seeing it too and fading into the trees, but his shadow was still cutting across the ground.

One man had peeled off from the rest, circling back. Not sprinting, but with purpose. And he was heading straight for the same bunkhouse Chunk was moving toward.

He was too far away to warn.

The red light kept drifting closer, steady and patient, while Chunk kept moving straight into its path—silent, unaware.

Then I lost Chunk slowly through the darkness.

It was on Chunk.

And just like that, the timing didn't seem perfect anymore.

35

Have to Fire—Chunk

Chunk hugged the wall, pistol low, breath steady. The door sagged on its hinges, and when the wind pushed it open another inch, he slipped inside.

The air hit stale and heavy—sweat, dirt, cigarette smoke. Eight bunks lined the walls, mattresses sagging, blankets twisted. Shirts strung over bedposts, socks stiff with filth, cans kicked into corners. It was a crash pad, not a barracks. Men lived here, but not cleanly, not disciplined.

Four bulbs hung bare from the rafters, buzzing faintly, casting enough light to show the mess. This bunkhouse was similar to the one he'd stumbled on earlier—the discovery that had set everything in motion—but nowhere near as tidy. A table in the back overflowed with cigarette butts and a half-empty bottle of whiskey. Boots lay abandoned in the aisle. Cards sat scattered mid-game. He was not sure what was worse, the mess or the smell.

Chunk moved quickly, pistol sweeping each corner. That's when boots crunched outside. The hinges groaned, the door creaking open wider.

He dove behind the third bunk, landing light, heart hammering against his ribs. If the man stopped short of this bunk, he'd be safe. But if he stepped past the second bunk, Chunk would have to fire. There'd be no other choice. And one shot would blow the night open—flashlights flaring, boots pounding through the trees, fifteen armed men turning the woods into a grinder. Radios barking, muzzles flashing, and the three of them dead before the echo faded.

Three against a dozen wasn't a fight. It was a fast, ugly end.

The man shuffled in, boots dragging. He passed the first bunk, then the second. Chunk's finger brushed the trigger. Then the man cut right, reaching for something stacked on a pile of upside-down milk crates. A jacket, a radio—cigarettes, maybe. Then he turned and walked back out.

Silence collapsed around him. Chunk let out a slow, shaky breath and rose.

Time was short. He worked quickly.

Chunk scanned the walls first—looking for a pegboard, a hook, a nail, anything that might hold a set of keys. Nothing. Just blank plywood and shadow.

He moved on, eyes cutting across the room with sharp, practiced sweeps. Makeshift tables, cluttered nightstands, gear piles—his hands hovered just above them, shifting only what he had to, checking for the unmistakable jingle or glint of metal.

Every second felt loud, even though he barely made a sound.

But no keys. Not yet.

Under the third bunk he spotted a duffel with two fully loaded mags. He thumbed the rounds and knew immediately—they fit the rifle he'd taken off Zombie's kill and put one in each back pocket. The one Zombie had earned with a round through a man's chest.

But on the table with the whiskey and cigarettes, half hidden, he found a folded piece of paper pinned down by the bottle. Not random scribbles—a map. No time to study it. He snatched it, folded it once, and shoved it into his pocket.

Before heading out, he lifted the whiskey bottle, took a long pull, and set it back down. Screw it. He'd earned that. On the way out, a Zippo sat on a makeshift table. He flicked it open, thumbed the spark wheel, and fire jumped to life. He pocketed it with the map.

Chunk eased toward the door. Stilled. Listened. Nothing.

He slipped out sideways, hugging the siding until he hit the blind edge.

Then he moved. Quick. Quiet. Up the slope through the trees.

Halfway up the ridge, his boot slipped, rocks skittering down the slope. His chest locked tight. Had they heard? He froze, listening for shouts, for boots.

Nothing. Just wind.

He pushed on, slower now, careful, until the treeline broke.

U-Haul and Zombie crouched low, waiting. Both locked eyes on him as he dropped beside them, body thudding into the dirt.

For the first time all night, he believed they might actually have a chance.

36

Where We Need to Go

Chunk came out of the trees, sweat on his face. He dropped low beside us, chest rising hard.

"One of them came back into the bunkhouse—alone, half-asleep, just grabbing something before heading back out," Chunk said, voice low but steady. "He got close enough that I thought I was gonna have to put a bullet in him, but he turned off before he reached my bunk. The place was a wreck, and I didn't find any keys, but I did find loaded mags that matched the rifle, a Zippo, and a map. Whatever they're running, they're operating out of that bunkhouse and keeping everything close."

It was strange, but I could swear he had a slight smell of booze on his breath.

He unfolded the map carefully. The corners peeled back with a soft, wet crumble. It wasn't an old military topo or something weird and coded. It was a printed Google satellite map—cheap black-and-white ink, like someone had run it off at a library or a gas station printer. The kind of map a regular person might print before a lazy weekend hike.

What made it strange was the handwriting. Thick pencil. Uneven. Rushed. The kind of notes you scribble for yourself when you know you'll get turned around without them.

The concrete building, which we knew now was a bunkhouse, the first structure we ever stumbled across, sat in the lower left corner of the map. Someone had drawn a shaky rectangle around it and scrawled "BH1" above it in block letters. That was where this situation started with us. Sill thinking to myself, if only Chunk hadn't walk up that ridge to take a leak.

A narrow line led away from that corner, tracing the path we'd unknowingly followed—a dirt service road winding northeast through the trees. The bunkhouse was circled a few inches up the page, like a checkpoint. A crude arrow curved along the trail with the word "RD" scratched in jagged handwriting. Whoever made this wasn't drawing a plan. They were leaving breadcrumbs.

Above the bunkhouse, the river cut through the middle of the map like a black vein. Its shape traced over the printed image, thickening the bends in pencil so it stood out clearly. Two spots along its length were scribbled over so dark the paper was almost torn—the word "NO GO" written beside each. I remembered both places. The sharp bend with the fast current. The steep embankment where the water rose to the tree line. Someone else had learned those lessons too.

"Here," Chunk said, tapping one of the dark X's. "This is the first crossing."

Zombie leaned closer, his breath fogging in the cold. "That matches where we turned back. No doubt."

Across the ridge line above the river, faint contour shadows bled through the print—hills stacked in pale gray bands. Over them, thick pencil lines traced an old logging road that ran north along the spine of the ridge. The hand that drew it wasn't careful. It wavered, doubled back in places, like someone who had walked it and wasn't entirely sure where it ended.

There were X's scattered all around the map. Each one had a number scratched next to it—3, 6, 12, 15. No labels. No key. Just numbers. Some were circled. Others looked like afterthoughts, half rubbed out.

The one nearest the corner—right by the concrete building—was 3. The bunkhouses were 12. Everything beyond that was guesswork.

A faint note just above the last X read, "MTN," followed by a shaky arrow pointing into what looked like open space. But the top of the map had been torn away. Whatever lay beyond was gone.

On the eastern edge, a jagged line traced a ridge trail with a note that said, "FENCE." On the western side, near the river bend, there was a small scribble: "DOGS," underlined twice. A few other markings were too smeared to make out, only the dents of pencil still pressed into the paper.

"This isn't a patrol map," I said. "This is a lost guy's roadmap."

"Or somebody new," Zombie added. "Somebody who needed to know where to turn and where not to."

Chunk's thumb rested on the corner of the paper where the "BH1" label sat. "This matches us. This is where we came in. That bend in the river here—" he tapped the heavy black scribble, "—that's where we had to double back."

"It lines up," Zombie said. "Exactly."

The forest was still soaked and dark, but looking at that map was like someone had drawn lines on fog. We could trace our route without speaking it out loud. We could see where we'd gone and how far we'd pushed. And somewhere beyond that torn edge—past those numbers—was something. A road. A gate. Maybe nothing at all.

But it gave us a bearing.

Chunk folded the map carefully, slower than he did anything else. It went into the inside pocket of his jacket like a fragile piece of luck.

"This doesn't tell us what's out there," Zombie said, his eyes still on the trees. "But at least it tells us where we've been and where we need to go."

The concrete building. The bunkhouse. The river. Possibly an old logging road.

And a torn piece of paper with X's scattered like breadcrumbs leading into the dark.

As they were still looking and discussing the map, thunder rumbled low on the ridge—not rain yet, just the promise of it—and the last thing we needed was another deluge. Still, Zombie and Chunk traded a look that said the same thing: a hard downpour would be a curse and a gift. Cursed us with mud and cold, sure, but it would blind Deke's men, smear flashlights, and turn disciplined sweeps into chaos. If the storm came, it might be the one stupid, messy advantage we could use to vanish.

But storms have a way of changing more than the weather. If it hit, the night wasn't just going to get darker—it was going to shift. And whatever line we'd been walking out here was about to get washed away.

37

Edge Pointed Out

Just then the bottom fell out. Water pounded a short rock overhang we squeezed under, the sound loud enough to chew through thought as we climbed the ridge to figure out where the hell we were. Thunder rattled the trunks, water rolled down the slope in brown sheets that dragged pine needles, branches, even small stones. The earth beneath us softened, slick mud creeping closer to our boots. It felt like the ridge was dissolving under the weight of the sky.

We crouched tighter under the rock face, packs pulled close, rain shells hissing every time one of us shifted. Hunger gnawed at all three of us, sharper now that we couldn't outrun it with movement. My stomach burned, sour and empty, and I could see the same hollow ache in their faces. Though we'd eaten the dehydrated meals not long before, the caloric deficit was still deep. The food took the edge off, but it didn't replace what days of hard movement had already taken from us.

Zombie broke first. His voice was tight, clipped. "A storm this strong will keep men from making rounds, at least making meaningful ones. I think we need to move soon."

Chunk's head snapped toward him. "Move where? Down that slope? In this mess? You'll slip, crack your skull, drown in a runoff before you hit the trail."

"At least moving keeps us ahead!" Zombie shot back, louder than he needed to be. "Sitting here is waiting for them to tighten the net. You know that."

Chunk dipped his head forward, glare hardening. "And you think stumbling blind through mud is better? You want to gamble the rest of our energy on that? You break your leg in this weather, it's over, and not just for you. Us."

The words hit harder than they should have, sharper for the lack of calories. My own chest tightened with the storm, every rumble of thunder matching the rise of their voices.

Zombie squared his shoulders, ready to stand. "You'd rather rot here like a sitting duck? That's not survival, Chunk. That's giving up."

Chunk shoved a hand toward the slope, mud running like veins down its face. "And what you're calling survival? That's panic. That's death faster."

I saw it—saw them both leaning in, saw fists ready, eyes wild. For the first time, it wasn't the forest closing in on us. It was each other. The crack that could break the only thing keeping us alive.

I pushed between them, palms out, forcing space where there wasn't any. "Stop. Listen. This—" I jerked a thumb at the rain, the mud, the endless roar of water—"this is winning if we let it split us. The only way out is together. We fight each other—we don't need Deke. We don't need the sheriff. The forest will eat us alive."

Neither of them moved at first, breath hot against

my shoulders. Then slowly, Zombie eased back, dropping his gaze. Chunk did the same, muttering into the collar of his shell. Cooler heads, but not by much.

Zombie gave a curt nod, almost to himself. "It's the hunger. The tired. Gets in your blood."

Chunk rubbed his face, rain running down his fingers. "Yeah. That's all it is. We keep the edge pointed out, not in."

I let out a breath I didn't know I was holding. The wedge had been there, but it hadn't driven through. Not yet. The storm kept raging, but at least we'd held together—three men still on the same side, even if the cracks were showing.

We'd burned the edge off the fight, but the question remained, heavier than before—what next?

Zombie tugged at his hood, staring through the curtain of water. "We move when it breaks. First chance. Cover like this doesn't come twice."

Chunk shook his head. "Not until the slope drains. Mud's too soft, runoff's too strong. You try to cross a draw right now, you're swept."

I listened, weighing both. The storm gave us a mask, but it also boxed us in. Moving meant risk. Staying meant waiting for them to tighten their grip. Both roads looked bad, and yet one had to carry us out.

Finally, I spoke. "We wait out the worst of it. Let the ridge hold—let the water find its path. Then we move, but carefully. No wasted steps, no noise we don't need. We can't gamble on speed or stillness—we balance both."

They nodded, slow and reluctantly, but it was the agreement all the same. The plan wasn't perfect, but it was ours.

For now, that had to be enough.

38

Silence Stretched Between Us

The storm deepened until it didn't sound like rain anymore—it sounded like the whole ridge was collapsing around us. Water hammered the rock ledge, sheeted off the rock face, and poured downhill in brown rivers. The ground we'd trusted turned to paste, boots would sink just from shifting our weight.

Branches cracked in the storm, trees groaned, and every snap made us flinch.

No one wanted to say it out loud, but we all knew the truth—the forest was dangerous now. One mudslide in the wrong spot and we'd be buried or swept away.

Zombie hunched forward, knees to his chest, hood dripping steady streams onto the mud. "This is cover," he muttered. "No people will see us. No ears hear us. They'd never know we moved."

Chunk glared through the curtain of water. "And where do you plan to go? Everything's slick. Draws are flooding. You try to climb out of here, the slope'll take you down faster than any of Deke's guys."

Their voices carried the same sharpness as before, but lower, almost buried under the storm. I sat between them, the roar pressing so loud it felt like it was inside my skull. Hunger made my chest feel hollow. Fatigue pulled at my eyelids. And for the first time, the thought crept in—maybe the forest was going to kill us before Deke ever had to.

Another crack split the air—louder, sharper. We all froze. Then, through the curtain of rain, a pine tilted, its root ball ripping out of the ground in a spray of mud. It crashed downslope, tearing smaller trees with it, the sound lost in thunder.

We stayed still, hearts pounding, as the earth settled. That tree could've been on top of us if the wind had bent differently.

The shelf felt smaller after that. Nowhere safe. Nowhere steady. Just three men, packs pulled tight, waiting for the storm to decide whether we stayed standing or slid into the valley with the rest of the debris.

Time crawled. Water found every seam, trickling down our sleeves, creeping down our backs, pooling at our boots. My legs burned from crouching, but standing felt impossible—too much chance of slipping, of showing a silhouette if someone still had eyes through the rain.

Chunk shook his head. "Moving blind's worse. We wait it out."

Zombie cursed under his breath, pulling his collar tighter. "We can't sit like this forever. Shelter's turning on us."

Their words felt heavier than the storm. Every option costs something—time, strength, safety. I felt the wedge of their earlier argument still sitting between us, and all I could do was grip my pack straps and hope the storm broke before we did.

Zombie pulled his phone out. The screen cast a pale glow against the rain and mist. The screen flickered, the blue dot that marked us jittering across ridges we weren't on. "It's trash," he said. "Storm's bouncing the signal, canopy too thick. Can't trust it."

Chunk didn't even reach for the map. It stayed buried deep in his pack—our one real shot at finding a way out. He wasn't about to risk it getting soaked and turning to mush.

He brought the screen between us, zooming and swiping with his finger. The lines lagged, then jumped, as if the trail was moving. He shook his head. "Might as well be guessing. Shows us where we aren't more than where we are."

I waited, then pulled mine out anyway, a little past one. Part habit. Part hope. I don't know. The screen lit, nothing but a slab of green with a few blue veins running through it—water, rivers, creeks. All swollen now, all changing faster than the map could keep up.

I clicked it dark and shoved it back into my pocket. Better to save the battery for the time.

Lightning lit the valley in a blinding flash. For a split second, I saw it all—the swollen creek raging below, mud pouring into its banks, trees whipping in the wind, close to breaking. Then darkness slammed back down. The image burned into my eyes, worse than not seeing at all.

For a fleeting instant, it sounded like the thunder was carrying something underneath it. A motor? A voice? My stomach knotted, but the storm swallowed it before I could be sure. Maybe it was just my mind twisting the noise. Maybe not.

Silence stretched between us, filled only by the

storm. I wanted to say something to break it, to remind them we were still a team, but the words stayed locked behind my teeth. All I could think about was the map and Zombie's intel. If it didn't lead us out, then we were just waiting here to die—whether by flood, hunger, or men.

The storm bore down, but under it a thought formed—when it eased, we'd have to move. And when we moved, we'd need a plan—not guesses, not debate. Something sharp, deliberate, a path worth the risk.

39

Pushed Downhill

Zombie broke the silence. "Now's the time. Storm this heavy, any trail eyes are blind."

Chunk shook his head. "Or they're not."

"They can't see through walls of rain," Zombie pressed. His tone had an edge—maybe conviction, maybe desperation. "Noise discipline's gone, anyway. If we're going to check for the road out, it's now."

They both looked to me. My gut twisted, but the decision was already made. Sitting still wasn't safety—it was slow drowning. I nodded once. "We move. Storm's our cover. Let's see if we can get down that ridge."

The mountain wasn't a rumor anymore, we could feel it on our backs. It had been sitting on our phones since yesterday, a wall drawn in contour lines stacked tight together. North was sealed—east and west funneled us back toward the trail and the rivers. If those ridge lines really were accurate, we were boxed in. We had to see it with our own eyes.

Chunk and Zombie pulled their phones, shielding the screens with wet hands. The storm made the blue dots jump, bouncing half a mile off and then back again, but the ridge lines held steady. Steep. Sheer.

Impassable unless the map was lying. A mile south, though, the lines bent wider, hinting at a break— maybe a shoulder, maybe just false hope. We wouldn't know unless we checked.

We agreed first to verify the wall. Then, if it held, gamble on the south. Either way, sitting still wasn't an option.

We pushed downhill.

The slope had turned to muck, boots sinking, pulling at every step. Runoff carved thin channels across the hillside, ankle-deep torrents that shifted and grew while we watched. Each was a new crossing, a new stumble.

Zombie led, planting his trekking poles carefully into the mud-slick slope. Every step made a wet, sucking sound as the rain chewed at the ground beneath us. One jab hit soft, the pole sinking instead of biting. His arm snapped sideways to catch balance, the pole joint cracked, and in a blink he was down.

A grunt, a sharp thud, then the sound of him sliding—boots scraping, poles clattering, mud tearing loose as he went five feet downslope. Halfway down, his right foot jammed against a buried root, twisting hard inward. There was a sickening crunch of leather and joint, followed by a strangled yell as his ankle folded beneath him. His knee buckled, his hip slammed sideways, and he started to tumble—but his left hand shot out, snagging a slick root that bowed but held.

For a second he hung there, twisted and straining, mud streaking down the slope beneath him. The pain showed plain on his face—teeth bared, eyes wide but focused.

"Got you!" Chunk barked, and we lunged forward,

locking onto the straps of his pack. The slope fought us the whole way—slick mud, sliding boots, shoulders on fire—but inch by inch we wrestled him back onto solid ground.

When we finally got him upright, he stayed bent over, both hands gripping his knee, trying to steady his breath. Mud streaked his entire left side. His right boot, caked thick with wet clay, hovered just above the ground, toes barely touching—the way someone does when every ounce of weight feels like a knife.

He gave it the slightest shift, just enough to see if it would hold. The ankle trembled, wobbled once, then steadied. His breath hissed through clenched teeth. "Not broken," he muttered, his expression barely shifting. "Just rolled."

Not broken didn't mean fine. Every step after would be slower, heavier, more dangerous.

To make things worse, the storm didn't seem to be letting up anytime soon. Soil gave way under us in sheets, small slides pulling rocks and branches downslope. Each one sounded like pursuit, like boots breaking cover. And above it all, the wind howled, releasing a widowmaker from the canopy. The branch came down like a club, snapping against the ground ten or so yards off. We dropped flat, hearts pounding, waiting for shouts that never came.

When we rose, packs were heavier from the water, straps biting into our shoulders. The mud sucked at our boots with every step, thick and cold. I was afraid I would lift my feet and my boots would come off in the mud.

That's when Zombie noticed that the fall cracked one of his trekking poles.

Chunk didn't say a word. He planted his own trekking poles in the dirt, then unlocked the shafts and shortened them down to fit Zombie's height. When he held them out, it wasn't dramatic—just simple, trail born practicality.

"Take 'em," he said quietly.

Zombie hesitated, then nodded and took them, gripping the handles like a man who knew how much they mattered. He handed his one intact pole to Chunk, with a look of defeat on his face.

Chunk collapsed the sections down fast, twisting until they clicked. I slid it along the outside of his pack and fed it through a gear strap, cinching it tight so it wouldn't rattle or catch brush.

I stepped up, took the broken pole from Zombie, and crouched near a downed log a few feet off the trail. A quick scan, then I slid the fractured sections under a mix of wet leaves, branches, and moss—buried just deep enough to disappear. No shine, no trace.

The swap didn't change the terrain, didn't make the mud any less cruel. But it shifted the balance just enough to keep us moving. Out here, that was everything.

40

Herded

There was no moving silently. Our boots sank with every footfall, squelching, ripping free. We couldn't silence the noise. We couldn't erase the tracks. The storm might have blurred us from searching eyes, but it left a trail behind us as loud as any shout.

Finally, the trees thinned, mist curling in heavy sheets. Through it, we saw another mountain. Sheer, black, slick as glass with the downpour. Even from this distance, we knew—no handholds, no ledges, no rope long enough even if we'd had one. With real gear, maybe. But with what we carried, it was a wall.

We ducked into a shallow clearing, rain pounding straight down, no canopy to soften it. Phones came back out, screens smeared with water. The storm made them lag and shiver, dots dancing, but the contour lines still showed the dip—a mile south, a break between the mountains.

Chunk frowned. "Could be nothing. A topo line looks wide on the screen, but out here it could still be vertical."

Zombie shifted his weight off the swollen ankle, voice low but sharp. "It's the only sign we've seen that the ridge breaks. If there's even a chance, we need to try."

I stared at their maps—the storm distorted it like everything else. "If it's a real gap, we could slide out without ever having to tangle with Deke again," I said, though even as the words left my mouth, the truth was catching up. If that break between the ridges wasn't passable, we'd burn energy for nothing—maybe worse. If the terrain turned bad, it could be more dangerous than cutting straight through their camp at dinnertime. And out here, every wasted step was a step we might not get back.

Silence followed, broken only by the roar of runoff. None of us liked the gamble. None of us liked the alternative more.

They killed the screens and slid the phones away. Chunk said, authoritative and steady, "We go south. See what the ridge gives us."

Every small rise was another waterfall. The ridge didn't slope so much as pour. Rocks slick with moss and rain blurred together into one long cascade. Every foothold felt like soap, every reach a gamble. One slip and you'd be gone, dragged downslope where branches jutted like spears.

Zombie limped harder on his ankle, leaning heavier on us. Chunk muttered darkly, "If this is the easier side, we're screwed."

I didn't answer. The thought already gnawed at me—if the mile south yielded nothing, then we would be soaked, drained, and weaker than before.

I bumped him with my shoulder. "Hey, look at that. Full-form Zombie mode."

"Yeah," Zombie groaned. "Real proud moment."

The joke hung there for a second, then went flat.

The storm hadn't hidden us.
It had herded us.

41

The Storm Gave No Answer

The mile south took everything from us. When we reached the dip that the phones had hinted at, we were soaked, bruised, and carrying forest debris from head to toe

The ridge funneled us into a hollow where the wall reared up again—lower than the cliff face we'd seen before, but no gift. A chute of black rock rose above us, water streaming down in curtains. It looked less like a slope and more like the inside of a dam spillway.

We stood under it, rain pounding, runoff splashing in our eyes. No one spoke at first. The mountain had an answer, and it was laughter.

Chunk broke the silence. "Lower, yeah. But I don't see a path. That's not climbing—that's swimming uphill."

Zombie shifted, ankle swollen inside his boot. "Still better than walking into Deke's arms. We've come this far."

I stepped closer, pressing a palm to the stone. Slick, cold moss giving way like wet felt. My fingers searched for purchase and found none. The rain blurred everything, running over grooves that might have been cracks or just scars from older slides.

Chunk picked up a rock, fist-sized, and pitched it upward. It smacked the slope and bounced—once, twice—before clattering all the way back down to land between us. He said nothing more. He didn't have to.

Zombie lagged a step behind as we trudged into the hollow, his weight shifting wrong even when he tried to hide it—favoring the bad ankle, each step shorter than the last. He would stop whenever possible and lean on his trekking poles trying to get some weight off his ankle, even if only for a few seconds. The storm masked plenty, but not the rhythm of a man walking on one good leg. He never said a word, stoic, but the limp was there. The mountain had already picked its target.

When Zombie caught up we discussed our next move. Zombie argued we had to try—the storm gave us cover, the ridge was lower here, and if there was ever a moment, it was now. Chunk countered that an attempted climb in this weather would break us faster than any patrol. His voice was calm, but the look in his eyes said more.

Chunk and I used to climb for sport. Crags in Tennessee, sandstone bluffs out west, trad pitches where a rope was all that stood between adrenaline and a crater. We'd clipped cams into seams, locked nuts into cracks, trusted our weight to steel teeth and nylon rope. Most walls gave you something—an edge to crimp, a crack to wedge, a pocket you could own.

This wall gave us nothing.

I thought about my spine—the metal hardware that kept me walking now—and how one bad fall here wouldn't just slow me down, it would finish me. C5 through C7, fused years ago. A climber's injury. Belayer's neck, they called it.

Chunk and I used to laugh about it. We were convinced it happened because he was never the fastest climber, and I spent too much time on belay, head tilted back for several minutes at a stretch. I could feel the rope through the belay device, sure—but I always trusted my eyes more. I watched him the entire climb.

That habit cost me later. And up here, on this ground, it meant there would be no second chance. Still, the thought of turning back—of slipping into the net, into patrols—was worse.

"We test it," I said finally. "Not all in, not yet. One at a time, slow, no higher than we can get back down. If it gives, we take the shot. If it doesn't, we save our strength."

We stripped off packs and set them against the base, rain hammering down on the nylon. I moved first, pressing hands into slick grooves, boots sliding for purchase. Every step was water, every handhold a lie. Twice I almost lost it, saved only by leaning into the stone and letting it scrape my forearm raw.

Six feet up was all it took to know. No finger crimps, no cracks, no edges to pinch—nowhere you'd even think of slotting a cam or hex. Even with seventy meters of rope, harnesses, and a full rack of trad gear, this chute would have been a nightmare. With nothing but paracord and will, it was suicide.

Below me, Zombie and Chunk watched in silence. I heard nothing but water and my breathing. I eased back down, with Chunk bracing me peeling off the wall, boots skittering, hands shaking.

Zombie searched my face for the answer he didn't want. I gave it anyway. "It's not climbable, it's suicide," I said, voice flat. Chunk exhaled, slow. "So what's worse—this wall, or walking through camp?"

The storm gave no answer. Only the mountain, black and slick, daring us to choose.

42

More Than Weather

The packs drank the storm like sponges, straps cutting deeper with every step. Clothes and sleeping bags sealed in dry bags—but everything else was soaked. The packs drinking up rain until they felt like anchors dragging across the mountain. Ditching them was never an option. Without those packs, we were done.

The worst was our feet. Socks long past soaked, skin wrinkled and soft, every step grinding grit into flesh. The water never let them dry, just churned them into raw weight we couldn't escape. We carried the storm in our boots with every step.

The wind picked up, bending the treetops, shoving curtains of rain sideways so hard it felt like the storm wanted to peel us off the slope. Hail mixed in now, sharp pings bouncing off our packs, off the stone, stinging against raw skin. The chute blurred to nothing, a silver torrent that swallowed sight and sound.

We tried edging back toward cover when it hit—a flash so bright it erased everything for a blink, followed instantly by a crack that didn't sound like thunder. It detonated. The air seemed to rip open, a pressure wave slamming through my chest hard enough to make my ears ring and my teeth ache.

A tree up on the mountain took the strike. The trunk blew apart with a sound like a gunshot times ten, and a branch the size of a battering ram sheared loose, tumbling downslope. It smashed into the ground yards away, sending bark, mud, and splinters spraying like shrapnel.

Zombie jerked back, his bad ankle folding beneath him, nearly yanking Chunk down with him. For a split second, I thought they were both gone—washed straight into the runoff below. But Chunk caught the wall, one hand white-knuckled on a slick seam, the other locked around Zombie's arm.

The smell of ozone and burned wood hung thick in the air. My ears rang so hard it felt like the world had gone silent except for the rushing water.

When they steadied, none of us spoke. The wall wasn't an escape. It was a grave waiting to be filled.

Lightning flared white all around us, burning the ridge into our eyes. Thunder followed like artillery, shaking the ground under our boots. For a brief, trembling instant, I imagined the mountain splitting and taking us into its dark. The storm wanted us gone as much as Deke did. Maybe more.

By the time we pulled back from the tree line, the decision was behind us. The wall wasn't ours to take. The storm had seen to that. We weren't climbing out. Not here. Not south. The mountain had spoken, and it left us with fewer choices than before.

It felt like more than weather. Mother Nature herself seemed set against us, each gust and downpour a hand shoving us back, each rumble of thunder a warning not to push further. Surviving the storm was its own trial, as if escape would not be granted lightly. And we knew that once the skies cleared, we'd face another gauntlet—the aftermath of the flood and the mud it left behind. Another obstacle waiting, one more test we'd have to take together.

The storm kept us hidden, but not for long. Once the night bled away, so would our cover—and with it, any chance of getting out unseen.

43

One That Sucked Less

The storm didn't end so much as sag. The hammering quit, but the sky never gave anything back. No stars. No moon. Just a low, swollen dark dripping mist into the trees. Runoff still ran hard, the sound threading through everything. Creeks we'd once stepped across in a stride had become brown ropes hissing around stone and root. Every hollow held water. Every slope ran.

We'd waited too long to make another push. The south was a dead end—sheer ridge, no line out. That truth had settled over us heavy, like the wet air. There was no clear path anymore. Just options that narrowed with every hour.

We hunkered on the lee side of a blown fir, the root ball rising behind us like a wall of mud and stone.

The night pressed close, the forest breathing around us. Chunk pulled the phone from his pocket, the pale screen cutting through the black like a knife. The dot pulsed north, faint, stubborn.

"We're not getting through down here," he said quietly, shaking his head. "It's a wall."

"Then we go back," Zombie said. His voice was flat, no question in it. "Bunkhouses. The road. Only way left."

"Back where they'll expect us," Chunk muttered.

"Yeah," Zombie said. "But expecting and finding aren't the same thing."

The three of us sat there listening to the water run. None of us said what we were thinking—that turning back meant threading the same ground we'd bled to get away from.

I rubbed at my face, feeling grit and rain. "We move before first light," I said finally. "Stay low. Hit the road quiet. If they're there, we skirt. If they're not, we move fast."

Chunk stared at the map another few seconds. "They'll have eyes on the road," he said. "They'd be stupid not to."

"They're not bulletproof," Zombie shot back. "We just have to be ghosts."

"That ankle's not exactly stealth mode," Chunk muttered, flicking a glance at the swollen boot.

Zombie's face went still. "I'll manage."

"You can't manage if you can't run," Chunk shot back.

"Then I won't stop," Zombie growled.

The quiet that followed wasn't just from exhaustion. It was calculation. No good options. Just the one that sucked less.

"Look," I said, my voice low. "We stay here, we get found. We push south, we get lost or break our necks. That road is the only thing still pointing out. So we use it."

Chunk finally nodded, the kind of nod that didn't come from agreement—just inevitability. "First light," he said. "No noise. No fuckups."

Zombie leaned back against the root ball, eyes half-closed, rain dripping off his hood.

That's when we saw it.

At first, it read like a shadow in the faint red glow of Chunk's headlamp. Then the lines sharpened into angles that the woods don't make when left alone. We moved toward it slowly, warily, ready to find it rotten to the ground or worse—recently used. But as we closed, it became what it was, an old hunter's cabin, long dead and dying slower.

Most of the roof was gone, pitched inward and caved, the ribs of old beams black with rot. One wall had slumped outward into the brush, a picket pile of logs spiked with moss. But the corner nearest the rise still stood true enough: two walls thrown up against each other, a crooked right angle of stacked timbers that had kept their shape by stubbornness, or luck. Above them, a slice of roof clung from a ledger, boards warped and gapped, but enough to keep the sky off a man sitting close.

We made a slow loop around the spot, eyes low, looking for anything new—tracks, chopped branches, an old tire rut. Nothing recent. Just the smell of wet wood and old smoke buried deep in the grain, the kind that never leaves a place that's sheltered men from weather.

In the corner, the dirt had packed to something like a floor. The place held the wind back and took the edge off the mist. We set the packs down with the care you give to things that might not lift again if you drop them too hard. Sitting felt like theft.

Chunk stood under the slice of roof and looked out through the missing wall toward the dark trees.

"This'll hold," he said. It wasn't a promise. It was a measurement.

Zombie didn't speak. He leaned his head back against the log, eyes closed, hands resting on the tops of the poles like a man at a prayer rail. The swelling above his boot had climbed another notch. I pretended not to see it for a minute so he wouldn't have to pretend it was nothing.

We were still a couple of miles from the place that would matter in the morning. But we weren't totally exposed anymore. We had boards at our backs, something above our heads and a little flat ground to stretch on. The forest had stopped trying to knock us down and started letting us hide, if just for a bit.

"We stage here," I said. "We eat what we've got, we get heat if we can manage it low, and scout the bunkhouses. We'll need a line in and a line out and a place to vanish if they come off the road."

Chunk nodded. Zombie opened his eyes and gave the smallest tilt of his chin in agreement. The cabin didn't answer. It just held.

Outside, the runoff kept speaking in its thousand small voices. The sky didn't lift, but it didn't lower either. For the first time since the wall, the world wasn't pushing us backward.

It wasn't safety. It was a pause. And right now a pause was worth more than anything the mountain had offered all day.

We settled into the corners like stones—quiet, heavy, shaped by the night. Chunk crouched near the opening where a wall used to be, headlamp snapped off, eyes tracking the dark like it might shift if he blinked too long. Zombie leaned against the stacked timbers, his ankle stretched out in front of him, hands folded over his chest, breathing slow but tight. The cabin gave him just enough cover to pretend it didn't hurt.

I lay back against my pack, the dampness at my spine still warmer than the air outside. Above us, the scraps of roof creaked now and then, a tired sound that belonged to old things trying to hold on. The rain had dulled to a whisper in the trees. Runoff threaded through the brush in a low, constant murmur—like the forest had gone from shouting at us to whispering over our heads.

And as we sat there in the half-ruined cabin, listening to the water rush through the dark, our minds began to move—each in its own direction.

Chunk's eyes fixed on the tree line like he could will it to break. Zombie leaned into the dark with the weight of pain and old ghosts. And me... I counted the choices that led us here and the few that might still get us out.

The silence didn't comfort. It coiled. And in that stillness, every thought felt louder than a scream.

44

Mother Nature—Zombie

Zombie didn't let them see how bad the ankle really was. Every step felt like someone driving a screwdriver into the joint and twisting slowly. Not sharp enough to cripple him outright, but steady, relentless—like the storm. He'd rolled worse before, back when boots and pain were all he knew, back when you either walked it off or got left behind. But out here in this swamp-soaked hell, every ounce of weakness dragged the whole group closer to failure.

He could tell they knew, though. U-Haul's eyes kept cutting over, like he was measuring him, weighing whether to call it out or let it slide. Chunk never said a word, but he shifted his pace just enough that Zombie could keep up without making it obvious. That was how Zombie knew they saw him slipping. They weren't fools. Hell, they were the sharpest guys he'd ever run with.

And that gnawed at him worse than the pain—the idea that he'd become the weak link.

Sitting here now, rain licking the walls of the half-dead cabin, it almost felt like they'd carved out a pocket of safety. Almost. Every throb in the ankle was another whisper: you're dragging them down.

So he did what he'd always done—ran a mental inventory.

Rifle: dry and ready. Couldn't afford anything less. Pack: heavy but holding, straps digging into his shoulders.

Food: low. Two meals. Enough for one final push, but hunger was already chewing at the edges of his patience.

Water: plentiful in theory, runoff everywhere—but filtering mud-thick streams took time they didn't have.

Knife: sharp, but not magic. Lighter: safe in Chunk's pocket. Gold. Maybe the most valuable thing they had.

The gear was fine. Solid. He was the part that was failing.

He tried not to dwell on it, but the truth had a way of creeping in when you sat still. His ankle wasn't just sore—it swelled and stiffened by the minute. In a few more, when they'd need speed, he'd be slower than both of them. And worse, they knew it. He saw it in their silence, the way they didn't mention it. Silence was louder than words when you'd been around men long enough.

Every crack of thunder was a reminder—Mother Nature didn't give a damn about their plans. It felt almost personal, like the storm had thrown its lot in with Deke—both working together to pin them in. Childish maybe, but real. The storm wasn't random. It was hostile.

They had a roof—half a roof anyway—and that was more than most men could have claimed in a place like this. And Zombie had to admit, for all the hell the storm had thrown at them, they hadn't broken yet.

U-Haul with the steel in his spine—not just the rods holding him together, but the grit that pushed them when they had nothing left.

Chunk with the brain and the stubbornness, always two steps ahead, turning panic into strategy.

They'd both carried him more than once over the past three days, even if they never said it. He knew it. And knowing it twisted something deep inside him—pride and shame breathing the same breath.

Because he respected the hell out of them. And he hated the thought of being deadweight to men like that.

Zombie told himself he'd push until something snapped. That he wouldn't give them the choice. But he'd seen men swear the same thing, and in the end their bodies didn't care about pride or willpower. Flesh and bone had their limits.

So did the mind.

He hadn't meant to think about the man again, but the name wouldn't stay buried. Reed.

He'd learned it after. Too late to matter. Too late to change anything.

It had been clean. Fast. Self-defense. No hesitation.

But knowing the name made it different. Made it heavier.

The wind hissed through gaps in the roof, threading cold air between them. U-Haul sat across from him in the dim, eyes locked on the dark like he could drag tomorrow closer just by staring hard enough. Zombie had always known U-Haul was strong—anyone who spent ten minutes around him picked that up—but he hadn't known this kind of strong. Not until now.

U-Haul didn't have the bulk of a man who moved weight like he could, but it was there, coiled quiet under the skin. Zombie had watched him climb slick boulders like they were nothing, haul his heavy pack when Zombie's felt welded to the earth. Saw him muscle through terrain that should've buckled him. He'd heard the stories—how U-Haul climbed crags on his fingertips, how he pulled iron in the gym that guys twice his size wouldn't touch. He'd never fully bought it.

Until this place proved every word true. U-Haul's strength wasn't loud. It just showed up when everything else started to break.

Chunk, meanwhile, was steady—grounded—the kind of man who could make a plan out of chaos. He didn't just see what was in front of him. He saw what came next, what it meant down the line. You could rely on him to turn fear into strategy. That mattered. More than either of them probably realized.

Together, they were stronger than Zombie felt he was. But maybe that was the point—being stronger together than any of them deserved to be alone.

The ankle pulsed again, nerves crawling up his calf. Zombie clenched his teeth and leaned back against the half-wall, letting the joint rest as much as possible before the final push out. The next few hours scared him more than he'd ever admit. But if he had anything left to give, he'd burn every last bit of it before letting those two go down because of him.

They weren't out yet. Hell, they weren't even close.

But they were still here.

Later today—storm or no storm, ankle or no

ankle—Zombie would be on his feet, getting out of this fucking place.

45

Plenty of Weight—Chunk

Firelight played across wet stone while rain still whispered against the tarp overhead. Chunk's shoulders ached, his back stiff, thighs cramped from miles that hadn't given them an inch. He could still move—hell, he could always move—but every step now felt heavier, the kind you borrowed against tomorrow because today had already taken everything.

He forced himself to take stock. Not gear first—body first.

His head was clear enough, though the storm's pounding still echoed like drums behind his eyes. His arms were solid, hands cut but steady. Legs were the real question. They burned, but they held. His stamina ran thin, but not empty. Hunger gnawed sharper than the cold. A few calories left between the three of them. Nowhere near enough, but enough to put one foot in front of the other. He could keep going. For now.

Then he checked gear. Pack soaked through, clothes damp but not ruined. Sleeping bag still dry—small miracle. Water filtered. Guns functional. Boots waterlogged.

That was the rhythm of this place—gain an inch, lose it to the storm, fight to steal it back.

His thoughts drifted toward Zombie. The man was hurting worse than he let on. Every shift of weight on that ankle gave him away, no matter how hard he tried to mask it. Zombie would follow them straight into hell without complaint, but the truth was the mountain had already taken a bite out of him. If that ankle failed at the wrong moment, they'd all pay for it. Still—he hadn't quit. Not once. That counted.

Then U-Haul.

Chunk had worried about him early on. But something had shifted out here. Maybe it was the storm. Maybe the danger. Maybe the realization that no cavalry was coming. U-Haul had started pulling his own weight in a way Chunk hadn't expected. Not perfect, not seasoned, but steady. He had the eyes now—the eyes of someone who understood the only way forward was through.

Chunk trusted him more tonight than he had yesterday. That mattered too.

Chunk's boys at home would never see him like this. They knew the dad who shouldered anything and carried everything. Out here, he was close to the line where willpower runs out and the body takes over. It scared him. Not for himself—but for us. If he folded, these two didn't stand a chance. That was the truth he carried, heavier than the soaked pack on his back.

Chunk had carried plenty of weight in his life— packs, loads, jobs that didn't let you break. But this was different. This wasn't about muscle or miles. This was the line where things either held—or snapped.

He shifted against the wall, letting the ache settle into bone, then forced the thought down—they had one shot.

And if the ridge wanted them broken, it should've done it already.

46

Own Line to Hold

I forced myself to be honest. My shoulders were rubbed raw where the straps had dug trenches into the skin. Hips ached, skin chafed, and my legs weren't moving on strength anymore—just stubborn rhythm, one step after the next because stopping wasn't an option. My hands were swollen, the cuts along my knuckles burning where the rain had worked its way in. My stomach was hollow, that thin, sharp ache that settles in once hunger stops shouting and starts whispering. My head was clear enough, though the weight of it all pressed from behind my eyes like a hand waiting to shove. I wasn't broken. Not yet. But I could feel the edge creeping closer.

The pack was soaked through, clothes damp but still serviceable. Sleeping bag still dry—our one mercy. Food nearly gone, two more meals between the three of us. Water clean, at least. Boots and socks were still on, soaked through, no way to dry them, no chance to warm them. The cold had worked its way in and stayed there, part of me now. Guns still worked, though every click and chamber check felt heavier in the wet. We had nothing extra. Nothing to spare. Every piece we carried was the line between walking out or not walking at all.

Zombie came into my thoughts next. I'd seen men hide pain before, but his ankle told its own truth. Every step was off. Every shift came with a flicker of pain he couldn't mask. He thought he fooled us, but I saw it plain. And yet he never complained, never hinted at stopping. He was still here, still pushing. That strengthened him more than the pain he carried.

Then Chunk. The one who anchored us, whether or not he meant to. He'd taken the weight every time we faltered, carried it like it was his alone. But I could see it gnawing at him too. The storm, the hunger, the endless fight against ground that wanted to swallow us whole—it was eating at his edges. But he never bent. Never let us see him crack. That steadiness was the rope we all tied ourselves to, even when he didn't know it.

And me. For too long I'd questioned what I brought to this fight. They had their strength, their experience, their fire. I felt like the odd man out—slower, less steady, more a burden than a brother. But something has shifted. Somewhere in there I found my own line to hold. Maybe they saw it, maybe not, but I felt it. I wasn't just following anymore. I was pulling too.

But beneath all that—the pack, the storm, the pain—sat the truth I couldn't shake. My wife. My daughter. Faces that hadn't left me once since this nightmare began. Every step I took was a promise to them, a thread stretched thin but unbroken. I'd told myself over and over I'd see them again. I'd retire with my wife on our mountain property already purchased, and one day walk my baby girl down the aisle. This wasn't the end of my story, or theirs. But the fear was there too, gnawing at the edges—what if I failed them? What if tomorrow came, and I didn't? That thought weighed heavier than the storm, heavier than the mountain, heavier than anything I carried on my back.

We had come this far. Three men still together. Still alive. The ridge had thrown everything at us— storm, hunger, the wall itself—and we were still here. The morning wasn't just another test. It was the hinge.

I thought of my wife's smile, my daughter's laugh, and the truth settled in. If I failed them, I wouldn't be coming home.

47

The Last Supper

We split the last two meals from Zombie's food bag. Nobody joked about "The Last Supper," but I knew the thought had crossed their minds. It had crossed mine too. The silence made it worse—just three men staring into the faint light of red, pretending the food was more than it was.

When the food was gone, Chunk pulled out the map and flattened it on his knee. Tonight wasn't about taking anything. It was about making sure we were ghosts moving forward from here. No second chances.

That's when Chunk and I laid it out—we'd leave our packs, keep only what we needed, and make a quick run to the bunkhouses in the dark. Quick there, quick back. Hopefully not much more than a mile each way. The point wasn't to fight or dig in—it was to know. When the push came at first light, we couldn't afford to be lost.

Zombie listened but didn't argue. He knew as well as we did—a bad plan could get you killed, but no plan would do it faster.

Zombie wanted to come. But the limp was too obvious. Every step risked him slowing us down and burning what little strength he had left. He would stay.

It stung him, but it gave us speed and gave his ankle another few hours to rest.

The forest closed in as we moved. Rain hung in the air, thin and cold, clinging to everything. The ground was soft and slick, making silence impossible. We moved light without the packs, keeping close, heads down, every branch brushing wet against our shoulders.

It didn't take long to find the old path again—a shallow cut through the undergrowth that curved along the ridge line. Even soaked and beaten, it carried the faint memory of a road. The closer we got, the heavier the air seemed to settle.

Then the shape emerged through the mist. The bunkhouses sat exactly where Chunk remembered them, low and squared against the treeline, roofs glistening dark with rain. Headlamps still made their rounds, thin white beams slicing across the compound in slow, steady arcs. The place hadn't moved. The danger hadn't either.

We stayed just far enough back to count structures, trace movement, and fix the bearings in our heads. No maps. No guesswork. If we made the push in the dark, we'd need every step clear.

When it was burned into memory, we turned back. The trek uphill bit harder than the way down. Mud pulled at our boots like hands, the ridge slicker than before. The forest swallowed the last thin beams of light behind us until there was only mist and the sound of our breathing.

We didn't talk. The plan was set, the route marked in our minds. Every step back through the trees was just gravity and grit, carrying the weight of what waited come morning.

By the time the cabin emerged from the dark, both of us were mud to the knees, socks and shoes waterlogged again. The red glow of Zombie's headlamp bled across the ruin, catching stone and broken beams like blood on bone.

He sat exactly where we'd left him.

His hands were dark. A knife lay across his palms. For a breath, there was nothing else in the world but the shine of blood in the red light.

Zombie didn't move.

His eyes were open—empty, fixed on nothing.

The thought came before I understood why—that he might be dead.

48

Measured in Seconds

Then my eyes slid right.

A body lay ten feet away, crumpled in the mud, half-hidden by shadow. Still. Too still for comfort. The shape of him was wrong—limbs folded in on themselves, head tilted at an angle that made my stomach tighten.

Chunk stiffened beside me. I felt it more than saw it. The map slipped in his grip, paper whispering as it sagged toward the ground. None of us spoke. None of us breathed. The cabin seemed to lean in, listening, waiting for the sound that would give us away.

For a heartbeat, the world narrowed to that body in the mud.

Then Zombie blinked.

It was small. Easy to miss. But a slow breath followed—ragged, uneven, real. Relief hit hard enough to make my knees weak, but it didn't last. Not with the knife still resting across his palms. Not with the dark sheen on his hands.

He didn't look at me. He didn't need to. His silence carried more weight than words ever could. Whatever had happened here was already decided. Whoever this man had been, he wasn't going back to his people. And when they realized he hadn't returned, the woods would close in even more.

Tonight, everything had shifted. The rules we'd been playing by were gone. Eyes were on us now—closer than ever—and the clock wasn't measured in hours anymore. It was measured in seconds, in footsteps, in how long we could stay one move ahead of the dark.

The question wasn't what we'd do at dawn.

It was what we'd do to survive the night.

49

Shelter to Signal

Chunk said it first, though the words were about to leave my lips. "What the fuck happened?"

"He came around the wall fast. Didn't say a word—just bum rushed me and reached for his belt. I didn't think. Training took over. Close the distance, break the grip, blade up. By the time my head caught up, he was already going."

Zombie stared at his hands and flexed them like he could still feel the resistance. "Wasn't clean. Wasn't planned. It just... happened."

I looked at the body. We weren't staging that as anything but what it was. A blade writes its own truth.

"We can't hide it," I said. "Even if we could, drag marks, blood—the whole thing screams us."

Zombie's voice steadied. "Doesn't matter. He's going to miss a check-in. The question is how long until they come."

My eyes dropped to his belt. The radio clipped there wasn't like the cheap handheld we'd lifted before—this one was square, heavy, the kind that has long range and more security features. Chunk scowled.

"They swapped rigs," I said, turning it in my hand. "That's why the old one went dead. New radios, new frequencies, new rules. They knew one was missing, so they pulled the plug."

"Which means they already suspect," Chunk said. "And now one of theirs isn't coming back."

The weight of it pressed heavier than the mountain had. We needed rest and energy. What we had now was a corpse and a clock.

Chunk said it out loud. "When they notice he's missing, we'll be lucky to see dawn."

I could feel it in my bones. Dawn might offer a way out, but it wouldn't come clean, or easy. They'd come looking—and when they did, suspicion would press down harder than the heaviest pack.

"We burn the cabin," I said, before either of them could.

Chunk's eyes narrowed. "Torch the cabin?"

"Let it scream," I said. "Let's lure them here. Then we move for bunkhouses and wait."

No one liked it, but no one argued. Motion buys moments. Standing still gets you caught.

Chunk flicked the lighter once. Nothing. Twice— just a spark. On the third strike, a thin, sickly flame fluttered to life, barely holding. It wasn't much, but out here it might as well have been gold.

Before he tried it again, we worked the cabin like scavengers. Not for big pieces—those would come later—but for anything small enough to give the flame a chance. We snapped brittle slivers from fallen beams, broke chair legs down into pencil-thin lengths, and shaved splinters until our fingers ached. Anything thicker than a finger went into one pile. Anything that still felt damp was tossed aside.

Zombie tested each piece before it went in—bending

it, snapping it, listening. Dry wood cracked sharp. Wet wood bent and died. The rejects piled up fast.

Chunk turned to the interior wall next, working the knife slow and careful. He peeled back the outer layer until the blade found something pale and dry beneath. Thin curls fell away, soft as paper. He crushed one between his fingers, then nodded. Tinder.

We built the stack small and deliberate—curls first, then the thinnest twigs laid loose above them, air left between everything. Too tight and it would choke. Too loose and it would never catch.

Chunk knelt low, cupping the lighter close, shielding it from the drafts sneaking through the broken walls. The first curls blackened and shrank, smoke rising, but no flame. He added another shaving. Tried again. A weak flame crawled along the edge, threatening to vanish with every breath of air.

Zombie leaned in and blew, slow and steady, careful not to kill it. The ember brightened, spread, and finally licked at the twigs. One caught. Then another. The wood hissed and spat water as steam pushed out ahead of the heat.

The flame faltered. Chunk fed it again—another twig, then two—waiting each time, counting breaths, letting the fire prove it could survive before giving it more. Smoke pooled at ankle height, thick and bitter, before slowly touching the walls.

Only when the twigs burned clean did we dare add something thicker. It took time. Adjustments. Patience we didn't have, but forced anyway.

At last, the flame stood on its own—small, stubborn, alive.

We'd lit it to speak louder than our boots—to make

the woods look where we weren't. But smoke is a loud liar. It announces itself. We had a few ragged breaths of time before it became a beacon.

The fire caught faster than we expected. A seam along the side wall blackened, then split, the orange glow crawling out like it had been waiting for the chance. Dry pine went up with a low crack, and the cabin began to feed the blaze.

"Few more minutes, then we move." Chunk said.

We didn't wait to see if the fire won or died. Wait too long and the smoke would lead them straight to us. Leave too soon and the flame would sputter out before it could do its job. That seam was razor-thin, and we couldn't miss it. With the tongues pushed shoulder-high, the roof edges smoldered, and we moved.

Packs up. Heads low. Into the trees.

The ruin behind us cracked and popped, the sound following like a warning. Smoke climbed into the canopy, dark and thick—the right kind, the kind that travels.

We'd barely made a hundred yards before the woods changed. Engines uncoiled through the trees, not a patrol but a pack. ATV's tore past, lights slicing the pines white. We went flat in the brush, mud in our teeth, the ground trembling under us. They didn't stop. They had a heading.

A minute after the last motor faded, the radio we'd taken came alive, sharp enough to cut.

"Control, Delta One. Reporting smoke—three klicks north of the bunkhouses. Repeat, smoke north of the bunkhouses."

"Copy," a second voice said. "Units en route."

The ATV's circled back slower, lights probing.

The men dismounted, radios overlapping. We lay still and listened. At first, the talk was procedural—who had eyes, who held the perimeter—but it turned personal fast.

"Control, it's the cabin that's burning," a man said, voice gone tight. "One down inside."

A beat. "Say again?"

"Affirmative. One down."

The reply came clipped and furious. "ID."

"Charlie," the first voice said, and the channel went quiet enough to hear the static breathe.

Then a steadier voice cut through, hard-edged and methodical—"Canvas around the cabin, they can't be far. Find those motherfuckers and string them from a tree!"

Chunk's mouth pressed into a thin line. Zombie shifted, his face going rigid, the limp tugging at our pace even in stillness. My thoughts wouldn't quit. Had we just opened a path—or killed our last chance? The smoke bought us time, sure—but it also woke them up.

"Sweep the trails. Hold the spur. Nothing leaves south."

Smoke thickened behind us, blotting the sky.

We eased south, using the shallow ruts where tires had pressed the earth. The radio hissed in Chunk's hand, quiet now except for breath and the occasional clipped command. The cabin had turned from shelter to signal. The surrounding men sounded like a net knitting itself closed.

We didn't say it out loud, but the truth rode on our backs with the packs: dusk might be our last shot—or the end of the line. If the road gave us a way out, we might live. If it didn't, the smoke we'd made would be the last mark we left in these woods.

Behind us, the cabin roared. In front of us, the trees waited without an answer.

And over the radio, just before the trees swallowed us, a voice cut through the static: "Tracks are fresh. They're close."

We didn't look back. The forest would either keep us—or betray us.

50

We'd Been Marked

We dropped in a half crouch, pulled forward one step at a time, mud slick against our knees and packs dragging low. A mile isn't far until you try to do it on your knees. Out here, low to the ground, knees pressed into roots and rocks, every lunge felt like a fight. My stomach was as hollow as the surrounding forest, the ache gnawing in time with my pulse.

Every push forward took something from me I wasn't sure I had left. Arms shook. Boots slipped. The pack bit my shoulders and dragged like an anvil. It wasn't just weight anymore—it was everything we owned. If we had to run, we'd have no choice but to carry it all. There were no do-overs. Leave it behind, lose it forever.

Chunk crawled a body-length ahead, head low, moving with the same steady rhythm he always had. Even here, crawling through mud in the dark, he seemed to find lines and angles where I only felt chaos. Zombie pulled himself behind me, his ankle grinding like a broken gear. I could hear his breath hitch whenever he had to brace against it. Still, he never said stop. He never said rest. The silence between us was its own kind of pact—no one wanted to be the first to admit just how close to empty we were.

The night wrapped around us like wet wool, thick and heavy. Every snap of a twig under our bellies felt like a flare. My face was inches from the earth, nose filled with rot and damp pine. The woods swallowed every sound, but it also magnified them, made it feel like the scrape of my jacket against mud could echo for miles.

Halfway across a shallow draw, the radio came alive. Static first—thin, nervous—then a voice too clear and too calm to belong to the woods.

"Darren, Robert, sweep east from the hunting cabin. Full perimeter. Report all signs."

I froze. The word cabin wasn't just sound—it was accusation.

Another voice bled in, tighter, clipped.

"Copy. Cabin's down. Smoke's still hot. No movement inside. But—" static cracked. "—Charlie's been drug out of the cabin. Knife wound. Heavy bleed out."

A third voice cut through the static, clipped and controlled.

"Tracks confirmed. They're still moving south."

Another voice followed, low but steady. "Copy that. Sweep wide and push them toward the bunkhouses. Don't lose the trail. We'll be ready for them."

Chunk twisted his head just enough to glance back at me. Even in the dark, I could see it in his eyes.

They weren't guessing anymore. They were hunting.

The half crawl turned into a full on hike after that. The mud pulled harder at my boots. Every root scraped deeper. My body was already drained, but now my head filled with worse things—what getting to the bunkhouses meant to them, whether they were already circling it, and whether the fire had bought us minutes or just lit a beacon that doomed us.

Zombie's breath caught again behind me. He shifted weight wrong and groaned, dragging his ankle like dead weight before catching rhythm again. Pride was keeping him moving, not strength. I knew it. Chunk knew it. But neither of us told him to stop. Stopping meant death.

Static hissed.

"Yeah, we got their trail again. Boot marks in the mud."

Another voice came through, steady.

"Copy. We'll have 'em boxed in before they reach the bunkhouses and force them into the creek. These guys aren't amateurs. Shoot on sight."

Chunk's scowl set. We'd been marked.

They weren't even pretending anymore—they knew. Knew we were heading south to the bunkhouses. Three men. Armed. Not lost. Not local. A threat.

I dragged forward anyway, mud swallowing my boots, grit grinding into the cracks of my skin. The fire at the cabin was supposed to buy us time, but maybe all it did was confirm everything they suspected. Knife wounds. Fire. Three sets of prints. Heavy packs. Trained. Not stranded.

The march stretched on, every yard heavier than the last, not just against the mud but against the seconds slipping away.

The voices on the radio had shifted—no more idle chatter. Just clipped commands, confident. Like hunters closing the distance on something that couldn't run.

We couldn't out hike them. Not now.

Chunk glanced back, eyes hard. "New plan. No straight south. No noise. No light."

He didn't have to explain the rest—we all knew why.

Hiking from the cabin had bought us time, but heading south now was a death sentence. If we didn't stop going straight for the bunkhouses, they'd be on top of us in minutes. We needed speed. We needed distance.

Sprinting would light us up, but being too slow would hand them our necks. What was left sat in the narrow strip between: low, quiet, and fast enough to disappear.

Chunk crouched, scooping a double handful of muck from the creek bed. "Predator up again, final push" he muttered. We smeared it on thick—arms, neck, faces, straps. Cold mud slid down my collar. Shivers couldn't be avoided. Zombie clawed leaves and pine needles from the ground, pressing them into the mud across his shoulders and back until he looked more like wreckage than a man.

Head to toe, we covered ourselves in the forest— mud, leaves, bark scrapings. The muck wasn't comfort; it was armor. Crude, wet, and the only edge we had left.

Chunk went into a crouch, shoulders rounded, head down. "Stay low," he whispered. He moved first, sliding with the lay of the ground, not cutting across it. I followed, pack cinched tight, mud slick over everything that made me visible. Zombie's steps whispered behind mine.

We moved in a staggered line, shapes broken up by the gunk we wore. Every step curved us slightly east—still heading for the bunkhouses, but never giving them a straight bearing. No clean line. No easy chase.

Behind us, engines growled. Radio chatter sharpened—search grid tightening.

Then, through the dark, a voice snapped over the net.

"Got movement."

Not a shout. A confirmation.

And it was us they'd found.

51

Toward the Ridge

The woods held its breath with us.

Engines rumbled beyond the treeline, low and steady, like a storm closing in. A flashlight beam cut across the ridge—too far to tag us, close enough to make my chest tighten.

"They don't see us," I whispered.

"Not yet," Chunk murmured.

But they thought they did. Someone on the radio had said "movement", and that was enough. Enough to make boots hammer down, enough to get ATV's chewing at the mud. Enough to make the night feel small.

Chunk didn't move, but I saw the math flicker across his face—distance, slope, time. "They think we're still angling south," he whispered. "Good. We're not."

Zombie's breath hissed through his teeth. "Then where the hell are we going?"

Chunk's expression changed. "Away. Deeper. We stop giving them a line."

I shot him a look. "That means losing the bunkhouses."

"That means not walking straight into a kill box," he said.

The engines swelled, closer now. A sharp voice snapped through the radio: "South movement confirmed. Push to the creek."

"See?" Chunk whispered. "They're already chasing it."

We turned without a word—no trail, no decoy, no footprints to dress up. Just a quiet pivot off the expected line, sliding into the heavier woods. The ground here was slick and uneven, but it swallowed sound. Branches brushed my face, wet and cold.

Chunk kept his voice low. "We arc a touch northeast. Enough to stay off their grid, not enough to lose the bearing entirely."

"Northeast?" Zombie whispered. "That drags us toward the ridge."

"It drags us away from the flashlight pointed at our backs," Chunk said.

I bit down hard on the inside of my cheek. We'd been moving all night—burning calories, bleeding time. The road sat somewhere beyond the trees, but not close. Not close enough.

Zombie limped over a root, breath catching. "We even make it before dawn?"

Chunk didn't answer.

He didn't have to.

The forest was thicker, darker, more tangled. Every step forward felt less like progress and more like hiding. Behind us, the engines barked and voices tightened. They weren't searching anymore. They were closing.

"Stay low," Chunk muttered. "No higher than the brush. If you can see the sky, they can see you."

A flashlight beam swept the old line to the south,

cutting clean through the mist. They were still committed to the wrong direction—for now.

I leaned close to him. "Even if we keep this pace, we're not making the road before the light hits."

"I know," Chunk said.

"So what's the plan?"

"Keep moving until we don't have a choice," he whispered. "And hope we're not standing in the open when the sun finds us."

Zombie gave a low laugh, more breath than sound. "Yeah. Real solid plan."

No one answered. There wasn't anything left to say.

The radio cracked behind us—another bark of orders. "Southeast team advance. Dogs out front." Engines roared to life, a sound that carried through the trees like a fuse being lit.

We pressed on—low, deliberate steps through a forest that felt like it was closing in around us. Each step north was another step between us and the road. Another second closer to daylight.

52

Corpses By Morning

The trudge had lost all meaning.

No direction. No finish line. Just one boot after another through mud that sucked and slurped at every step. The storm had finally bled itself dry, but the quiet it left behind wasn't peace—it was punishment. Every drop that fell from the canopy hit like a clock tick. Every snap of a branch sounded like something finding us.

We didn't talk. We didn't need to. The plan was dead.

Probably not reaching the bunkhouses by dawn. No more pretending we had a route.

Now it was just survival—bare, ugly, and stripped of purpose.

Chunk led the way, rifle across his chest, every motion slow and deliberate. Zombie limped behind, leaning hard on the trekking poles, his breath sharp and uneven. I stayed between them, eyes down, counting steps in clumps of ten to keep my mind from unraveling.

Finally, the ridge leveled into a small hollow—a pocket in the hillside half-swallowed by rock and roots. It wasn't much. A crack in the earth, a place forgotten.

But it was cover. And that was enough.

Chunk ducked inside first, sweeping the light once across the ceiling before killing it. "We'll hold here," he said.

No one argued. We dropped our packs like corpses. My spine screamed when the straps released. Zombie slid down the wall, groaning as he stretched his ankle out.

I sank against the stone, head back, eyes closed. The cold crawled through my clothes fast, like it had been waiting for permission.

Chunk crouched near the entrance, listening to the woods. "They'll sweep the trails and the bunkhouse path first," he murmured. "We're too deep now. That's the only good news I've got."

"Bad news?" I asked.

He looked at me, deadpan. "You can see your breath."

He wasn't wrong. It was getting colder by the minute—air thin and wet, the kind that chews through layers. My hands were already stiff.

Zombie rubbed his arms, teeth clicking softly. "We're gonna freeze our asses off."

Chunk nodded. "Fire's a risk. Smoke rises, heat shows."

"Yeah," I said, "but hypothermia doesn't care about stealth."

That earned me a glare. "You light one, and anyone within half a mile sees it. We might as well hang a sign."

I held his stare. "You want to spend the night sitting in wet boots with no heat? We'll be corpses by morning anyway."

Zombie lifted his head. "What if we dig in? Shield it behind the rocks. Keep it low."

Chunk considered it, something working behind his eyes. "Maybe. But if the air shifts and that smoke catches…"

"It's better than dying slow," I said. "We keep it tight, small as a candle. Enough to keep the blood moving."

Silence. Just wind sighing through branches outside.

Finally, Chunk gave a slow nod. "Fine. But we stay sharp. First flicker of noise, it's out."

Zombie closed his eyes, muttering, "Thank God," as if we'd just negotiated with death itself.

Chunk didn't relax.

"If this doesn't catch," he said, already unstrapping the nylon tarp from his pack, "we pull the sleeping bags. They might get wet. Doesn't matter. Survival."

Nobody argued.

He snapped the trekking poles out and planted them tight into the mud behind the miniature fire pit, angling them low. We tied the tarp across the tops and staked the back corners with rocks, creating a shallow lean-to that hunched over the flame.

"Keep it under that," he said. "Low. No flare."

The tarp sagged under the weight of rain, but it broke the wind and held the heat close. Smoke curled sideways instead of climbing.

The fire wasn't comfort.

It was permission to keep going.

Chunk rose, slinging his pack against the rock. "We'll grab what dry wood we can find. You stay here," he told Zombie. "Keep your foot up. No heroics."

"Don't plan on any," Zombie said, leaning back against the stone.

Chunk motioned for me to follow. "Come on."

53

Trembling Now

No moon, just clouds dragging their bellies across the treetops. I kept behind Chunk, watching the faint outline of his shoulders move through the dark. The ground was slick with moss and mud, each step a gamble.

We worked in silence, collecting deadfall, pulling fallen limbs off trees too stubborn to drop them.

When we stopped moving, I could hear my own pulse thudding in my ears.

"Keep close," Chunk whispered over his shoulder.

"I am," I muttered, though my focus had already drifted.

Something caught my eye down the slope—a glint, faint and silvery, maybe frost on stone, maybe water catching light through the trees. It wasn't anything, probably. Still, it tugged at me. I eased a few steps off the trail, more curious than cautious.

The ground dropped out sooner than I expected. My boots skidded on wet leaves and I slid the rest of the way down on my ass, scraping through dirt and leaf litter before coming to a stop against a sapling. Not hard. Not enough to hurt. Just enough to knock the breath out of me and leave my ears ringing for a second.

I pushed myself up, brushing off my pants, half-grinning at my own clumsiness. By the time I looked back toward the trail, the slope hid it from view.

"Chunk?" I called quietly, certain he was just out of sight.

No answer.

Water somewhere below, the soft hiss of leaves settling where I'd slid. No footsteps. No movement.

"Chunk," I tried again, sharper this time, then froze, the sound carrying farther than I liked. I stood there listening, pulse climbing, realizing how easily I'd let the ground steal him from me.

Okay. Breathe.

He can't be far. Don't lose your head.

I cupped my hands to my mouth and gave our whistle—two sharp notes we'd used since the start of our trip. But my lips were cracked, the sound thin, like whistling along to a tune no one else could hear.

I tried again. Louder.

Still nothing.

The cold hit harder now, mixing with the heat rising in my chest. I turned again, then again, unsure which way I'd come. Every trunk looked the same, every rock repeated itself.

The panic built in tiny layers—first in my gut, then in my throat, then behind my eyes.

"Chunk!" I hissed, voice shaking. "Zombie!"

No reply. Not even an echo.

I started walking—slow at first, then faster, pushing through branches that slapped my face. I tried the whistle again, but it came out pitiful, barely louder than my own breathing.

A sound stopped me.

Not far away. A branch snapping under weight. Then another.

I froze, crouched low, pulse hammering.

"Chunk?" I whispered again.

Silence.

I could feel it now—the forest wasn't empty. It was watching.

Listening back.

Something about that thought made the fear shift from sharp to suffocating.

Another sound, farther off. A rustle.

I turned toward it, unsure if I was going the right way or walking straight into something else. My hands were trembling now. My breath came fast and shallow. "Okay... okay, think," I muttered to myself. "North. Ridge. Find the hollow. Find the—"

Then I saw it.

Through the trees, maybe fifty yards out, a flicker of light.

Not headlamps. More orange.

Moving.

It blinked once, then again.

Almost rhythmic. Like a signal. Or a flashlight sweeping across trunks.

I held my breath.

The light stopped, lingered, then went out completely.

My skin prickled. My first thought was relief— Chunk. It had to be.

But the longer I stared, the more certain I became that it wasn't him. Too far. Too deliberate.

I whispered, barely audible, "That wasn't Chunk…"
And the forest swallowed the rest.

54

Bring Him Back

Back at the pocket, the fire had burned to a tired pulse—orange coals pushing back the dark just enough to be cruel about it. Smoke clung low, refusing to rise. The air smelled like damp earth and regret.

Zombie sat close to the flames, poking at them with a stick, eyes half-lidded from exhaustion. Every few moments he'd glance toward the tarp—covered entrance, listening for the crunch of boots or the low hum of voices.

When the brush outside snapped once, then again, he straightened fast, rifle half-raised.

"Chunk?" he called.

The tarp flapped aside, and Chunk stumbled through, breath ragged, mud spattered to his thighs. He dropped the bundle of firewood against the wall, the sound too loud in the small space.

Zombie frowned. "Jesus, you trying to bring the whole forest with you? You were gone forever."

Chunk didn't answer. He just stood there, eyes on the ground, chest still rising and falling. His hands shook when he finally wiped sweat from his face.

Zombie's tone sharpened. "Where's U-Haul?"

Chunk looked up slowly, and for a moment, Zombie

saw something he hadn't seen in him before—fear.

"I lost him," Chunk said.

"What?"

"U-Haul," Chunk rasped, voice breaking in the middle. "He drifted off when we were grabbing wood. I turned around, and he was gone."

Zombie blinked, not understanding at first. Then the meaning sank in like cold water down his spine.

"You mean... lost lost?"

Chunk nodded once, his face going still. "I called. Whistled. Nothing. I searched until I couldn't tell which way was back. It's blacker than sin out there, Zombie. I couldn't see my own goddamn hands unless I was using my healdlamp."

Zombie threw a stick into the fire, embers scattering. "You left him?"

Chunk's head snapped up. "Don't start."

"You left him," Zombie said again, louder now. "You were supposed to keep eyes on each other!"

Chunk stepped forward, voice cracking under the weight of his own guilt. "I know! You think I planned it? He was ten feet away one second, gone the next. It's a maze out there—wet, silent, and it eats sound. I couldn't find a damn trace."

Zombie's breathing quickened, his face pale beneath the glow. "He won't find his way back. Not in that mess. He doesn't even know which way the ridge runs."

"I know," Chunk said, quieter now. He raked a hand through his hair, pacing. "I should've just gone on my own."

"Yeah," Zombie muttered. "You should've."

Chunk stopped pacing and stared at him, anger

flashing for a second before fading into something worse. "Don't you think I know what this means? Out there, alone, in that cold? He's as good as—" He cut himself off, swallowing the word.

The silence after that was brutal. The only sound was the faint hiss of sap boiling in the wood.

Finally, Chunk grabbed the rifle from Zombie and slung it tight. His voice came out low but shaking.

"I'm going."

Zombie shifted, pain ripping across his face as he tried to stand. "You won't find him."

"I have to try," Chunk said. He looked back toward the forest. "I can't sit here and get warmth from that fire while he freezes in the dark."

Zombie leaned forward, the firelight catching the sheen of sweat on his temples. "You think I want to sit here either? But if he finds his way back and we're both gone, we'll never regroup."

Chunk hesitated. The words hit like stones—true, but unbearable.

Chunk's voice softened, rough around the edges. "You want to do something for him? Keep this fire alive. Make sure he can see it if he makes it out. That's our only play."

Zombie exhaled hard, nodding once. He crouched, feeding a few branches into the flame. The orange light brightened for a second, catching both of their faces— the fear, the guilt, the quiet resignation.

Chunk rose suddenly, the decision already made in his eyes. He slung his rifle, tightened the pack straps, and grabbed his light."I'm going after him," he said. "No waiting, no debating. If he's lost, I'll find him."

Zombie looked up sharply. "Chunk—"

He cut him off with a shake of the head. "If I'm not back in an hour, you assume something happened to both of us. You don't come looking. You stay put, you hear me?"

The words landed heavy between them, no argument left to make.

Zombie stared at the fire, then back at him. "You're not doing him any good by getting yourself killed."

A surge of tension ran through Chunk. "He's out there alone. I'm not sitting here while he freezes or runs into one of them. That's not who we are."

Zombie's throat tightened, but he managed a nod. "Then go bring him back."

Chunk didn't answer. He rested a hand on the rock wall beside the cave, took one long breath, and stepped into the dark.

The fire cracked behind him, a single ember leaping free, flaring bright—and dying just as quick.

55

Silence Pressed Harder

The night had a weight to it.

Cold seeped through every seam of my clothes, but it wasn't the cold that had me shaking. My face burned hot, the kind of heat that comes from panic, not weather. The forest closed in until the world was only the red beam of my headlamp and the drum of my heart. Every sound felt personal—the shift of branches, the drip of water, the whisper of wind that might have been voices.

This was the worst-case scenario.

The one we never said out loud.

I tried to breathe slow. In through the nose, out through the mouth.

Didn't help. My chest still stuttered, tight as wire. I turned, half certain I'd see a light or a silhouette—anything human—but there was only the dark.

Then I smelled it. Smoke.

Faint at first, a thread slipping through the cold. Then stronger, thicker, enough to taste on my tongue. I froze, every sense clawing for meaning. Smoke meant fire. Fire meant people.

Chunk and Zombie. It had to be.

They knew I'd never find my way back in the dark.

They'd know the only way to pull me in was a fire—a flare against the black. That thought steadied me, gave shape to my steps.

"Good," I whispered. "They're thinking."

I followed the scent, angling through the trees, feet sinking into the soft ground. The wind shifted, carrying more of it. Definitely close now. I told myself the rhythm of my breathing was better—more control, less panic—but my pulse still pounded in my ears.

Then the smell changed.

Heavier. Sharper.

Too much fuel, too much burn for what we'd risk.

A flicker of unease crawled up my neck. Chunk would have kept it small, hidden under a tarp or stone lip.

Zombie wouldn't have let the flame breathe this wide. This was open fire, careless heat.

I slowed, crouching instinctively, one hand on the pistol.

"Maybe the wind's wrong," I muttered. "Maybe it's drifting."

The words didn't sound convincing even to me. The smoke thickened, curling low through the brush. It shouldn't have been that strong—not unless I was right on top of it.

I moved another ten yards. The glow appeared—thin and orange between the trunks, quivering the way a warning does before it fully shows itself. Relief pushed in hard, desperate. I wanted it to be them so badly my brain started to fill in their shapes—Zombie hunched over the fire, Chunk standing watch with the rifle.

But as I edged closer, something didn't sit right.

The color was wrong—too bright. And the smoke bit at my throat.

I stopped breathing.

That wasn't ours. Couldn't be.

I dropped low behind a fallen tree, heart rattling in my throat. The forest pulsed with that light, orange bleeding through the fog. I strained to hear voices, footsteps, anything—but the night was too still. The only sound was the faint hiss of burning.

"Chunk?" I whispered, barely air. "Zombie?"

Nothing.

Nothing but silence, so heavy it hummed.

Then, through the haze, something moved—a figure cutting between the trunks, backlit by the orange glow. Not broad-shouldered like Chunk. Not limping like Zombie. Taller, thinner. The movement is not deliberate, not searching, not lost.

My mouth went dry.

He turned. Slowly.

The firelight caught metal at his hip, the curve of a mask or glasses—hard to tell through the shimmer of heat. Then his head lifted, and though I couldn't see his face, I felt the weight of his attention find me.

I froze, every instinct screaming don't move.

He took one step forward. Then another. No hurry. Just certainty.

I backed up until bark pressed against my shoulders. My hand found the pistol grip, slick with sweat.

The figure stopped. The flame behind him guttered, throwing everything into a strobe of shadow and light.

Then the beam of a headlamp—red, narrow, searching—snapped on and cut through the dark straight toward me.

I couldn't breathe. Couldn't think. Every nerve begged to run.

And then—a hand clamped down on my shoulder from behind.

Cold ripped through me. Reflex screamed to pull the trigger, but I bit it back, teeth clenched, waiting to see if the voice that followed was one I knew—or one I'd been running from.

56

Unspoken Rule

The hand landed on my shoulder hard enough that my breath stopped. The pistol came up before I even thought, trigger finger grazing the curve of steel. My body braced to fire—until the whisper cut through.

"Easy."

The voice was low, steady, familiar. Chunk.

Relief hit so hard it bordered on pain. My knees buckled, the pistol sagging at my side. He leaned in close, his face set in a hard, unmistakable line even in the firelight bleeding through the trees.

"You almost got yourself shot," I whispered.

He gave me a look that said I wasn't wrong, but I wasn't right either. "Put it away. Before you make noise we can't take back."

I holstered the pistol, though my hands wouldn't stop shaking. The fire popped again ahead of us. Laughter carried through the trees—slurred, careless, the kind that came after long hours drinking under the stars. It twisted something inside me. Sounded too much like the nights that had made me love the woods in the first place.

"Four tents," I whispered. "Ultralight. Like ours. They're drunk. Loud."

Chunk crouched beside me, eyes narrowed on the glow. "So, they're either the luckiest hikers alive—or they're standing dead in the middle of a crossfire they don't even know exists. Maybe both."

The fire cracked again, laughter rising with it, and for half a breath I wanted it to be safe. Wanted to believe we could walk out of the treeline and share the code of the trail—hikers helping hikers. Water, food, a place by the fire. That was the rule out here.
But the woods had already chewed up men who tried to play kind.

"They don't know," I said. My throat felt raw. "They haven't stumbled upon it yet. The operation. Deke. Any of it. They're blind."

Chunk didn't answer right away. His silence was heavy. Because we both knew what the unspoken rule said—you don't leave hikers stranded. You help. Always.

Finally, he exhaled slow. "We need to get back to Zombie. But leaving them…" He shook his head. "It'd be like walking past a man bleeding out on the trail."

I swallowed hard. "And if we warn them? We drag them into our nightmare. Maybe get them killed."

A hard look settled over Chunk. "Or maybe they're the numbers we need. Seven's harder to kill than three."

The glow pulsed through the trees, the laughter curling around it. It didn't sound like killers. It sounded like hikers. But in these woods, sound lied.

My hand drifted back to the pistol on instinct. Because if I walked toward them, it wasn't just about saving strangers. It was about betting everything—our survival, our escape, maybe our lives—on the chance that they were exactly what they seemed.

The fire was no longer just theirs. It was ours too. A signal. A risk. A test.

The choice pressed down on me.

Do we step into the light? Or do we leave them to burn when Deke finds them?

My pulse wouldn't slow. The laughter didn't fade.

And in that moment, the woods whispered the cruelest truth: either way, the fire was going to cost us.

We crept closer. The fire growing from a faint flicker into a steady pulse against the trunks. It painted the underbellies of branches orange and made the nylon tents glow like lanterns. Four of them, pitched sloppy but solid, clustered around the blaze.

A small Bluetooth speaker hissed in the dirt, spitting out some cheesy 80's track—synths and drum machines just clear enough to recognize, just loud enough to carry. It clashed with the woods, sounded wrong out here, like the forest didn't want to listen.

Their camp was a mess. Packs half unzipped, boots tossed in a pile, trash already collecting in a black plastic bag that sagged near the fire. They'd strung a tarp overhead but didn't bother staking one side—rain had puddled and sagged it into a hammock of water.

"Man, that's my song," one of them slurred, too loud. Another told him to shut up and pass the whiskey. Their laughter rolled easily, carelessly.

Chunk's hand brushed my sleeve, a silent warning—see them for what they are, not what you want them to be.

But my eyes stuck to the pile near the fire—food wrappers, a corner of something vacuum-sealed, maybe trail meals. Calories sitting in plain sight.

I leaned a little to get a better look. That's when it happened.

Crack.

Just a twig. Just one. Surely not loud enough for them to hear I thought.

"Hold up," a voice said. Not drunk now. Sharp. "Lights."

White beams flared. Headlamps snapped on in unison, four beams cutting the woods apart. They swept like searchlights, slicing through the trunks, sliding closer to where we crouched. Methodical.

My breath caught, pistol trembling in my hand. The beams worked exactly as we would've done—back and forth, wide sweeps narrowing down.

And in that moment, I knew the game had changed. They'd heard us. We weren't ghosts anymore.

The fire popped, the music hissed, but all I could feel was the weight of the light crawling toward us.

No option now but forward.

57

White Beams

The snap under my boot was a cannon shot in the silence. Laughter cut, the thin speaker still leaking music into the night, but every voice had gone hard.

Alcohol dulled their balance, not their suspicion. I pressed lower, pistol tight, finger stiff along the frame.

"There!" one voice cracked. "I saw movement. Ten o'clock."

"Hands up!" a third slurred, wobbling but steady enough. "Whoever's out there, come out now!"

The white beams swept closer. My chest tightened. Any second now, one of them would cut me wide open in white light.

Then a voice rose steadily from the dark. Chunk. "We're hikers!" he called. The words were intelligible, pitched just loud enough to carry. "Off-trail. Lost the blaze. Cold, hungry, not looking for trouble."

The headlamps faltered, the beams catching on bark instead of pushing forward. Muffled voices carried by the fire.

"Lost hikers? Out here? At this hour?"

"Bullshit."

"Let's see your hands or we don't listen."

Chunk didn't move. His voice came again, harder this time. "We're not walking blind into four lights. We've had guns pointed at us already this week."

That sparked them. A couple laughed—ugly, uncertain. One voice sharper than the rest cut through: "What's that supposed to mean?"

Chunk took a gamble. "We stumbled onto something we weren't meant to see. A drug operation—remote, organized, well supplied."

His voice stayed calm, clipped. "They know we found it. And now they're trying to make sure we don't walk out."

The beams wavered. Silence stretched, broken only by the crack of the fire.

Then one hiker spoke, slower now, sobered by memory. "Hold up. Remember that smoke? The plume we saw, back over the ridge?

"Yeah," another muttered. "And the lights—ATV's, couple nights back. Heard engines and gunshots, thought we were just camped close to locals."

"Locals don't patrol the woods with headlamps at three a.m.," Chunk snapped.

The banter shifted. Suspicion remained, but doubt had cracked.

Chunk pressed. "That's who we've been dodging. That's why we don't walk into beams. If you've seen it too, you know it's real."

A pause. Then, softer: "Alright. Red beams. Ours first, then yours. No white. Nobody blinds anybody." The harsh white flared down. In their place came four dim red cones, softer, eerie, bleeding across the trees instead of burning them. Seconds later, Chunk flicked his lamp to red. I did the same. The forest took on a fresh glow, everything bathed in a blood-hued haze. Shapes were still vague, faces shadowed, but it no longer blinded anyone.

A voice from the fire: "Now—step out. Hands where we can see. Slowly. No guns pointed our way."

Chunk and I could peer around the tree and see that they were not carrying weapons. Upon seeing that, we slowly stepped out.

"You've not seen what we've seen. Not one or two men, but a network. There are multiple large grow houses for weed and buildings for cooking meth. They run ATV's through the woods at all hours."

The hikers shifted uneasily, red beams jittering. One of them muttered, "Christ."

Chunk leaned a little closer, his voice low but sharp. "And now you're burning a fire big enough to beacon a mile in every direction. If we can see you in the dark, then so can they. These boys grew up here— they know every rock, every ridge, every shortcut. You're a bonfire in their backyard."

The drunkest of the group tried to laugh, but it came out weak. Another swallowed hard, his light shaking over us before cutting back to his friends. The air between us felt thick.

That's when the loud crack came echoing through the pines. A large caliber round we have heard too many times the past three days.

"We don't have time," Chunk pressed. "If you believe nothing else, believe this—if I could find you, they can too. And if they do, you'll wish we were the only strangers in these woods."

The silence that followed was heavy enough to bend branches. Their fire popped, spitting sparks into the dark. One of them cursed again, softer this time, like the truth was finally catching hold.

Chunk followed by saying, "if you don't believe us, fine, we are heading out to get the rest of our hiking party."

One of them—tall, stubbled, with his hood down—finally said, "Even if half of that's bullshit, it's not worth sitting here waiting to find out the other half."

The decision spread fast through their group like a cold front. Heads nodded, lips tightened. None of them wanted to be the last to move.

I stepped forward just enough for my voice to carry. "We've got a third. Bad ankle. He's holed up. We need to get back to him before first light."

That sealed it. Whatever doubt they had left, it wasn't enough to gamble. They turned in unison, moving with the urgency of people who'd just realized the woods weren't neutral ground. Packs were yanked from the ground, poles collapsed, stakes ripped from earth without care for the gear.

One of them kicked through their fire, then upended his Nalgene. Another followed, pouring the last of their water onto the coals. Steam hissed up, thick and white, rolling into the canopy like a signal flare. It didn't hide them—instead, it made the smoke rise sharper and thicker, as if someone had just punched the forest.

We all went still, letting the hiss echo out. The woods beyond were dead quiet—quiet in a way that felt more dangerous than an engine roaring up on us.

Chunk's voice came low, steady. "Now we move. Before that smoke becomes the only landmark anyone needs."

The hikers looked at us differently now—not like strangers, but like people tied to the same fuse. Their fire was out, their nerves were raw, and for the first time, I realized we weren't alone anymore.

One of them lifted his chin toward the dark trail.

They shifted, glancing between each other and then the trees, as if they expected them to split open. Before anyone could take a step, the radio at Chunk's hip crackled—sharp, alive, too loud in the hush.

A voice bled through the static. Calm. Certain. "They're not far. I can smell smoke."

Every head snapped toward Chunk, wide-eyed, caught in the same dread. He told them that we were able to find one of their radios, helping us keep tabs on their movements.

Chunk broke the silence, voice even but heavy. "We don't want a fight. We just want out of these woods alive."

One hiker swore under his breath. "Jesus. That smoke—we thought it was just other campers. And those engines? We figured they were hunters."

Their beams softened, cutting across us less like searchlights and more like signals of understanding.

Step by step, we fell into line and started down the trail, our lights overlapping as we hiked into the dark—unsure if we were walking toward help, or another kind of trap.

58

Names in the Firelight

Chunk fell into the line like he always does—instinct first, speech later. He moved slower now, feet picking the soft route through the ruts we'd made earlier, eyes on the ground as if the trees read their own map aloud. "Left at the two finger cedar," he murmured. "Then a wash that splits—take the bed left. You'll know the stump I mean."

He kept glancing over his shoulder, checking that we were following.

We followed.

The red beams bobbed behind us, painting the trunks with a weird, bloody light that made everything look soft and dangerous. The hikers moved with us, packs cinched, poles in hand. They were quieter than they'd been at the fire—no more jokes, just the clack of boots and the hiss of breath. The atmosphere between our groups felt delicate and new, like an agreement stitched fast with thin cord.

As we walked I started to talk. That's what you do when the dark presses in—you give shape to the fear by naming it. "I wanted five nights of quiet," I said, more to myself than anyone. "We left the trailhead, thought we were just getting away from the world."

One hiker, kept his head down as he listened. His red beam swung over the path like a slow pendulum. Now… the smoke you said? We saw a plume earlier this evening back on the ridge. Thought lightning, then it kept burning for a couple of hours. Didn't make sense." He sounded small saying it, like he'd been a fool for ignoring the pieces.

We told them the rest in broad strokes. Enough to explain why we couldn't stay where we were, what we'd learned from the radio, and how everything had shifted once we crossed a line we hadn't known existed. We didn't know them—not at all—and we kept our guard up, careful not to say anything that could come back on us later. Less was more. The hikers listened without pressing, the way people do when they understand that some truths are safer left unfinished.

That's when they told us who they were.

One of the hikers with close-cropped hair finally spoke, not stepping forward—just letting his voice reach us.

"I'm John," he said. He pointed with two fingers, slow, deliberate. "That's Thomas. That's Patrick. And the little guy, he's Jeremy."

He didn't wait for approval, didn't try to sell it.

"We served together. Army Recon. Long time ago now." He exhaled through his nose, a tired, almost embarrassed sound. "Doesn't mean we're heroes. Just means we know what it looks like when things are turning bad."

Thomas nodded once, his features fixing into something firm.

"We came out here to drink and sleep under trees," John said. "Not to end up in someone else's fight."

Patrick shifted his weight, eyes never leaving the tree line. "And when it does," he said quietly, "it usually doesn't announce itself first."

He looked into the dark, the way the woods seemed to breathe.

"Guess the woods didn't care what we wanted."

The last man hadn't spoken yet. He stood a little behind the others, shoulders drawn tight, like he wished the trees would swallow him.

Jeremy, said. "I didn't serve with them. We all grew up together back in Jasper, Georgia—same bus stop, same ball field, same dumb trouble." He gave a small, tired shake of his head. "They went Army. I didn't. Just stayed home, got a job, life, routine."

He looked from John to Thomas to Patrick—friendship, yes, but threaded with guilt.

"I come on these trips so we don't lose each other," he said. "Supposed to be a weekend. Campfire, catching up, passing around old and new stories."

His breath caught, not dramatic—real.

"This... isn't that."

Thomas gave him a look that was half affection, half warning.

"He doesn't run drills. Don't expect him to move like we do."

Jeremy bristled a little, but his voice stayed even.

"I can carry my weight. I just didn't sign up for... whatever this is."

John answered for all of them—quiet, flat: "None of us did."

Hearing it shifted something in my chest. Recon meant discipline—it meant pattern recognition—it meant men trained to move without being seen. It didn't mean they were looking to shoot us. It meant that if it came to guns and quads, it would feel like a fight with rules—less chance of a blind, chaotic ending.

Chunk didn't show relief, not exactly. But his shoulders eased a fraction. "Fairer than being jumped by guys who know the woods like breath," he said. "That's what I meant earlier."

One of them—Patrick—snorted, half laugh, half a hard breath. "We're not stupid. We carry trauma just like anyone else. But we know how to read tracks, how to hold a perimeter, how to move silently when you can't risk a sound. If we help you get out, it's not because you told a good story. It's because we know what a bad one looks like."

Water ran in a low voice off leaves, a steady, patient sound that made the hike feel like a procession. I watched the way Chunk's face tightened when we came to the wash he'd called—the one with the split bed. He stepped to the left as he said, "You see the flat rock with the dark line? Keep left there. Watch the root system—the big root that looks like a torn hand. That's the one that caught Zombie."

My throat closed. We'd been moving on a string of landmarks—threaded memories that meant more than a topo map could show. The hikers followed without question. Recon or not, they were good at following a man who knew the land.

Halfway back, Thomas finally spoke, voice low like he was afraid the trees might hear him.

"Why didn't you just keep moving? I mean—if you knew people were out here."

Chunk didn't even slow down.

"Because there's no direction that isn't death."

The group went quiet.

He kept his tone level, just facts:

"The ridge runs east and north. Straight up. Wet rock and dirt with nothing to grab. You don't climb it. You just slide back down and break something. Doesn't matter how tough you are—you can't fight gravity when the mountain says no."

No one argued.

Chunk shifted his pack and continued.

"The river's west. And it's running high. Fast. Cold enough that once you're in, your body locks up. You don't swim out. You drown. That's not a maybe."

Jeremy stopped breathing for a moment.

Thomas swallowed.

"And south?" John asked.

Chunk finally looked at him.

"That's the camp. The bunkhouses. Their ground. Their trails. Their people. You walk south, you walk into them."

"So we're in the middle," Thomas said, voice barely audible.

"Yeah," Chunk answered. "Pinned between a wall you can't climb, a river you can't cross, and the men who will kill you for trying."

I added, because it was the truth we had been living: "We didn't stop because we were tired. We stopped because anywhere we move has to be the right move. If we guess wrong, that's it. No second shot at it."

No one spoke after that.

They understood now.

We weren't lost.

We were contained.

John spat a piece of mud and swore. "If that's true, we're already past calling in uniforms. This becomes—what it is now. Get out or get taken." His voice had that edge Recon kids keep—no sentimental gloss.

We were a ragged, dangerous little convoy—three of us who'd been pushed hollow by the woods and three former soldiers with a civilian friend drinking beers under the stars. We might be enough.

Either way, there was no turning back now.

We moved without speaking, retracing our steps through the trees.

When our beams cut through the trees, Zombie's head snapped up. The moment he saw shapes behind Chunk and me, his whole body changed—rigid, eyes flat, pistol rising on instinct. He was exactly where we'd left him, fire guttering low beside him, the weapon loose but ready in his hand. His ankle was swollen, his face hollow in the red light.

"Hands!" he barked. His voice was hoarse but carried the edge of someone who'd already been forced to kill twice. "Get your damn hands where I can see them!"

The hikers froze. Their red beams scattered across the ruin, cutting Zombie's face into hard lines. One of them swore under his breath.

I stepped forward, palms high, voice fast. "Zombie, it's us—me and Chunk. They're hikers. We found them—"

But he didn't lower the gun. His eyes burned into the strangers behind us. "They with you, or they got you?" His finger tightened just enough to show he wasn't bluffing.

The night went dead quiet. No fire crack, no shuffle

of boots—just breathing and the sound of the pistol's metal shifting as Zombie locked his wrists.

Chunk moved then, calm but sharp, stepping directly into Zombie's line of sight. "Easy," he said, voice like a steady hand on a shaking shoulder. "It's me, brother. If they were holding us, you think I'd be walking point? You think I'd leave a rifle slung behind me?"

For a second, Zombie didn't blink. His chest rose, stalled, then dropped. His hand trembled once before he let the barrel dip.

Chunk crouched low, palms still open. "They're hikers. Four of them. Three Recon boys, Army, same unit. Not Deke's crew. We heard their music—we saw their fire. We vetted them. They chose to move with us."

Zombie's eyes slid to me. I nodded, slow and deliberate. "They're clean. Packs and poles. Just like us, they stumbled into this and didn't know."

The silence stretched, and for a second I thought the pistol might rise again. Then Zombie let out a long, ragged breath, lowered the gun to his lap, and dragged his free hand over his face.

"Goddamn it," he said. "You don't roll up with shadows behind you at two in the morning and expect me to clap."

Chunk allowed himself the faintest grin. "Fair. But you're not wrong to be jumpy. If it'd been me in your seat, I'd have done worse."

Zombie's eyes flicked past us to the hikers, still frozen near the treeline, beams down on the dirt. "And them? They buying this nightmare?"

Thomas, stepped forward just enough to be seen.

"We're buying it," he said simply. "Because we've heard the engines too. Because we've smelled the smoke and heard the gunshots. And because your hands are shaking like you've been through hell."

For the first time since we'd left him, Zombie laughed—short, sharp, bitter. He set the pistol on the ground beside him. "Welcome to the circle, then. Hell's got room for a few more."

The tension broke—not gone, not by a mile, but fractured enough to breathe again. We moved inside, the hikers fanning along the wall, Zombie leaning forward like he'd never quite stop watching them.

And that was when I realized trust wasn't a thing you built out here. It was something you borrowed, moment by moment, hoping it didn't collapse before dawn.

The hikers stepped closer, beams all red. For the first time, I could see them properly: stubble, wet jackets, tired eyes. They looked as wrung-out as we felt.

Chunk leaned forward, elbows on his knees, his frame filling half the circle. His voice came steady, carrying like he was laying down rules.

Zombie shifted against the rock, pain tightening his face, but his voice was steady.

"Trail names are fine out here," he said. "But I want real names. If we're walking together, we need to know who we've got at our sides."

The four hikers exchanged a look—quick, silent, the kind shared by people who have been through things together. Packs rested in a heap near the wall, boots steaming from the miles, faces tired in the fire's low glow.

John spoke first.

"I'm John. Retired Army, Recon, 101st Airborne. Guess some habits don't die."

Beside him, the broad-shouldered man gave a gravel laugh. "I'm Thomas. Not a medic, not officially. But I patched more knees and ankles in the field than most of the medics. Hail from Jasper like the rest of them."

The third leaned forward, restless even sitting still. "Patrick," he said. "Army 101st with John and Thomas. It doesn't matter how long I served—they made sure I never forgot where I started. In the hills of the Blue Ridge Mountains."

The smallest of the four shifted, his voice quieter but quick. "Jeremy. No military, but I've been friends with these bozos since we were kids."

Their words settled into the circle, heavy as boots.

Then Chunk nodded once, stepping into his moment. The firelight under the stone roof threw his size into stark relief, cutting his face into sharp lines. "We'll start with trail names," Chunk said. "That's just what we use out here. Habit."

"They call me Chunk. I've been big all my life, bigger than most. Cardio for days, lungs that don't give out. One guy said I was built like a damn Sasquatch. The name stuck." He tapped his chest. "Name's Steve. Air Force Linguist once. Just Steve now when not on the trail."

Zombie leaned forward, pistol resting casually in his lap now, eyes hollow but sharp. "Zombie. Got it on a climb years back. The trail was near vertical, switchbacks cutting like knives. I was so gassed I looked like I was dragging a leg, like one of those old movie zombies. Nobody let me forget it." His lips pressed thin. "Name's David. Still dragging, I guess. But I'm moving. Ex-Marine."

They all turned to me then. The fire popped, and I felt the eyes. I swallowed once. "They call me U-Haul. On the first hike I ever did with these two, I brought too much of everything—stoves, clothes, backups of backups. They said I looked like a moving truck. The name stuck. Extra gear usually slowed us down. On this trip, my spare water filter was the reason we didn't. That's me." I exhaled. "Real name's Joe. Just Joe. No military.

The circle held for a beat, all of us sitting in the orange-red glow with names laid bare.

John gave a slow nod. "Fair. That's enough. We're not strangers anymore."

The others nodded with him. Thomas poked at the coals with a stick. Patrick rubbed his hands together. Jeremy kept glancing out into the dark, as if he could already hear what was coming.

We weren't safe, not by any stretch. But danger widens its teeth when you're alone. With others beside us, the woods felt a little less hungry.

The fire hissed low. Outside, the woods waited. Dawn wasn't too far away. It felt less like safety and more like a deadline.

I stared into the tiny flames and thought about what the morning would demand: decisions, not calories.

Tracks to follow, not rest. Survival, not comfort.

Names in the firelight didn't mean we'd make it out. But without them, we'd already have been lost. Names in the firelight didn't mean we'd make it out.

But without them, we'd already have been lost.
    When the sun came up, one of those names might not answer back.

59

We Were Seven

There was more smoke than flame. None of us moved to feed it. The tarp kept the embers hidden, but we all knew the clock was ticking. By morning, the woods wouldn't just be dark and wet—they'd be alive with men who already knew too much about us.

Silence stretched after we had laid out our names. The fire popped, but nobody reached for it. Thomas' hand never left the stick he'd been prodding at the coals, like he needed the excuse to keep one fist closed. Patrick's eyes kept cutting to Zombie's pistol, measuring the distance. And Jeremy—he might have been the youngest, but he was the one who whispered something sharp that I couldn't catch, drawing a warning glance from John.

Chunk shifted, his size filling the space on purpose. "Names don't mean trust," he said, voice low. "Not out here."

For a second, I thought the circle might collapse before it even formed.

John broke the silence first. His voice was quiet but clipped, the way orders sound when you don't want them to echo.

"We're seven now. That's enough to move as a

squad. Enough to fight. We need to think stealth, not force."

As he spoke, I noticed it for the first time—each of the three veterans carried pistols, holstered tight against their hips. Not bulky hand cannons like something from a movie, but practical, serviceable sidearms. Glock 19's, by the look. Compact, reliable, built to run wet or dry.

Thomas shifted on the rock, his jacket tugging just enough for the polymer grip of his to flash in the firelight. Patrick's rode inside his waistband, tucked low but unmistakable. John rested his palm on his without even thinking, like it was part of him. It hit me then—they weren't just hikers—they were operators who'd never really shed the muscle memory.

Only Jeremy was visible bare. No pistol, no knife big enough to count. He didn't seem ashamed of it, just practical—like he knew three men armed and trained were more than enough when they went hiking. And maybe, on some level, he didn't want to carry the weight of pulling a trigger out here.

Thomas rubbed a thumb along the edge of his knee. "Rule one: no fire after this. It's warmth, but it's a beacon. We can't afford to look like we're dug in."

Zombie's face went cold and practical. "Fire's not for comfort. It's for keeping my core temp up and my ankle from locking solid. We try to move at first light without it, I'll slow you down before the ridge."

Chunk's eyes cut to him. "Then we chew faster. Pain's cheaper than bullets."

John leaned forward, elbows on his knees, eyes darting. "We've got one priority—exfil." He paused. "Everything else is secondary."

I swallowed hard and nodded. The language was sharp, tactical—still a step ahead of me—but I was getting there. Exfil. I didn't know the term exactly, but I understood the idea well enough: get out, clean and fast, before everything collapsed. My role was shifting—less dead weight, more voice. "If it doesn't get us out of here," I said carefully, "then it doesn't matter."

Patrick's laugh was humorless. "U-Haul gets it." He leaned back, tapping a stick against the rock. "Only thing these boys can't hide is the way they come and go."

Chunk adjusted his position. "I already pulled a bearing from the bunkhouses. South slope, low grade. If we shadow that path from a distance, we'll find where it spits out."

John turned toward him, eyes steady. "Bearing's not enough. You need eyes on the tire ruts, proof of exit. Otherwise you're chasing shadows in a forest full of them."

Chunk didn't flinch. "I'll get eyes. But we need to time it. Hit the path too early, they're still crawling it. Hit too late, we lose the element of surprise."

Zombie's voice was low, almost a growl. "So when?"

That's when all four of them—the ex-Recon boys and Chunk—looked at one another and answered in unison.

"Right before first light."

The words hung there like a verdict. First light meant no shadows to hide in, no red beams to cover us. It meant exposure. But it also meant visibility—our chance to spot tracks before they faded into the mud and underbrush.

Thomas leaned over the fire, nudging a stick through the embers until the sparks died.

"We move staggered. No bunching. Point and rear set, everyone else centered. Five meters spacing."

He glanced up once. "If we take contact, we break contact immediately—split left and right. Regroup after sixty."

John added, "Noise discipline. No chatter unless it's hand signs. Radio stays on low listen-only unless absolutely necessary. One crackle at the wrong time could pin us."

Chunk rumbled low, his voice like gravel. "And I'm not walking some Recon playbook just 'cause you wrote it. If it makes little sense out here, I call it."

John's eyes held steady, but Thomas leaned in. "Then make it make sense. Or we all die loud."

Silence started until Jeremy finally broke it.

Jeremy's face was pale in the dim light. Unarmed, relying on the others, but he didn't waver. "Then it's settled. We become invisible. Get on trail only when it's suicide not to."

Patrick finally leaned in, voice low but sharp. "We all know the real risk. They've got more men, more eyes. Maybe drones, dogs. We're a needle in their haystack. The only way we win is if we don't act like hay."

Zombie exhaled hard, ankle stretched out, swollen but stable. "Then it's simple. We don't stop until we're out. No matter how bad it gets."

The fire cracked, a last pop before it fell into quiet ash.

John looked around the circle, meeting each set of eyes. "This is it. No more discussing. Before first light, we move. We ghost their road, we find where it spits out. We get out of these woods."

No one argued. Because there was nothing left to discuss.

I sat there with the warmth fading from my knees, heart heavy but sharper than it had since this hell started. We weren't just three men anymore, stumbling half-dead through mud and fire. We were seven.

And six of those seven were armed. Five trained. Dangerous in a way that finally felt like it might balance the scales.

But dawn was coming. And dawn would show whether seven was enough.

60

Deadlier Than Firepower

John and Thomas still carried the weight of the bottle in their faces, a faint edge to their words, but they admitted it outright. "We've been through worse," Thomas muttered. "Adrenaline does the sobering for you."

John grunted. "Few hours' sleep and a hard march will finish the job."

All agreed we had maybe three or four hours of night left, and that was all the rest we were going to get. There was no world where seven bodies slept through until dawn. Instead, we settled on the obvious: no shifts, no formal guard duty. Everyone would lay down, but everyone would stay ready to move at the first crack of a twig.

John and Patrick checked their watches and set alarms for 0500. The faint green glow of tritium markers pulsed softly in the dark—steady, familiar, grounding. No signal, no satellite, nothing to sync with or call home. Out here, time was the only thing that still worked.

When we were settling in, John unfolded a paper map from a waterproof sleeve. The edges were soft, creased from years of use, the ink lines faint but still sharp enough to trace ridges. He was the only one with his headlamp on, red beam angled down so it wouldn't cut the dark. His eyes never left the terrain as he whispered bearings under his breath.

It was obvious he wasn't new to this. Every mark, every fold of the paper was treated like gospel. He wasn't reading a map—he was reading the woods themselves.

We sagged back against the stone, exhaustion settling over us like weight. My pistol sat on my thigh, Chunk's rifle leaned close, and Zombie stretched out with his ankle raised, his expression pinched with pain. The Recon boys loosened their holsters—no one planning to let go of a weapon, even if sleep got the better of them.

The overhang shielded us from the night sky, but not from the truth waiting outside: first light would strip us bare. No shadows left to hide in. No red beams to blur the world. Just seven men, one plan, and the thin hope that stealth would be enough to carry us out.

And as John traced the ridgeline with his finger, I wondered if the woods would let any of us leave at all.

John

The map was the only thing holding John steady— not the paper itself, but the lines burned into it, routes he'd traced in another country with different men who never came home. Terrain spoke to him the way faces spoke to other people. A ridge's slope was a raised eyebrow. A dry creek bed was a scar. The woods had moods, and if a man couldn't read them, he didn't last long out here.

They had seven now. Enough bodies to matter. Not enough to make mistakes.

If they stuck together, they'd move too slow. If they split, the wrong set of eyes would find them first. Classic problem—numbers without weight.

John traced the south slope again, the one Chunk had insisted held the road out. Chunk wasn't wrong. Tire ruts followed the path of least resistance, and a loaded truck didn't gamble on steep ground unless the driver was a fool. The north-facing grade made sense— low angle, natural drainage channels, places a rig could crawl without spinning out. But sense wasn't proof. Proof was seeing it with his own eyes before someone wiped the evidence clean.

He marked a point where the ridge flattened near a stream. If he were the one running this operation, that's where he'd cross. Water chewed up tracks fast, but if you hit it early—before the mud settled—you could see everything. They needed to reach that spot at first light. No sooner. No later.

Tactics were the easy part.

The men were harder.

U-Haul: listened, watched, absorbed more than he realized. He hadn't cracked. There was grit under that skin, coiled and ready.

Zombie: John didn't like that ankle. The man was tough, stubborn in a way that sometimes helped and sometimes killed. An injury was a bleed—slow or fast made no difference. The clock started the second it happened. Still, Zombie kept his pistol close even in sleep. John respected that.

Chunk: John trusted him most. Big men weren't supposed to move quiet, but Chunk did. He carried himself like someone who'd been in a different kind of fight once—maybe not in these woods, but somewhere breathing wrong got you killed. That mattered.

His own men weighed on him too. Thomas would find his footing once the whiskey fog lifted—he'd hiked worse under worse conditions. Patrick stayed steady as stone, his silence sharper than most men's words. Jeremy worried him, but not from lack of a weapon— sometimes the unarmed ones saw cleaner than the men gripping steel. Sometimes restraint was deadlier than firepower.

Still—the math sat heavy.

Six armed, one hobbled.

Two with no military background.

All stacked against mountain men with home-field advantage and whoever lurked above them in the chain.

John dragged a hand through his beard, feeling the stubble, feeling the weight of command creeping back in. He'd thought he'd put that burden down years ago, but out here, old instincts clawed their way to the surface the moment people looked his way.

The woods outside were black, but dawn was moving under the horizon, pushing upward. First light would come soon. And with it, the moment when every assumption he'd made would either carry them out—or bury them deeper.

He leaned back against the cold rock wall, pistol pressing against his thigh. No whiskey left in his system now. Just the mission.

U-Haul

John hunched over the map, red glow washing the creases like dried blood. His lips moved with the bearings he whispered to himself, a steady cadence:

ridgeline, creek bend, slope angle. His pen scratched every so often, noting details that only he seemed to see.

Zombie was the first to drop off, pistol resting loosely near his waist. His breathing came ragged at first, then smoothed into the rhythm of a man too exhausted to keep fighting sleep. Chunk leaned back against the rock wall, not out, but his eyes shut longer between blinks. Even I felt the pull, eyelids heavy. At some point I might've snagged a handful of minutes— nothing like real rest, more like falling into a dark hole and clawing back up before you drown.

The fire had long since gone to ash. The rock overhead hid us, but it also made the night seem heavier. Every time I stirred, John was still there, bent over the map like a priest reading scripture. My eyelids are finally getting heavy. I could feel myself drifting off.

61

They Were Hunting Us

I stirred awake, bones stiff from the cold rock. The red glow of John's lamp was gone. Only the faint digital green of Patrick's watch ticked down the hours.

Somewhere behind me, Zombie shifted in his sleep and groaned. Chunk exhaled slow, steady, not quite asleep but saving his strength.

I closed my eyes again, trying to find a scrap of rest before the alarms screamed us back to life.

But I knew—when they went off, when pre-dawn cut the woods open—we'd find out whether John's bearings would save us, or whether this rock overhang would be the last shelter any of us ever had.

The alarms snapped us out of whatever half-sleep the cave had let us borrow. High, thin beeps cut the dark. Watches slapped silent. For half a breath we stayed where we were—then the cave filled with motion.

John was already folding the map after one last look. The red glow from his lamp clicked on, then off, it was indeed about to be first light. "South slope," he said, voice flat and exact. "Two ridgelines over. Stream at the base. If we see any vehicles, that's where we'll see proof. That's our line."

The words landed like an order and a promise. Hope didn't come cheap—it came in bearings and angles and the cumulative weight of someone who'd navigated worse and survived.

Before we left, we settled the water situation. Jeremy and I loaded the filtration kit—my fill bag flattened in the pack, the filter where my hand could find it without thinking. We worked our way to a thin run of water at the draw's entrance, that deceptive little stream that seems innocent until you understand the whole slope empties into it. It slid by cold and brown, fast enough to feel like a message.

"Filter and go," John said. "No hanging around. We'll lose the dawn window."

Jeremy dunked the fill bag, pulled the handle until his forearms burned. Water poured into the bladder, and I watched the clear pulse steady into the bag like it was buying us minutes. Eight bottles were topped, my own bottle filled, one spare kept for emergencies. The filter spit a few weak bubbles and then sang clean.

While we worked, Thomas dropped to one knee beside Zombie. His hands moved with the practiced calm of a man who'd done this before—in desert heat, on mountain trails, maybe in worse places. He unzipped his battered first·aid kit, pulling out a roll of gauze, a thin aluminum splint, and a strip of elastic wrap.

"Boot off," he mumbled. Zombie grimaced but didn't argue, tugging at the laces until the swollen ankle came free. The joint was puffy, skin stretched tight and ugly, already darkening along the sole.

Thomas' fingers probed gently, finding the limits of pain, then worked fast. He padded the ankle with gauze, braced the outside with the splint, then wrapped it snug with the elastic—tight enough to give support, loose enough not to cut circulation. When he finished, the ankle looked bulkier, but stable.

"Try it," Thomas said, leaning back.

Zombie slid his foot back into the boot. The fit was stiff, but it held. He stood slowly, testing the weight. His face twisted, but he stayed upright.

"That'll keep you moving," Thomas said. "Not pretty. Not perfect. But it'll hold."

Zombie's face went firm, pride trying to outrun what his body couldn't. He hated the limp, hated the attention, but the brace held him together well enough to move. And for now, that was all we needed.

He hated being a burden. Everyone could see it.

We checked weapons once—again—and Chunk slipped the dead man's radio into a pocket and thumbed the power button out of reflex, feeling the hollow click like an accusation. Static was all it offered. Worthless for talking, maybe useful for a moment of recon later. For now, it was ballast.

John tapped a spot on the map one more time, then slid it back into its sleeve and tucked the sleeve into his jacket where it wouldn't sweat or tear. He looked at all of us, slowly and carefully, not with the warmth of a leader but the weight. He repeated the strategy from earlier. "Five-meter spread," he said. "One on point, one on rear, center stays tight. Hand signs for threat or silence. If it goes sideways, break left or right. Regroup at sixty."

It wasn't a debate. It was a rhythm.

There was a weight beneath the tactical certainty— something colder than the morning air. We had made enemies of men who knew the woods. None of that was on the map lines, but it wrapped around us like wet canvas.

"You ready?" Chunk's whisper was close enough that I felt the breath.

The confidence in his voice wasn't smart—just earned, the kind that comes from carrying stupid loads and coming back anyway. I nodded, steadied by it more than anything else.

We left the cave the way we'd come into it—quiet, practiced, all seven of us fell into step like we'd been born to this rhythm. The forest at first light was a different animal, gray and wet, every leaf a mouth. Our feet made noise, but there was no hiding that. But the spread and the silence kept the sound from forming into anything that mattered. They read tracks like a language: deer, fox, and then man.

John led, eyes forward, the route already mapped in his head. The rest of us stayed tight in the middle—Patrick and Thomas moving with practiced calm, Jeremy light and careful, learning the pace as he went. I stayed close to Zombie, who was hobbling but holding together better than I'd expected. Chunk brought up the rear, unhurried and deliberate, old instincts—climbing, hauling, reading terrain—settling into something that looked a lot like security. We weren't separating. Not now. Not for anything.

We crossed the small draws John had marked. Water running hard enough to steal a boot if you misjudged it.

By the time the ridge's shoulder came into view, the woods had thinned just enough to show one track we'd been hunting. A shallow groove, water-licked and fresh. It didn't feel like victory—only a narrow fact. Proof that the tracks had been this way. Proof that a road in meant a road out.

John's face went calm and cold. He didn't lift his eyes. "This is where we watch," he murmured. "Not now. Not yet. We read the pattern. Wheels tell us where. Men tell us how many."

We sank into the dark line on the side of the ridge—five meters, spread—and the morning wrapped around us. I felt the old fear and a new one braided together—the kind that comes from cold strategy and the kind that comes from knowing how much you have already risked.

The march wasn't the end. It was a promise. Following the tracks would be our action. We would learn the pattern. We would not stop for anything until we were out—or until the woods made the choice for us.

Zombie stayed on his feet, wobbling just a little, but the brace gave him enough strength to stand tall. His pride carried what the splint couldn't.

Nobody clapped him on the shoulder or called it good—we all just exchanged the looks that said we knew the truth. He'd move, but it would hurt, and every step would test how far grit alone could take a man.

We were still catching our breath when we heard them.

Three sharp cracks. Rifle fire that rolled through the trees, faint but close enough to freeze every muscle. Two more followed, faster, like punctuation to a sentence we didn't want to read.

Every head turned the same way, though none of

us could be sure. In the woods, direction was a liar. Sound bounced off the ridges and came from everywhere at once. All we knew was the shots were out there—close, deliberate, and in the path we thought we had to take.

John's voice came low, grim. "Fuck, they are close!"

Thomas's hand hovered over his pistol, his expression going still. Chunk slid the rifle off his back and brought it into a tactical ready position.

My stomach sank hard. We weren't just in danger—we were in trouble. The shots were coming from the direction we needed to go, at least we thought, but it was hard to tell for sure out here. Still, one thing was certain: we were close to something bad.

Deke and his boys weren't just nearby. They were pissed about the loss of their two men, wanted revenge, wanted our heads on poles.

This was no joke.

The only hunters in these woods weren't after animals. They were hunting us.

What they didn't know was we are now seven, not three. Regardless, shit was about to get real—real fast.

62

Crack Between Us

The last shot still echoed when Patrick hissed through his teeth.

"Screw watching. We should move on 'em now. Hit the bastards before they box us in."

John didn't even look back. "No. That's noise we can't take back."

Patrick shifted, his Glock already in his hand, knuckles white. "They already know we're here. Crawling through the woods just makes us prey."

Chunk's expression flattened. "Or it keeps us alive."

The air turned sharp, heavier than the gunpowder still hanging in it. For a moment, it wasn't us against Deke's men—it was us against each other.

Thomas raised a hand, trying to cut through it. "Save it. We're exposed here."

But Patrick wasn't done. He jabbed a finger toward John. "This isn't the Army, man. You can't keep us in a holding pattern while they stack bodies on us. Out here, aggression keeps you alive."

John turned on him then, the mask slipping just enough to show the steel underneath. "Don't preach survival to me. I buried more men overseas than you've ever stood next to. You want to rush twenty rifles with a sidearm? Be my guest. But don't drag the rest of us into your suicide plan."

Patrick stepped in, close enough that the barrels of their pistols nearly kissed. "Always the officer. Always the damn playbook. You think they'll give us time to measure bearings and watch patterns? They'll hit us the second they smell hesitation."

John's brows pulled together. "And they'll gut us if we charge like amateurs. Discipline is what keeps us breathing."

For a moment I thought one of them would swing, not at Deke's crew, but at each other.

Chunk muttered low beside me. "Hell with this. We were better off when it was just us."

Zombie nodded, shifting his weight off his splinted ankle. "At least we knew where we stood. Now it's seven bodies pulling in two different directions."

I kept my eyes on John and Patrick, but my voice was for my own. "We follow them, we inherit their fights. We break off, we're three against the ridge. Either way, it's a coin toss."

"Three was working," Chunk said. "We were still moving. Still breathing."

"Barely," Zombie shot back. "But yeah—less noise, less liability."

I felt the words heavy in my chest. These weren't allies, not yet. They were four strangers with guns, and one of them looked like he'd rather fight Deke head-on, than take another cautious step forward.

The argument between John and Patrick kept sparking, Thomas trying to keep it cool, Jeremy hovering uncertain. But the truth was evident even in the dim morning light—this wasn't one group. Not really. It was two. And the crack between us was only getting wider.

63

The Woods Exploded

They were still at it when the ridge narrowed, voices low but sharp enough to cut bark.

Patrick's words came like gunfire, fast and hot. "You keep waiting, John, and they'll circle us like wolves. Every minute we sit is a minute they close the net. You want to die cautious, fine—but don't drag the rest of us down with you. You talk like you've still got rank. This isn't a platoon, and you're not my CO. Out here, orders don't mean shit. Results do."

John stepped in, chest to chest now, with the kind of quiet fury that makes men nervous. "You want results? Discipline gives you that. Patience gives you that. Not tantrums and itchy trigger fingers."

Patrick's hand twitched near his Glock, not quite drawing but close enough to make everyone tense. "You think you're the only one who's seen combat? You don't own survival. You don't own me."

Thomas's voice tried to break through, calm but tight. "Enough. We can't afford to split. Not here."

But it was already too far gone. Thomas shifted, ready to step between them if it went hot. Zombie muttered, "This is bullshit—we were better off three against the ridge than seven with this circus."

I couldn't argue. Watching them posture, I felt the same question grind at my gut: are we safer with them, or safer without them?

And then everything froze.

A murmur drifted up the ridge—two voices, low but close, the sound that carried wrong in the trees. A patrol.

John's hand went up, fist clenched. Halt.

All the arguing, all the posturing, stopped in an instant. Weapons raised, eyes wide and scanning. The only sound was the wind echoing across the pines.

We sank low, boots digging into pine duff, bodies pressed against the slope. The divide between us was still there, hot and sharp, but for the moment survival crushed it flat.

The voices sharpened—crunching steps, snapping twigs. We stayed stone-still, breath locked. Every second dragged itself out, slow as fear.

Patrick's hand tightened around the Glock, and for a moment I wasn't sure who he wanted to point it at— the patrol or us.

We were prey trying not to be heard.

Two of them. Maybe three. Close enough to hear their boots scrape rock. They were sloppy. Sloppy meant vulnerable.

My thumb flicked the safety without thinking. One squeeze, then another, and they'd be down before they knew we were here. Clean, fast, efficient. Predators don't wait. Predators strike.

But I caught the others in my peripheral. John stood motionless, as if sheer patience could turn bullets aside. Thomas crouched low, knuckles pale but controlled. None of them wanted this fight.

And that was the problem. With them around me, there were seven bodies to give away the ambush. One flinch, one noise, and it'd be a bloodbath.

Still, the itch stayed in my finger. Waiting felt like suffocating.

From my angle, I could see Patrick's shoulders rise and fall, every breath ragged like he was one decision away from pulling us all into the grave. His eyes kept flicking between the patrol and us, like he was trying to decide which way the balance tilted.

My own lungs burned from holding back air. The world shrank to creaking boots, the smell of sweat, and the terrifying truth: survival didn't just depend on Deke's men not spotting us. It depended on Patrick choosing not to fire.

The voices moved on, slowly at first, then fading down the slope. Only when the sound bled into silence did I realize I was shaking.

But Patrick still hadn't lowered his pistol.

The voices grew louder. Branches cracked, leaves hissed under boots. Then again appeared—two shapes moving just thirty yards downslope, rifles slung casual, like they owned the ridge.

I could see their faces in the gaps between the trees. Sweat, cigarettes, the easy arrogance of men who thought the woods belonged to them.

Every muscle in me screamed to stay still. John's fist remained raised, his message clear: wait. Thomas's eyes flicked from us to the patrol, his lips pressed thin. Chunk's knuckles whitened around the stock of his rifle. Zombie hovered over his brace, one hand trembling despite himself.

But Patrick was shaking for a different reason.

His Glock was up, muzzle steady, chest rising and falling like he was holding back a scream. He scanned their path, then scanned us—reading every twitch, every breath, every ounce of hesitation. And I saw it in his face. He was done waiting.

"Fuck this waiting shit," Patrick growled.

And before John could grab him, before any of us could breathe, Patrick surged out of his crouch, weapon leveled, breaking cover like a wolf finally loosed from the chain.

The men's heads snapped toward us.

The woods exploded.

64

Running for Survival

Patrick came up from his crouch like a spring released. Two shots fired almost together—center mass, precise, unforgiving. The first patrolman fell back into the dirt, dead before his rifle even lifted.

The second man staggered, eyes wide, his rifle slinging wildly as he stumbled. He wasn't aiming—he was running, crashing through brush with panic firing each step.

"Get the fuck back here hillbilly!" Patrick roared, tearing after him, Glock spitting fire into the trees.

"Down!" Chunk's voice hit like a hammer as his hand shoved me flat. My cheek ground into damp leaves, heart beating so hard I swore it was making the dirt tremble. Gunfire roared overhead—Patrick's pistol, the panicked rifle, then heavier rifles deeper in the woods, snapping branches and shredding bark.

"Cover your head!" Chunk barked, pressing me lower as rounds cracked blind through the brush. I tucked tight, arms over my skull, waiting for the hot punch of a bullet that never came.

Then—silence. Just for a breath. The silence that isn't peace, only pause.

Chunk hauled me up by my collar, voice sharp and raw: "Zombie! Let's get the fuck outta here!"

He didn't wait for an answer. He took point, rifle high. I fell in behind him on instinct, legs running before my brain caught up. Zombie pulled the rear, no limp now—adrenaline had burned it out, replaced with something savage.

We weren't running a trail. We were running for survival.

Their training was all that was left.

65

My Gut Clinched

Branches whipped across my face as we tore downslope, every step blind, every breath a gasp of wet air. Chunk drove the pace, shoulders low, cutting through the brush like a plow. I stumbled after him, boots slipping on moss and loose rock, the world nothing but motion and noise.

"Keep up!" he barked, not looking back.

Zombie crashed behind me, heavier but steady, no limp, no hesitation—just raw adrenaline. The brace, the pain, all gone.

Rounds cracked somewhere behind us, but muffled now, the fight collapsing into echoes. Patrick's voice wasn't among them. We didn't have the luxury of caring.

Chunk veered sharp left, then dropped, pulling us down into a shallow draw. We skidded in on our stomachs, packs scraping rock, mud soaking our chests. He raised a fist—halt.

We froze.

Every muscle screamed to keep moving, but instinct knew better. Running made noise. Noise brought bullets.

I pressed my face into the earth, trying to slow the hammering of my lungs. Zombie dropped in beside me, wide-eyed, nostrils flaring like an animal still tasting the chase.

For a long, breathless stretch, nothing. Just the drip of water off leaves. Just our blood roaring in our ears.

Chunk finally whispered, voice buried in the dirt. "We need cover. Not just trees—terrain. Somewhere they can't see down into."

I nodded, though he probably didn't notice.

Zombie's mouth cinched shut, breath hissing out between his teeth.

Chunk pointed up-slope to where a ridge spine slanted jagged, rocks stacked like broken teeth. "There. If we belly into that, they'll walk right over without seeing us."

We crawled, slow now, every inch a fight. Pine needles worked into my palms. My chest rasped against wet moss. The ridge face grew above us, steep enough to blot the gray light, and then we were under it—wedged in a pocket where roots and stone formed a hollow.

We pressed deeper into the hollow, mud and rock swallowing us whole. My chest still heaved from the run, lungs burning, when a new sound cut the silence—footsteps crashing through brush, reckless, fast.

"Shit," I hissed, hand inching toward my pistol.

Then the voice—loud, panicked, too close.

"It's Jeremy, It's Jeremy! Don't shoot!"

My gut clenched.

Chunk and Zombie both spun, eyes wide with fury.

"Shut the fuck up!" Chunk spat, voice a low growl.

"Jesus Christ," Zombie hissed, "you trying to get us

lit up?"

Branches snapped, and then he was there—Jeremy, breaking into the clearing, eyes wild, face pale. He didn't slow. He launched forward as if he were diving for his life, arms outstretched, body hanging in the air for an instant before he slammed into the mud beside us. The breath blasted out of him in a grunt.

"I didn't want the fight. Patrick's out of his mind—charging patrols, looking to die. That's not me. Survival makes sense. Fleeing makes sense. If they're dead…" He sucked air, voice breaking. "If they're all dead, I don't owe them an explanation."

Silence followed, only the rasp of four men sucking air, pressed shoulder to shoulder in a space built for ghosts, not fugitives.

I didn't say it out loud, but the math had already shifted.

We were now four.

They were now three.

And the men hunting us…they were looking for three.

I lay there in the dark, the thought heavy in my chest. Could Patrick's rash decision—the one that split us apart—be the one thing that finally gave us a chance to escape this hellhole?

66

Dying Slow

We stayed buried in the hollow, the forest breathing above us.

Chunk broke the silence first, voice low. "We figure it here. Not running blind. Not again."

Zombie's whisper was sharp. "Figure what? We're still outnumbered. Still hunted."

"We're four now," I said, surprising myself. "That changes the math. They're hunting three, not four. That's an advantage."

Chunk gave a slight nod. "Maybe. But advantage don't mean shit if we waste it."

Jeremy shifted, mud sucking at his sleeve. His voice came out shaky, louder than it should have been. "So we wait? Just lay here until they sniff us out? Patrick wanted to fight, yeah, but at least he picked a direction. This—this feels like dying slow."

Chunk's head snapped toward him. "This feels like staying alive. You follow orders, or you shut your mouth."

Jeremy's eyes darted between us, frantic. "I'm not built for this, man. I'm not military, I'm not trained. I fix tents, I read maps, I—fuck—I don't know how to sit here quiet while they sweep the woods. I can't." His breath quickened, voice climbing higher with each word.

Zombie's hand shot out, gripping his arm hard enough to make him wince. "You can. Or you're dead. Those are the only choices."

The silence that followed wasn't peace—it was Jeremy's ragged breathing trying to wrestle itself down. His fear sat heavy, spreading to the rest of us whether or not we wanted it.

Zombie leaned closer, his breath hot against my ear. "Tell me the truth—are we better with him, or without? 'Cause I'll tell you right now, I don't trust him. Not with my life. Not with yours."

Chunk's eyes stayed locked on the ridge above. "I'd rather haul dead weight I know than carry wild cards. And Jeremy? He's a wild card."

I didn't answer. My throat was tight. Zombie was right. But so was Jeremy—waiting here wasn't a plan. It was just stalling.

Chunk tapped the mud with one finger, marking time. "We give it five more minutes. If the woods stay quiet, we move. Not before."

Nobody argued.

So we lay in the dirt, four men pressed shoulder to shoulder, waiting to see if five minutes could buy us the difference between life and death.

The forest went taut again—then the low growl of an engine bled through the ridgeline.

ATV.

The sound rolled across the trees, bouncing off trunks, crawling down into the hollow where we lay pressed into the mud. It was close, then closer still, gears whining as the machine clawed uphill, then fading as it shifted away.

We froze, lungs burning, until it thinned into nothing but a distant echo.

A crow barked once from the canopy, and then even that fell silent.

Chunk's expression shifted. He raised one finger, holding it in the air like a fuse waiting to burn out. We listened for gunfire, for boots, for voices—but nothing came. Only the rustle of wind through pine trees, the slow drip of water off stone, the sound of the woods remembering themselves.

Finally he leaned close, whispering sharply. "When it's just birds and wind, that's when we move. Not before."

Zombie frowned. "Move where?"

Chunk's eyes flicked downslope toward the tree line, then back to us. "Intel. Recon. We've been guessing too damn much. I'll go eyes-on, see how many, see how spread out. If they've pulled back, we need to know. If they're circling, we need to know that too. If I'm not back in thirty…" He didn't finish. He didn't have to.

Jeremy swallowed, mud streaked across his cheek. "You're going out there alone?"

Chunk's whisper was steady, not up for debate. "Better one set of boots in the leaves than four. We sit tight until it's clean again. Then I slip out. Quiet. You three stay dark."

He settled his rifle against his chest, eyes scanning the ridge, waiting for the last trace of the engine to die.

And just like that, he started to crawl out of the embankment.

Mud. Roots. Darkness. One inch at a time.

I pressed my face into the dirt, listening to his slow

retreat, praying it didn't snap a twig or draw a shadow.

The silence grew heavier. The wind shifted.

And then, faint—too faint to be sure—boots on gravel. Voices carried low.

Patrol. Close.

I gripped the earth, heart hammering. Jeremy's breath hitched like he was about to scream.

Chunk was still out there, moving blindly toward them.

67

One Heartbeat—Chunk

Chunk hugged the mud, inching forward through needles and roots, every movement measured against the breath in his lungs. Two boots in the leaves, not eight—that was the plan.

Voices bled through the ridge before he saw them. Boots sloppy on gravel, rifles hanging loose—the kind of walk men carried when they believed numbers kept them safe.

"Reed ain't the only one down," the smoker said, words muffled around his cigarette. "That outsider dropped one clean. Two in the chest. But he caught lead himself. Saw the trail—blood on the rocks."

The second man grunted. "So he's done?"

"Maybe. Maybe not. Deke says it don't matter. One's gone, one's leaking, leaves one more to clean up."

Laughter followed—ugly, nervous. "One more to go. Ain't much of a fight now."

Chunk held still. They weren't talking about his Ninjas—they meant the other three. One of their men was down; Patrick was probably wounded, maybe gone. But where were John and Thomas in that count? Deke believed only one outsider was left breathing.

Relief flickered—slight comfort—but it meant

nothing if they found him now. He'd be the second dead hiker this morning.

He slid another yard forward, pressing deeper into the brush until the shapes came into view. Four of them in a staggered line, rifles dangling over their shoulders, discipline long gone to hell. But numbers and noise could still kill.

Chunk kept his eyes low, tracking more than the men. The ground told its own story. Deep ATV ruts cut into the mud, carving down the slope toward a low draw. From there, the tracks arced east, away from the spot where his group had holed up. A serviceable path—worn, traveled often—something heavy moving in and out.

If they followed the ruts straight, they'd walk into the patrol head-on. But if they curved wider, took the ridge spine southeast and bent back around, they could shadow the trail without crossing it. They could get back to the spot they'd occupied that morning—higher ground, with an angle to watch without being seen.

He filed it all away—numbers, weapons, routes, terrain. Enough to get them out, if luck held.

The patrol shuffled past, still talking too loud, still walking too close. The last man dragged his boots, then stopped short.

He turned, squinting upslope.

Right at Chunk.

"Stop," the man muttered, voice low, "thought I saw movement."

The others chuckled, dismissing him, their steps fading downslope. But he lingered, staring into the brush where Chunk lay pressed flat against the earth.

One heartbeat. Two.

If he took a single step closer, the mud would give Chunk away.

68

Line in the Dirt

The minutes stretched like wire pulled tight. Every crack in the woods, every birdcall, every twitch of Jeremy's breath felt like the one that would give us away.

Then I caught it—movement low to the ground.

At first I thought it was them. A patrol swept back through, eyes sharp now, rifles ready. My hand clenched my pistol so hard my knuckles ached.

But then the shape took form—broad shoulders, crouching low, slow as a shadow. Chunk.

He made it into the hollow, mud streaking his face, his expression carved into that stone-cold look he wore when things got bad. His rifle stayed tight to his chest, his eyes sweeping past us to check the light gray behind.

I wanted to whisper, to ask, but the look on his face killed the words before they left my throat.

Finally, he slid in beside us and pressed his back to the roots. He stayed quiet a long moment, listening, like he was making sure he wasn't dragging danger in behind him.

Chunk spoke low. "I heard them talking. They think one of us is dead. One wounded. The third they can't find."

His eyes flicked toward the fog. "If they're right, they think the three of us are accounted for—dead, wounded, and one still running."

Jeremy swallowed hard, but Chunk wasn't finished.

"Four-man patrol. Sloppy. No spacing, loud. But they're out there. ATV ruts cut south through a draw. Service path. If we arc wide, ride the ridge spine southeast, we can shadow the track without ever touching it. Puts us back where we stood this morning—higher ground, with eyes."

His eyes locked on mine. Hard. Unblinking. "That's our way out. But if they catch our scent…"

He let silence say the rest.

Zombie's expression tightened inward. Jeremy shifted like he wanted to shrink into the ground.

My throat dried up. We weren't just staying alive now—we were trying to outmaneuver men convinced they had us boxed in.

And the margin between the two was razor thin.

That's when Chunk's intel hit me like cold water. Patrols. Tracks. A way out if we were smart enough, quiet enough.

But it was Zombie who broke the silence, his voice low, steady, carrying a weight I hadn't heard in days.

"We're still making it out today. One way or another. By the time the sun goes down tonight, we'll either be out of these woods—or in holes. No in-between."

His eyes cut across the group, daring anyone to argue. Nobody did.

He yanked his bootlaces tight and swiped a streak of mud across his cheek. "We go now. No waiting, no bright sun, no second chances.

He scanned the tree line like it was already closing on them.

"Our job's simple: get to the arc of those tire tracks before they figure out four of us are still breathing. We move fast. We stay low. We stay unseen. No camps, no breaks, no circling back. Daylight's only good as long as the trees swallow us."

He pointed downslope, his face going hard.

"Once we hit that road, we ride those tracks out. Flank parallel in a straight line. No wandering. No heroics. We're not fighting for sunset—we're fighting one hour at a time."

Jeremy shifted, eyes jumping between us. "No packs? Just... nothing?"

Something cold settled over Zombie's face. "Weight slows you. Gear rattles. We're done camping. This is the last push. You want to walk out of here? Drop everything that doesn't keep you alive."

I stared at him—at the streak of mud drying across his face, the ragged steel in his voice. For the first time since we'd been cut out of our food bags, Zombie didn't look like the man limping behind. He looked like the man he must've been before—trained, hardened, built for this kind of hell.

Chunk gave one slow nod. "He's right. We ghost this. We hit that arc before the sun's fully up, and we're off this ridge as fast as we can move. It's today... or it's nothing."

That was the line in the dirt.

The sky was still pale and cold, the woods barely waking up, and we had a razor-thin window before Deke's crew figured out their numbers didn't add up.

We weren't surviving until tonight.
We were surviving the next few hours.

69

Nothing Back

Chunk's voice cut through the trees, low but hard. "Leave nothing that IDs you. No names. No addresses. No trail names. If they find our gear, it dies with us."

He wasn't being dramatic—he was being right.

If they found anything that pointed back to who we were or where we lived, they wouldn't shrug and let it go.

They'd come looking.

For payback.

For silence.

For closure.

And the kind of people who run an operation like this?

They don't miss twice.

That was the line.

I touched the things that still felt like me. Knife first—small, honest weight in my palm, kept it clipped on my front right pocket. The phone next—screen cracked but not dead. Still powered off and slid it deep in my left side pocket and zipped it closed. The waterproof wallet Chunk gave us years ago stayed in my zippered back left pocket. Everything else was just noise.

The question hanging in the air wasn't gear. It was

Jeremy.

I glanced at Chunk's holster, then at Jeremy's bare hands. "You giving him your pistol?"

Chunk shifted the rifle sling across his chest. "Better if he carried one."

Zombie shook his head immediately. "Better for who? He panics—we die. He yells—we die. He mishandles it—we die."

Jeremy flinched. "I'm not gonna scream."

"You already sound like you might," Zombie said flat.

I kept it blunt. "We don't trust you with a firearm. Not yet. Not in this. You're staying unarmed."

Jeremy's eyes burned, lips pressed tight, but he didn't argue. Offended, yeah. Dangerous? No. He swallowed it down.

Chunk settled it with the final word. "No pistol. You pull your weight in other ways. End of story."

That's when he gave the rest of the order. "Tags. Patches. Trail names. All of it—gone."

We obeyed.

The trail name tags—fabric rectangles looped with paracord—came off first. U-Haul. Chunk. Zombie. I got my knife back out and cut my tag loose, folded it small, and slid it into my back right pocket. Zipped shut. I needed to know who I was, even if no one else could.

Then the patch.

The Hike Ninjas patch wasn't just fabric. It was bold and loud—three hooded hikers with backpacks strapped tight, faces masked like ninjas. One in teal, one in red, one in mustard yellow, mountains burning orange behind them, the words **'HIKE NINJAS'** cut sharp across the bottom like a team banner. We'd plastered the design on clothes, hats, coolers, trucks, water bottles back home. It was ours. It was a symbol that made us more than just three guys on trails—we were a crew, a unit, brothers. Cutting it off our packs wasn't just losing cloth. It was gutting part of who we were.

I slid my knife under the stitches and worked it free. Threads popped like bones. The patch curled in my hand, colors dulled by dirt but still defiant. I couldn't drop it. I tucked it with the trail tag in my zipped pocket.

Joe, U-Haul, Hike Ninjas—gone from the surface, not from the world.

We shoved everything else back in our packs fast. Stoves, clothes, broke down our trekking poles—every comfort that had once made us hikers. Chunk's rifle stayed. My knife stayed. Pistols stayed. The filter and fill bag were mine now, folded tight and shoved deep. If we hit water, we'd pump straight into our mouths. Plastic bottles were too loud where one crinkle might as well be a gunshot.

"We don't just dump it," Chunk said. "Hide it right."

We dragged the packs fifty feet off the faint game trail into a tangle of blowdown. Pine boughs, leaves, dirt layered until no colors showed, no straight lines left. From five yards away it looked like nothing but storm fall.

Chunk studied it the way a hunter studies tracks. He gave one nod. "If they stumble on it, it better look like a windfall, not a campsite. Move."

Zombie crouched low, scooping mud in both palms. "Coat up, one last time. Head to toe. No shine. No skin. No smell if you can help it."

This wasn't camouflage. It felt like a burial.

I really did not want to do this for the third time, but we smeared mud across our faces, forearms, necks. Pine needles ground into hair, moss smeared green under eyes. Jeremy gagged at the smell, then slapped mud on his cheeks like he wanted to disappear. Chunk's glare pinned him until he shut up.

By the time we were done, we weren't men anymore. We were lumps of the ridge, grown out of its dirt and rot.

Chunk set the order: "I lead. U-Haul on me. Jeremy behind U-Haul. Zombie on six."

Zombie's eyes flicked to Jeremy, measuring him. Then he gave me a nod—he'd cover the rear no matter what. Always had.

We dropped low, heels lifted, knees bent deep, bodies folded tight to the ground. Dirt scraped our boots, sticks and vines brushed our shins. Knives tight. Pistols quiet. Chunk's rifle held close, barrel tracking inches above the earth.

We moved in a crouch, slow and deliberate. Chunk flowed ahead like the ground had shaped itself around him. I mirrored—step, pause, breathe. Behind me, Jeremy struggled to stay quiet, his boots scuffing mud too loud, his balance off. Twice he clipped my heels, a soft knock that sent a jolt up my legs. Zombie hissed once from the rear, sharp and final, and Jeremy froze, chastened.

We kept moving, thighs burning, calves screaming, sweat cutting clean lines through the grime on our faces—but we stayed low, shadows inside shadows, doing everything we could to disappear.

The forest gave us nothing back. No more engines.

No more shots. Just birds in bursts and the long sigh of wind through needles. It felt like the woods wanted us gone but wasn't ready to decide how.

Still, each pull forward dragged the thought with it— Jeremy wasn't weightless. He was weight. He was a liability, breathing too fast, too loud, clutching too close.

And in the dirt, pressed to the ridge, I couldn't shake the question chewing my gut—were we four, or were we really still just three?

70

Kill Box

We moved in a line bent low and tight, bodies folded but upright, knees flexed, backs angled forward to stay beneath the brush. Chunk set the pace—slow, deliberate, patient—his rifle cinched flat against his chest. I matched him step for step, the rhythm burning into my thighs: plant, step, pause, breathe. Jeremy drifted behind me, too close, too loud. Zombie guarded our six, the kind of quiet that makes you suddenly aware of your own breathing.

No packs. No poles. Pistol snug against my mud-black hip, my folded fill bag pressed flat in my side pocket. Every step scraped something—bark, grit, needle litter. Pine needles stitched into my shins. My calves trembled, and the tension in my jaw was the only thing keeping my teeth from chattering.

The forest wasn't quiet. It was busy. Sap gnats clung to the sweat on my neck. Something small skittered through the duff at my feet and vanished. A far woodpecker hammered a rhythm that sounded like someone knocking on a door we couldn't see.

We moved inside the sound. We had to. Anything else was panic.

Jeremy sneezed once, then twice.

They weren't loud—but in the stillness they

cracked sharp as snapped trees. My boots stopped on instinct. Chunk froze ahead of me, head turning just enough that I caught one eye, hard and bright beneath the brim. Behind me, Zombie's hiss sparked quick and quiet, like striking a match and killing it fast.

Jeremy crushed his mouth into his sleeve. "Sorry," he breathed, the word swallowed by dirt.

We held still long enough for the birds to come back, long enough for the wind to remember the pines. When the forest forgave us, Chunk lifted two fingers—move.

We went again. Step. Settle. Breathe.

The slope pinched, funneling us between a snagged blowdown on the left and a spine of rock on the right. It felt like moving through a choke point. The air grew close and damp. Needle litter darkened, sour and rotten. I caught the smell of iron in the soil—and something old and sharp beneath it. Ghosts of fuel, maybe. Old ATV scars buried under years of pinefall.

Jeremy clipped my heel again. Not hard—just enough to jar grit under my sock.

"Back off," I whispered.

"Can't see your feet," he whispered back, too quick, too honest.

"Then watch my shoulders."

Chunk stopped us short of a thin screen of laurel and held there, listening. I listened with him. The woods carried a soft shiver I didn't like, a kind of held breath that wasn't ours. Wind pressed from one direction only. Birds had cleared a lane somewhere ahead.

Through a net of green I could see a swale where water cut the ridge and left the ground smoother than it should've been. Not a stream. A track. The kind that goes wet-mud dark after rain and remembers tires. If we were right, this was one feeder that arced southeast toward the road out. If we were wrong, it was a lane men had used to drag bodies.

We watched it for a long time. Long enough for my thighs to throb. Long enough for a gnat to land at the corner of my mouth and crawl, and for me to let it, because batting at it would be noise. Long enough for Jeremy to start that thin, high breathing that means a person is winding himself into a panic.

Zombie broke the stillness with a whisper. "We slow for him, we die for him."

Chunk didn't turn. "We don't leave our own."

"He ain't our own," Zombie growled.

A silence like a blade edge.

"We don't leave our own," Chunk repeated, softer, heavier. "We move the way we planned: arc wide, never touch the cut, shadow it southeast until it bends. We do not cross open ground. We do not skyline. We do not hurry. We do not stop."

"Copy," I breathed.

"Copy," Zombie said, but it sounded like a warning more than agreement.

Jeremy didn't say "copy". He pressed his face into his sleeve again, like the word might come out wrong.

Chunk inched us forward, skirting the laurel screen. He took us high, above the swale, where the ground was meaner but thicker with cover. I followed the exact line of his shoulders. Behind me, Jeremy's boots found the same depressions my boots left, but he dragged one leg and left a smear I didn't like. Zombie would brush it with his feet as he passed. He always cleaned up what he could. He'd done it for me before, when I was new to fear.

We slid past a cedar blown down in the last storm. Its root ball had torn a hole in the earth big enough to swallow a man twice over. The hole was black and cool, the place that holds water and smells like stone. For half a second I wanted to crawl in and shut the world outside. Half a second is how people die though.

Chunk's hand rose—stop. He held it there, then rotated his wrist—listen.

At first there was nothing but wind and insects and the long low groan of trunk against trunk. Then a faint tick, wrong in the natural chorus. Another. Light, careful steps were barely noticeable. Not the heavy stomp of Deke's sloppiest boys. Someone who knew how to move quietly but didn't know the forest was listening.

They were in the swale. Close. Invisible through the laurel. The sound of a radio button depressed and released—a tiny plastic click that cut my spine in half.

Jeremy's breathing climbed. He tried to smother it and made it worse. Zombie's fingertips closed on his shoulder and squeezed once: "you breathe like us or you don't breathe at all."

The steps paused. The radio clicked again, two brief taps. A language we didn't speak.

Then they moved on, not toward us, not away— parallel, drifting east, deeper into the funnel the land had made.

Chunk waited a full minute after the sound was gone. Then another. Then a third. He counted them off on the knuckles of the hand that held his rifle.

Only then did he move.

The ridge changed under us as we arced. Brush gave way to low huckleberry and the lichen that makes rock look wet even when it isn't. We slid along a seam of stone scoured clean by rain and boots. Ancient flow. Recent traffic. My shirt stuck to my stomach. Mud dried and cracked at the corner of my mouth like salt.

"Speed up," Zombie whispered. Not to Chunk. Not to me. To Jeremy. "You breathe when he breathes. You stop when he stops. You touch his boots again and I leave you in the open."

Jeremy said nothing. He sped up.

We cleared the stone seam and dropped into a saddle where leaf litter had drifted deep. It was the quietest place we'd crawled through all day. It felt like someone had put a hand over the forest's mouth. I didn't like it. Silence can be mercy. It can also be design.

Chunk's shoulders tightened in a way you only see when you've watched a man too long. He felt it too.

He took us off the straight line that wanted to pull us into the middle of the saddle and dragged us up along the edge where the ground pitched and the trees grew in crooked because they'd had to fight for light. My boots slipped twice. Jeremy slipped three times. Zombie caught his shoulder the third time and held it until the panic left him.

Through a gap I saw the far side of the saddle: a narrow throat between two boulder heaps where the swale we'd been shadowing pinched to a single cut. The brush there had been broken chest-high, not by deer. Boot lines crisscrossed at the mouth. Fresh scuffs on stone. Above it, a limb hung with something that caught dull light—a strip of tape or a flag, or a bell with its tongue wrapped in cloth. A warning line for men who didn't trust their eyes.

"Kill box," Chunk whispered, calm and cold.

Chunk didn't look back, but his hand flattened, palm down—low. Then he pointed with two fingers along the upper edge, tracing a line that would keep us from ever stepping into the throat, from ever putting our bodies where their rifles could rake left to right and right to left and pick off all four of us at once.

"Learn it," Zombie breathed, the whisper so faint I felt it rather than heard it. "Ridges don't try to help you. They try to herd you."

Jeremy's touched my boot again, harder now, deliberate—as if to say, "here, I'm here." It still jolted me. It still said liability in my mind.

We inched on, away from the throat and its quiet and its promises. The swale kept pulling east. We kept above it, ghosts in bark and mud and breath.

A crow barked twice from downslope. Then once more. A pattern.

Chunk stopped so slowly that stopping was movement. His shoulders lowered by a hair. He lifted his fist—hold—and I felt the order run back through my arms and into Jeremy and then into Zombie.

Mud cooled against my skin. My pants twisted from the crouching. The patch and tag in my pocket pressed into my hip like a memory with edges.

Somewhere ahead, the quiet men waited for noise— patient hunters crouched in the brush, rifles resting on their knees, ready for the first careless branch snap.

We were caught between them, ghosts crawling through a throat that wasn't ours. One side wanted us to blunder forward—the other wanted us to hesitate.

Either way, the ridge was funneling us where it wanted: into a kill box.

We were between them, and the ridge wanted us in the middle.

We didn't know it yet, not the shape of it, not the count or the angles, just the pressure of a place that narrows because somebody decided it should.

Chunk's hand closed—back. Not a retreat, but a redraw.

We melted up, inch by inch, off the saddle's lip and into thicker growth, trading ease for cover until the throat disappeared and the world went back to green and brown and breath.

Jeremy's legs trembled.

For the first time all day, I understood the mistake we'd been making.

They weren't waiting for us to move forward.

They were waiting for us to decide which way to run.

71

Peel Like Bark

The engines came back before we even finished swallowing the last crawl.

Not a distant murmur. This time the roar of sound cut the ridge like a saw. ATV's, multiple, worked the high ground with a confidence that smelled like blood.

We hit the dirt, stomachs and forearms and faces pressed into wet needles. There was no shadow to hide in today, only stillness. Any movement would glitter in the light like a signal.

The two machines crested the rise opposite us. No covered faces on the riders. Both men sat upright, arms locked straight on the handlebars, like they were posing for a wanted poster. Rifles hung across their laps, easy as belts. They stopped their engines halfway up the rise, letting the machines idle and the words reach us clean.

"Reed bled out on our watch!" the first man shouted, voice raw and close. "You think you're sneaky? We're gonna skin you, peel you like bark, and hang what's left from the oaks so every hiker sees 'em in spring!"

The second man's grin was a sound. "We'll cut out your tongue and sew it to the signpost. Leave your boots for the dogs. Don't make us have to find you twice. Come on out and make it easy."

They revved in unison like a challenge. The motors barked, and the ridgeline threw its taunts back at us until the words came from everywhere.

Jeremy's body seized behind me. His breath went jagged, tiny sobs trapped somewhere in his chest. He scrabbled at the dirt as if he could push the ground between us and the men. His hands found my shoulder and slipped, clumsy and wet with mud.

Zombie was on him before I could move. The knife slid free with a soft sound of leather, then steel pressed cold under Jeremy's chin. The point barely dented skin. The threat was the pressure, the intent so close you could taste it.

"Calm the fuck down. You hear me?" Zombie breathed, voice like the blade in his hand. "You make a sound and this ridge is your grave. Do you understand?"

Jeremy's eyes rolled white with panic. He tried to form words and could barely catch them. "I—I can't..."

"Shut the fuck up." Zombie's whisper cut through his panic. "You scream, you make noise, you give them something to aim at and you die. Not a warning. A fact. You die right here and they will think you are the third dead hiker."

The riders barked out short, ugly laughs. One leaned forward and spat threats across the draw. "We'll gut you slow. Hang you where the river can see. Sheriff'll sign the death certificate himself."

Jeremy's face contorted, lips working in wet shapes. He buried his face in his sleeve, but his breath still hammered out—loud, frantic, counting the seconds for him.

Zombie didn't move the blade. He kept it there, steady as a vow. "Say it," he told Jeremy.

"I understand," Jeremy gasped, the words forced out like a rotten tooth.

"Say it again, like you mean it." Zombie insisted.

"I understand." The last syllable trembled like a question.

Zombie shoved the knife into a tree beside Jeremy's hand with a dull thud. The man on the second ATV, who'd promised to skin us like bark, let out an evil laugh and kicked his machine. The two ATV's revved away, looping the ridge, their motors a slow snarl in the trees.

Chunk leaned in close enough that I could feel his breath on my ear. "They really think there's one of us left," he murmured, voice low, almost reverent. "Just one. They don't know we're stacked four deep on this ridge."

Zombie wiped Jeremy's panic off his sleeve and settled beside us, eyes cutting through the dawn light like slits of steel. "That's the only goddamn break we've had in days," he whispered. "As long as they think they're hunting a single wounded deer, we've still got teeth."

I nodded, though my pulse hammered. "It's something," I breathed. We're harder to hit if they think we're just one shape in the trees."

Chunk shifted his weight. "They'll figure it out soon enough," he said. "But until then?

Zombie's expression didn't change, but his whisper cracked like cold bone. "Then let 'em hunt a ghost. Ghosts don't leave tracks."

Chunk never turned, but his voice slid through us

all, steady and cold. "We move. You make a sound, you die here. Not a story. Not a sermon. That's the rule."

We hiked out, slow as a funeral pace, each inch bought with a small prayer to nothing. The riders' threats hung in the air like tar—sticky, heavy: hangings, dogs, stakes, signs. No answer came from the forest. The trees only listened.

When the motors at last bit down the slope and faded, the silence that came after was thick, as if the woods had soaked up the words and let them sit there like poison.

Chunk moved like a machine, slow and precise. "Arc wide. Stay above the cut. Never cross open ground. Never hurry. Don't let them herd us." His breath was a plan. His eyes were hunting the next line.

Jeremy didn't speak. His chest heaved and his hands shook. He tried to keep pace, but once he slipped again and banged my heel with the side of his boot. It was a tiny thing, but in the math of this ridge it felt enormous.

We kept moving. Every scrape of a boot, every little wet whisper of breath behind me sounded like a noise we couldn't own. The riders' words had changed the ridge—the ground felt narrower, meaner. Jeremy's panic had become not just a problem to manage but a hazard.

And in the quiet stretch that followed, as we moved across stone and rotten duff, I felt something colder than fear: the sense that the woods had chosen who it would take next—and it was not gentle about its preferences.

72

Get Up Here

The woods went quiet in a way that felt intentional— like the whole ridgeline had paused to listen to the engines fade. The men's threats still clung to the inside of my skull, jagged and fresh, but the only sounds were our breath and the soft ticking of cooling metal in the trees below.

We needed distance. We needed direction.

We needed a way south.

Chunk crouched beside us, eyes tracking the dark rise above. A pale scar cut the slope where rock showed through the trees. Broken slabs stepped just enough to promise a way up. "We're blind down here," he murmured. "We don't know where the hell the road is anymore. We keep running circles and we're gonna run straight into those assholes."

Zombie's jaw flexed once—tight, controlled. "Elevation buys us sight lines," he said. "Maybe wind advantage. Makes it harder for them to sniff out sound."

Chunk nodded, still studying the rock. "And from up there?" He tapped the pale line with two fingers. "I might see a path south that won't get us gutted."

It was the best idea we'd had in awhile.

"I'll go," Chunk added before either of us could argue.

He wasn't wrong. The ridge wasn't a cliff, but it sure as hell wasn't kind. Roots twisted like knuckles, slick stone sweating cold humidity.

"You fall, we can't come get you," Zombie said quietly. "They'll hear us from a mile."

Chunk smiled without humor. "Then I won't fall."

"You sure?" I asked.

"Nothing about this is sure," he said. "But it's the only move I see."

And then he went.

Chunk moved with the kind of patience you don't get from the gym—you get it from years of trusting your life to whatever the mountain offers. He found holds we couldn't see until his hand was already in them, leaned into the stone like it was something he'd studied, not something he feared. Slowly, deliberately, he climbed until the ridge stopped looking like a wall and became a staircase only he could read.

We watched, barely breathing.

Halfway up, a flat ledge stole him from view.

Then another. Then nothing but the cold vertical scrim of granite and wet moss.

Minutes stretched.

Then doubled.

Then kept going.

By the tenth minute, my palms were wet, Zombie's leg bounced silently in the leaves.

"Come on, Coach," Zombie whispered.

Then—finally—faint scuffing. Chunk stepped into view at the ridge's edge. He didn't wave. He didn't whisper.

He hooked two fingers and yanked them toward himself—sharp, angry.

"Get up here. Now."

And with that, the three of us prepared to climb into the only silence the woods were willing to offer.

73

Bone-Splitting Thud

I went first. My legs remembered the route before my lungs did. Back in the day, I could sprint this pitch so fast Chunk had to holler at me to slow down so he could keep the rope taut with his belay device. That was another life. Now my hands and arms burned, my breath came quick and ragged, but I still pulled myself over the lip of the first shelf.

I peered down. Jeremy hadn't moved an inch. He stood at the base, shoulders tight, eyes wide as if the rock had teeth. His hands were clenched so hard his knuckles were white against the mud.

"I—" he stammered, "I can't. I can't do heights."

I could see Chunk look over the ledge and we exchanged a look that didn't need words. This was a problem the size of the ridge.

Below him, Zombie watched Jeremy. I could feel him there more than hear him—a stone in the grass, patient and brutal. He stepped closer until his shadow cut in front of Jeremy, and his voice slid up the face in a flat, hard edge.

Zombie

Zombie stood just below Jeremy, staring up at him. Even through the hardened mud streaked across

Jeremy's face, he could see the flush beneath it. Sweat poured off the man's forehead, dripping from the tip of his nose. He looked less like a climber and more like a man standing in front of a firing squad.

Zombie leaned close. "You either get up this wall or you stay here. You know what that means. We're not coming back down to get you."

Jeremy's mouth opened and shut, eyes flicking between Zombie and the rock. He looked ready to collapse right there in the dirt.

Zombie started his climb, not waiting for a response. At first the holds were generous, his body moving on muscle memory. But quickly, the rock changed. Jugs shrank into edges, ledges into smears that begged boots to slip. His forearms screamed with every pull. His bad ankle didn't help, but he ignored the pain, muttering his usual Marine mantra under his breath: Embrace the Suck.

He stopped to catch his breath, and that's when he looked down. Jeremy was moving—but barely. Slow as death, one shaky grip at a time. He'd frozen maybe twenty to thirty feet off the ground, pressed against the wall as if he thought it might swallow him whole.

"Climb," Zombie called down, low and sharp. "Don't be a bitch. Move."

Nothing. Just Jeremy's ragged, loud breath echoing off the rock.

"Climb!"

Jeremy twitched, lifted a hand, and froze again. His whole body started shaking.

Zombie sighed, cursed, and began working his way back down toward him. Every downward move was worse—holds smaller, body heavier. By the time he got close, Jeremy was crying. Not quiet sobs—wet, ugly sounds that carried farther than a rifle shot.

"Please," Jeremy gasped, reaching out with one trembling hand. "Don't leave me—pull me up—please—"

Zombie didn't move. He didn't trust him. One grab, one slip, and they'd both be dead. No harness, no rope. Nothing to save them.

Above, he could hear Chunk and U-Haul yelling—voices tight with panic but controlled enough not to echo down the mountain. "Shut him up or pull him up—just do something!"

Jeremy's cries only grew louder. His whole body shook so violently Zombie thought he'd peel right off the rock. Every second was a death sentence for all of us. Every sob a beacon—here we are. Come skin us like bark from a tree.

Survival took over. Zombie's muscles seized, breath locking in his throat.

Then Jeremy grabbed his boot.

Not steadying himself. Pulling.

Zombie's hands slid. The world tilted.

One more tug and they'd both disappear.

The thought barely formed before his body answered.

He drove his boot into Jeremy's chest.

Jeremy didn't scream on the way down. Just one grunt—and then the bone-splitting thud that rolled up the rock and punched straight into Zombie's ribs.

The woods froze. Even the birds went silent, like they had turned their heads to look.

Zombie clung to the wall, sweat burning his eyes, breath tearing out of his lungs. He couldn't look down.

Couldn't afford to. It was him or them—truth stripped down to its knuckles.

Hand over hand, he climbed higher, forcing his body to move. Above him, two shadows waited—his brothers, the only ones left.

The Hike Ninjas were intact.

For now.

74

Breathing Room

Zombie pulled himself over the lip of the ridge and collapsed onto his side, chest heaving like he'd carried more than his own weight up the rock. Mud streaked his face, sweat cutting rivers through the grime. He didn't look down. None of us did.

For a long while, the only sounds were the wind scraping the ridge and the pound of blood in my ears. Below us, the forest held still, heavy as stone.

Chunk crouched nearby, eyes locked on Zombie. Not angry. Not forgiving. Just steady, cold, measuring.

Zombie sat up, wiping at his face with trembling hands. "I killed him," he whispered. His voice was thin, as if he hadn't meant to say it out loud. "Boot to the chest. He was pulling me down... and I just..."

His words dissolved into the air. He opened his fists, then clenched them again, over and over, like he was trying to feel whether they were still his.

Chunk spoke first, voice flat and certain. "You saved us. Don't twist it into something else." Zombie's head snapped toward him, eyes hollow but sharp. "I murdered him."

I slid closer, crouching, so he had no choice but to meet my eyes. My throat was tight, but I forced the words out. "No. Jeremy killed himself when he froze. He was finished the second he locked up on that wall and grabbed your boots. You just made sure the three of us didn't go down with him."

Chunk leaned in, his voice steady, controlled. "You heard it. Every sob carried for half a mile. That was a beacon, and you shut it down. Don't confuse survival with malice. You gave us a chance."

Zombie's breathing slowed, but the weight in his eyes didn't fade. He rubbed the back of his neck, then muttered, "Felt too easy. One push. That's all it took."

I gripped his shoulder until he finally looked at me. "Easy doesn't mean wrong. If we make it out of here—if we ever see another sunrise—it'll be because you did that. That decision right there, that's what bought us a fighting chance."

Chunk exhaled, sun catching the sweat on his brow. "It's twisted, but it helps us. If Deke's crew finds Jeremy, they'll believe he was the final one standing. They will stop hunting us, we are now ghosts, but we need to stay invisible. We got a sliver of breathing room."

That landed heavier than anything else. Zombie blinked, the tremor finally leaving his shoulders. What felt like a nightmare choice had become leverage. A weapon we didn't have to carry.

Chunk finally sat back. "Three again. Maybe that's how it was always meant to be."

The words settled like stone. Heavy. Unmovable.

Zombie didn't answer. He just stared at his hands like they still held Jeremy's weight, like he could still feel the push in his boot. The surrounding silence wasn't relief—it was a shadow pressing closer.

Somewhere below, Jeremy's body was cooling in the dirt. And somewhere out there, Deke's men would find it.

They'd think we were done. All three no longer a threat.

They'd be wrong.

75

Miscount

Chunk's grin wasn't big, but it was real. "Good news now," he said. "You can see damn near everything. South is clearer than we thought. There's a path along that ridge—flat enough we can walk it for a good stretch without being seen."

"Line of sight?" Zombie asked.

"Clear. No engines. No buildings. No movement. If we get up there, we can make ground fast without touching the forest floor. Beats dodging hillbillies on ATV's." The ridge bought us sight, and sight bought us a choice.

From where we crouched on the ridge, the view opened just enough to read the terrain. Through the gaps in the branches, the line below wasn't narrow or clean like a hiker's path—it was wide, ugly, chewed apart. Twin tire ruts with a churned-up spine between them. A work road, plain as day.

Chunk leaned forward on his elbows, eyes narrowing. "See how it hugs that shoulder, then drops into the notch? That's the obvious line."

Zombie's finger followed the same bend. "Look beside it. Softer ruts. ATV's. Two machines riding wide. Not just a stroll—they're moving weight."

I caught it too: a pale patch chewed bare, stacks of

pallets slumped under a tarp. Not hikers. Not campers. A drop site.

"Traffic pattern," Chunk muttered, tapping where the track bent and vanished into shade. "They come from the west, cut north, park on that flat. That's their staging zone. We don't want any part of it."

Zombie angled his chin north. "But see that clay break? Culvert under the road, stream feeding through. If we flank, crawl, we can use it as cover. Once across, we hug the far treeline until the grade spits us out closer to the county road."

Chunk sketched the route in the air with a dirty finger. "That's the play. We flank north, drop into the lee, then move south to the culvert. We wait for a lull and slip through."

He paused. "Once we're on the far side, we stay in cover—hedges, shadows. If there's a fence, we climb it slow and quiet. If not, we cut across the fields and keep moving."

I asked the question anyway: "Timing?"

"Before dark," he said flatly. "Not after. Descent is suicide in black. We go down while we can still see footing. By dusk, we're staged near the road, not clinging to rock."

No one argued. Jeremy was still down there, broken in the notch. If Deke's boys found him, they'd think it was all over and would stop the hunt. That miscount might have been the only advantage we had.

So we stayed on the ridge long enough to be sure— long enough to scan every bend of the road for movement, long enough to let the map etch itself into our heads. The rock baked hot under us, sweat pooled beneath our shirts, cottonmouth drying our tongues.

The hours after that stretched thin and quiet. We moved when we could, stopped when the ground or the sound demanded it, measuring progress in yards instead of miles. Muscles cooled too fast when we held and burned too hard when we went again. No one complained. No one needed to. The ridge kept score for us.

Clouds stacked and unstacked overhead, light dimming by degrees rather than minutes. Wind slid along the spine of the land and shifted, never settling long enough to trust. Somewhere downslope, a branch cracked once and went still. We waited it out, knees bent, breath counted, until the forest decided it wasn't about us.

By mid-afternoon the air felt heavier, like it had learned something and wasn't ready to share it. Shadows shortened, then slowly began to stretch, reaching farther between the trunks. We adjusted without talking—staying off skylines, trading easier ground for cover, letting the ridge dictate our shape and speed.

When the sun tipped west and shadows began their long crawl across the treeline, Chunk finally spoke. "Time to get down," he said. "Ridge already claimed one. We don't give it two."

The climb was careful, slow. Roots became ladders, shadows became grips. Twice my boots slipped, and twice Chunk's hand clamped my wrist before I dropped. The ridge was hungry, and we weren't feeding it.

At the bottom, we didn't move far. First priority was water. We found a trickle running over stone, filtered straight into mouths. Just hands and lips and the bitter taste of iron. Enough to quiet the burn in our throats, but not enough to feel full.

We pulled back into cover, tucking ourselves near a culvert that gaped dark and wet like the mouth of a cave. That's where we'd wait, pressed into brush and mud until the light drained away.

Above us, the clouds kept thickening, dragging the day down faster than it should have gone.

Chunk's whisper carried in the damp air. "Make or break. We hold until dusk. Then we cross."

And with Jeremy behind us and the road ahead, we lay still. The woods crouched tight around us, waiting for the night to decide whether it would let us leave.

76

Noose Tightening

We didn't move right away. Chunk's plan was simple—study, wait, then move before full dark

That's when the first growl came.

At first I thought it was another engine, distant and low. But the sound rolled on too long, too heavy, too deep. Thunder. Out across the valley, crawling closer with every breath.

The air shifted sharply and metallic, the way it always does before rain. Zombie's face tipped to the sky. "Fuck, not again," he muttered, voice flat, like he'd already seen what storms in these woods could do.

The first drops came thin, splattering against rock and leaf. Then steadier. By the time the sun slipped behind the ridge, the rain was a curtain, soaking us where we lay. It wasn't a flood, not yet, but enough to turn dirt to slick clay and wash the sweat from our faces in cold streaks. We could tuck into the culvert a little to keep the rain from hitting us straight on the top of our heads.

Darkness came faster under the storm. The ridge that had stretched wide an hour ago shrank into a narrow gap of trees and water. The forest didn't feel like a map anymore—it felt like a trap closing.

Engines barked somewhere below, a quick rev, then

silence. ATV's. Close.

We froze. Every muscle is stiff. Bodies with that coldness you can feel in your bones. Rain drummed against the canopy, loud enough to make it hard to hear, hard to trust what direction the sound had come from. Then a shout carried up the road:

"We found the last one," a man called out, not triumphant—just worn out, like he'd been expecting worse. "Let's get this over with… damn thing's already stiff."

Another voice answered, irritated and impatient. "Hold the upper side. Lift him clean. I'm not draggin' this one all the way back. If he's really the last, we're done here before dark."

The phrasing hit us like a gift wrapped in horror— they thought Jeremy was the final body. They thought the ridge had taken all three of us. Just like we had hoped.

The words landed like stones. For a moment the rain drowned everything else. Then the meaning of what they'd said slid into place. Jeremy's body had been found. They'd counted us wrong. They had assumed we were all dead or critically injured.

Chunk's fingers dug into the dirt where he'd been lying. He didn't smile. He didn't need to. "Good," he said, quiet and hard. "Let them think that."

Relief slid through me—thin, cold, and gone almost as fast as it came. In the rain-blurred distance, we could hear their voices carrying that exhausted triumph men get when they're finally done hunting something they never wanted to chase in the first place.

If they believed Jeremy was the last of us, then as

far as Deke's whole crew knew, the job was over. No more sweeps. No more gridlines. They'd spread out lazy, pack in their gear, and start thinking about dry clothes and the long ride home.

That gave us air. Not safety—air.

Because even with the miscount working in our favor, the danger didn't shrink. The rain made everything unpredictable: sound bent, tracks washed out, and a patrol could drift the wrong direction without meaning to. If one of them wandered toward our real line with enough curiosity or bad luck, we'd be trapped on the ridge like fish in a net someone forgot to close properly.

Miscounts were a gift. But gifts in a storm came with a timer.

We had to move before the rain cleaned the truth and handed it right back to them.

We flattened lower into the mud, rain washing our faces into masks. The storm kept us soft around the edges. The miscount kept their attention elsewhere. For now, it was enough. We waited, every muscle coiled for the moment we had to turn the lie into escape.

The voices on the ATV's finally bled into the distance, swallowed by the trees and the rising weather. Their threats still echoed in my skull, but the woods closed back over them like nothing had happened.

Rain slicked across my shoulders, cold enough that shivers ran down my spine. My clothes plastered to my skin, every seam held water like ice. Fingers numb, teeth pressed together, I dug deeper into the mud, wishing I could dig into the earth itself.

We didn't talk. We didn't dare. All I could hear was

the storm building, droplets hammering leaves. Night couldn't come fast enough. Darkness was the only cover we had left, the only chance to slip past the noose tightening around our necks.

But the clouds made the day collapse early, and every second of gray light felt like a countdown.

I pressed my face into the wet ground, mud coating my lips. My chest rose and fell too fast. If night didn't get here quick—if we didn't move soon—the cold and the waiting would finish me before Deke's men ever had to tighten the rope.

77

Everything Went White

Rain softened the woods to a dull, trembling hush. Every branch black and slick, every shadow swollen with water.

We moved slow, letting dusk fold over us like a blanket. Chunk led, bent low, shoulders tight, taking each step like he could feel the ground thinking beneath him. Zombie followed, his breathing steady and close. I was third, trying to keep my feet quiet on dirt that no longer knew how to hold anything.

The ridge was just ahead—a dark, knuckled line through the trees. Then we heard them.

At first it was only a smear of sound—engines buried in the rain, the kind of noise you convince yourself you imagined. Then it came again—closer, angrier. The whine of clutched throttles. The grind of tires against wet stone. I'm so fucking tired of hearing ATV's.

Chunk froze, one fist raised. We dropped into the understory, into dripping laurel and black spruce, and waited.

Rain ticked through the canopy in nervous fingers. The engines grew teeth as they climbed, and the first set of headlights lashed across the trees like a blade. We flattened ourselves to the slope, trying to become part of the ground, part of the mess of roots, rot, and wet leaves.

The ATV's crested a hump of the ridge and idled.

Jeremy's body laid slung in the rear rack of the lead

machine, wrapped in a poncho, boots sticking out like afterthoughts. One of the riders slapped the tarp as if it were a bag of dog food.

"Deke's gonna be damn glad," the first man hollered over the rain. "About time this bullshit wrapped up."

"Yeah," the second said, exhaustion weighing his voice. "They say he's the last one. I'm done hunting these assholes."

They weren't celebrating. They weren't triumphant. They just sounded tired—men who'd been out too long, working a job nobody wanted to explain later. And hearing them talk like it was over for them put a cracked kind of relief in my chest.

Chunk leaned back toward us without turning his head. "Stay low. Stay still. They'll roll through."

Zombie nodded once. I swallowed hard, trying to make myself smaller.

But the rain had made the hillside treacherous. The mud slicked under my boots as I crouched, weight shifting just an inch too far. My heel skidded. My hands shot out for balance. The ground, waterlogged and eager, gave way beneath me.

I slid.

Not far, maybe six or eight feet, down a short, steep embankment that dumped me into a brighter strip of open ground. My shoulder clipped a dead limb on the way, snapping it clean. The sound was wet and sharp, loud enough to feel.

The ATV engines revved.

"Hold up!" one rider barked. "Something moved— downhill!"

Headlights swung. White beams tore across the slope and locked onto the raw smear of mud my slide had carved.

Chunk didn't hesitate.

"Run!" he barked. "Now!"

Zombie's boots scraped above and to my right, then

disappeared as he broke away. Chunk was gone to my left the same way—up and out of sight, swallowed by the embankment and the dark.

I tried to follow.

I lunged for the slope, boots slipping on slick mud and roots. I tried again, harder, and slid back down, rocks skittering loose beneath me. A third try would've just made more noise.

So I stopped.

Alone. Exposed. Headlights crawling closer.

I ran.

Behind me, an engine screamed. One ATV peeled off the road and came after me, tires digging into the mud, headlights bouncing like wild eyes.

Branches slapped my face. Rain blinded me, running into my mouth, my collar. My lungs went raw. Somewhere behind me a rider shouted—words lost in the wake of the engine.

Then…gunfire. A single shot cracked like the sky splitting. I didn't look back. I couldn't.

The engine died abruptly. The headlights snapped out. Boots hammered the ground, getting closer. He'd left the ATV. Now it was just him and me in the gray dark.

He crashed through a thicket and hit me full-on, a human battering ram. We went down together, skidding in the mud. His fist found my cheekbone. Stars burst behind my eyes. I rolled off the next strike, got under him, slammed a fist into his ribs—once, twice—felt something give.

He snarled and drew a knife. I caught his wrist, muscles burning as the blade hovered inches from my throat. Mud smeared up my arms, slicking our fingers. Rain poured over us like a curtain trying to erase the scene.

He was strong, but I had a different kind of strength: bone-deep, inherited. My father brought it home from Army Recon in the sixties, irony not lost on me now, and into a life where work didn't pause and showing up wasn't optional. My grandfather had lived the same way even earlier, a World War II Army Combat Engineer who crossed Europe doing jobs that didn't care how you felt that morning.

I grew up around men who didn't take days off from being capable, who didn't expect the world to cushion them, who believed endurance was the point. That kind of strength—old, unaccommodating, unfashionable— lived in me.

I thought of my father and my Grandpop, men who never quit just because something hurt, and I felt something inside me turn to iron.

I couldn't let go of his arms without losing the knife in my chest, so I did the opposite—I drove it toward him, shoving through his leverage until his arms bent and his balance broke. It pulled us chest to chest, the blade trapped between us. That was when my thumbs came free. I drove them into the soft give of his eyes. He screamed, instinct overwhelming strength, and his hands opened—the knife dropping between us.

But his other hand found his pistol.

A cold circle pressed against my ribs. My breath locked. He grinned, rain streaming over yellow teeth.

"Shoulda stayed dead with your buddy up the trail."

His finger tightened.

The forest ripped open.

One single gunshot—and everything went white.

78

It Made Him Blood

The world went silent after the shot—so silent it felt like the world had stopped. For a moment, I floated somewhere outside my own body, weightless, unanchored, waiting for pain to bloom. Waiting for the fire. Waiting for the truth of what had just been taken from me.

A heavy shape collapsed across my chest, hot and slack. Mud surged up around my face as we sank together. I couldn't move. Couldn't see. Couldn't hear. Couldn't tell where my body stopped and his began. I tried to drag in a breath and felt only pressure, wet and suffocating, like the earth was folding over me.

Something warm spilled down my ribs.

For one stretched-thin second, I was certain it was mine.

My fingers scrabbled through the mud, desperate, searching for the wet heat of a wound, my wound. Ribs. Stomach. Neck. My hands shook so hard I could barely feel what they touched.

No hole. No fire. No pain.

But I couldn't trust that—not yet. The world still felt too far away, too dim, too wrong. Maybe this was shock. Maybe the hurt hadn't reached me yet. Maybe I was already dead.

A hand grabbed my collar and yanked me upright, hard. I choked on air and mud at the same time. Another hand slid across my chest, checking, pressing, verifying something I still wasn't sure of.

"Hey—HEY—look at me."

A voice. Rough. Familiar. Close.

But I still couldn't see him. Not through the blur. Not through the ringing in my skull.

"You hit?" the voice demanded again, sharper now. "U-Haul. You hit?"

Only then did the shape on top of me roll away with a dead thud, giving me space to breathe, to see, to understand.

The blood wasn't mine.

And the voice wasn't a stranger.

Zombie's pistol came up as the beam cut through the trees. He checked the man's pulse—once, fast— then dumped the body to the ground. Satisfied, he holstered without a word.

A second figure stepped into view, the light catching half his face: John—mud-caked, bleeding, unreadable—pistol steady, smoke still curling from the barrel.

"Wasn't about to watch you die out here too," he said, breathless but cold. "And he'd have had you gutted."

Rain pattered harder on the leaves above us. My heartbeat finally began to slow, though it stayed louder than the storm.

I wasn't dead.

Not yet.

But whatever we'd been before that shot—three men scrambling for survival—wasn't what we were now.

John stepped in when it mattered.

Out here, that made him more than a friend. It made him blood.

79

They Were Still Hunting

John holstered slowly, eyes still locked on the dark where the man had fallen. None of us spoke. The rain carried the silence for us, pattering heavy through the canopy, dripping down our faces.

Chunk, rifle angled low, mud streaked across his cheek like war paint. He looked from me to the corpse to John, and for a long moment it was just breathing and rain.

"You good?" Chunk asked finally, voice hoarse.

I nodded, though my chest still felt hollow. "Thanks to him."

John's gaze flicked my way, sharp but brief. "Don't thank me yet. We're not out of this. We need to move."

The words sat heavy, colder than the rain.

Zombie wiped his blade on his pant leg, still keyed up. "What about you, Chunk?"

Chunk shifted his grip on the rifle, rain dripping from the barrel. "Guy came at me sloppy. Fired wild— panic fire, no rhythm, no control. He wanted to sound dangerous, but he was not trained." He shook his head. "First volley went over my shoulder. I dropped and rolled, bought space. Waited until he thought I was running. When he swung around to chase, I put him down clean."

He didn't say it proudly. Just flat truth. A military marksman's memory surfacing after years of dust.

"Not a soldier," Chunk muttered. "Not even close. Just a man with a gun. That's the difference." You could see that Chunk took the rifle off his kill, two slung around his chest.

We let that sit. None of us liked what it meant, but we were grateful it was true.

The rain thickened, drumming on leaves, soaking deeper into our clothes. I caught shivers climbing my spine, each one harder to push down.

John finally pulled his gaze from the corpse and turned it on us—mud smeared across his face, rain tangled in his beard, his expression hard as rock.

"Patrick didn't make it," he said. No wavering, no softness. Just the truth laid bare. "He charged that son of a bitch like he meant to break him in half. They cut him down before he ever reached the tree line."

The words landed heavy. Even the rain felt quieter for a second.

John shifted his weight, wincing as he did. "Thomas kept running with me after that. They clipped him during the push—took him low, through the calf. He couldn't move, I dragged him out as far as I could."

Chunk's face tightened. He didn't ask how bad—he didn't need to.

"There's an old shack down the line," John went on. "He's holed up there. I stopped the bleeding as best I could. He's alive, but he won't make another hike without help."

He stepped closer, close enough that rain pooled on his eyelashes. "I don't leave my people. Not ever."

His eyes flicked past us, searching. "Where's

Jeremy?"

The question landed heavier than the rest.

I didn't give details. I didn't dare. "He fell," I said. "Off a wall we were climbing. He didn't make it. They already have his body."

John held my gaze, reading what I wasn't saying. He nodded once and didn't ask for more.

Chunk cursed under his breath. "That's weight we can't afford to carry."

I turned on him, heat rising in my chest. "I wouldn't be breathing if John hadn't shown up. Thomas wouldn't either. We're going back for him."

Chunk's expression shifted, his eyes moving from me to John, then down the ridge where the last gunshot had echoed.

A long breath escaped him.

"Fine," he said. "Then we move fast."

The pistol was heavy and bitter cold in my hand now, but heavier still was the thought of what came next. Three of us could move clean, but Zombie was limping hard, and Thomas was still just a promise in John's mouth. The math didn't add up—we weren't five, not really. We were three dragging two shadows.

We pressed into the brush to rest a moment, catching our breath. That's when it came—not the high snarl of ATV's we'd learned to hate, but something deeper. A slow, deliberate thrum that carried through the ground as much as the air. Heavy tires chewing wet soil. A truck.

John froze, pistol held tight, eyes sweeping the darkened woods. Chunk stiffened, solid as stone. Zombie's face looked bloodless in the red glow, rain cutting thin tracks down his skin.

The sound cut out suddenly, leaving nothing but dripping trees and the rattle of my pulse in my ears. That silence was worse than the noise.

I swallowed hard. Gratitude burned in my chest. John had saved me, but it mixed with something colder. They were still hunting. We were still prey.

We were four again. But then the trees lit white—headlights cutting straight through the dark. The forest wasn't finished with us yet.

80

Last Pause

The shack wasn't much, it was four leaning walls, half a roof, and a smell of rot so deep it seemed baked into the wood. But it gave us what we hadn't had in days: a pause. No open sky. No ridge to slide off. Just four corners to catch a breath.

Thomas lay against the wall like a shadow pinned there, his face a pale mask streaked with rain and dirt. He had done what he could for himself with the scraps of gauze in his kit, and his belt was cinched tight high on his thigh, a makeshift tourniquet biting into the muscle. But the bandage was soaked, his shirt clinging dark to his ribs. Every shallow breath hissed like it hurt.

John dropped beside him, hands moving with muscle memory. He cinched the wrap tighter, pressed gauze into the wound until Thomas flinched. "You're a stubborn son of a bitch," John muttered.

Thomas's lips cracked into something that wanted to be a grin but didn't make it. "And you're late." His voice rasped like gravel.

Nobody laughed. The rain in the roof gaps pattered too loud, and the weight of what lay outside pressed too heavily.

Thomas shifted, jaw tightening. "That round didn't

just pass through," he said. "Felt it shatter something on the way in."

He swallowed, breath catching. "Leg's not holding right. If it's shattered, the bleeding's gonna get worse when it swells. I'm on a clock."

The words landed hard.

Chunk paced, rifle low but eyes always on the broken slats of the wall like he could see through them. "We can't sit here. Every minute puts them closer. We flank the road—now."

John bristled, one arm steadying Thomas upright. "He won't make two steps without us."

Chunk stopped pacing, squared up with John, his voice a low grind. "And if carrying him slows us until all five of us end up in the dirt?

The air in the shack turned sharp. Even Thomas tensed, his fingers digging into the dirt like he was bracing for a verdict he didn't like.

I broke in before the wire snapped. "Shelter's not safety. You both know that. They sweep ridges, they sweep cabins—this shack is no different. We move. Thomas included. End of story."

John's face hardened, but he gave one sharp nod.

Chunk said nothing. He shifted his sling and racked a round, the metallic snap serving as his answer.

The next five minutes passed in work. Real, heavy, quiet work. John and I stripped our undershirts and used them to pull a splint tighten and more substantial—sticks snapped to length, bound hard along Thomas's leg until it held straight enough to trust. Every time we cinched it tighter, his breath stuttered, the pain slipping past whatever discipline he had left.

Chunk moved through the gear with quick decisions, passing the newly acquired rifle off his kill to John without ceremony. Between them, they filled a single magazine each from the ammo Chunk had lifted out of the bunkhouses earlier—slow, careful, making every round count. They didn't bother loading more. If one full mag each wasn't enough, it wouldn't matter, we'd all be dead. Everything else got tossed aside as dead weight.

Zombie limped through a final check of his weapon, pain flickering across his face. The ankle brace held, but the stiffness in his stride said it was a thin line between walking and collapsing.

When it was time, John and I hauled Thomas up. His arms slung over our shoulders, his boots dragging but lifting when we lifted. The leg bowed when it took weight, wrong in a way that made my stomach knot.

He was deadweight one second, fighting to move the next. Pride alone kept him vertical—and it was clear pride wouldn't last the night.

Zombie took the door last. Even limping, he scanned the treeline like he expected it to peel open and spit men at us. The storm had thickened, rain falling steadily, turning the dirt into paste.

The shack vanished behind us in seconds, but its shadow stayed. It was more than just four rotten walls—it was the last pause we were going to get. From here on out, there would be no more hiding. Every step would be toward the road, toward the men waiting on it, toward the fight that was coming whether or not we wanted it.

The thunder rumbled closer, heavy and certain.

The storm was coming down on us, and so were they.

We weren't three anymore. We weren't four strong, either. We were three hardened men carrying two wounded. And the forest had no mercy for either.

Somewhere ahead, the men waited.

We had no choice but to walk into both.

81

Embrace the Suck

We didn't stop. Not once.

Chunk took point, rifle slung, his shoulders hunched like a man shouldering more than a pack that was discarded hours ago. The rain came steady now, not punishing.

John and I bore Thomas between us, his arms hooked tight over our shoulders. He stumbled, dragged, but stayed upright when we lifted him. Zombie limped in the rear, his face pinched with pain, pistol steady despite the hitch in his step. Every man carried something: weight, wounds, or fatigue, and the forest offered no mercy.

The mile stretched long, maybe longer. We talked little. Breath was too valuable to waste. Every now and then Chunk's voice cut through the rain and the grind of boots:

"Embrace the suck."

"Fight for what's waiting for you at home."

"Think of who needs you back."

He wasn't sermonizing. He was reminding. The reminders a man gave himself out loud so he wouldn't forget. I thought of my daughter's face, of the vows I'd broken just by being in this situation. The weight of it all pressed harder than Thomas across my shoulders.

The forest never gave us clean miles, but it gave us cover. No engines. No flashlights hunted the tree line. Just the wet pressing of boots and the low hiss of rain in the needles. It almost felt too quiet—like we were walking through a space where the enemy had already passed, leaving silence as a trap.

Then, ahead, light. Not a sweeping headlamp. Not a truck beam knifing through the dark. But a dull glow, steady and rooted.

We slowed for the first time. Hearts and feet and lungs had been one machine for that long mile, but the light broke the rhythm.

Through the trees, shapes took form. Not bunkhouses, not shacks like the ridge had been littered with. Bigger. Two mobile homes, side by side, their siding dull, their windows leaking pale light like sick eyes. The glow pushed out into the wet night, haloing in the rain.

Chunk dropped to a crouch, raised a fist. We froze and sank with him.

He studied the shapes for a long while, silent, water dripping from his nose. Then he leaned close, his whisper a rasp.

"Not the bunkhouses. Not a grow shed. That's residential. Maybe staging, maybe worse. We hold here."

John and I eased Thomas down against a pine, his back pressed to bark slick with rain. Zombie shifted behind a trunk, pistol steady across his lap, his ankle stiff but his eyes sharp.

Chunk squinted through the trees, tracking shapes we couldn't see.

"I'm going to swing around and get a clean read on

the backside," he said. "Signs of movement, engines cooling, anyone laying low and waiting to tag whoever comes through. If there's a blind spot, I want to find it before it finds us."

He tapped his chest twice—habit, not bravado.

"Ten minutes. Stay quiet. Stay ready."

I objected, silently, but the look in his eyes shut me down before saying anything. He wasn't asking permission. He was already gone.

We watched him slide into the dark—the forest swallowing him one step at a time until even the rain covered his sound.

And then we were still. Waiting. The waiting that chewed nerves raw. Every creak in the trees felt like boots. Every flicker of light in those trailer windows felt like eyes staring back at us.

Thomas coughed under his breath. John steadied him with a hand on his shoulder, murmuring something quiet. Zombie's expression twisted, as if he were grinding the pain into submission.

And me—I just tracked the passing moments, fighting not to picture what Chunk might be walking into.

82

Noise Was Death—Chunk

Chunk moved through the rain, rifle in the ready position while he swept left to right, the sound whispering against the leaves as he broke from the group, rifle held tight across his chest. Every step was measured, deliberate. Noise discipline mattered more than speed now. He didn't bother looking back—he knew the others would be watching, counting the minutes he was gone.

The glow from the trailers bled stronger with each yard. Not headlights. Not lanterns. Electric light. That meant a generator, and a generator meant permanence.

He slipped between two oaks and eased onto his stomach in the muck. From there, the angle opened. Vehicles. More than one. A beat-up pickup sunk to the axles. Two ATV's. A third shape under a tarp—too square to be a car, maybe crates.

One trailer's door stood open just a crack. The light inside was yellow and ugly, shadows moving against the wall. Men, at least two. Their voices carried faintly, softened by rain, but the cadence was all wrong for casual talk. Orders. Arguments.

Chunk tracked the line of mud prints around the steps. Fresh. Recent. Boots with deep treads. One set came straight from the treeline, not the road. A patrol returning. Maybe the same pair they'd crossed earlier.

He steadied his breath, memorizing the layout— where the lights bled, where shadows pooled, where cover broke. This wasn't a shack. It was a hub. A node in their system. And if his group was flanking the road on the right, they had just stumbled onto its artery.

He started sliding back—then froze.

A shape at the far edge of the light caught his eye. Long, boxy, mud-caked, but familiar enough to pinch his lungs tight.

No. Couldn't be.

Chunk crept two yards closer, squinting through rain and shadow. The tarp had slipped just enough for a beam of trailer light to kiss the metal beneath. The dent in the fender. The half-peeled sticker on the bumper.

His truck.

They'd stolen his goddamn truck and hauled it up here like a prize.

A hot wave of anger surged in him, but he forced it down. Rage made noise. Noise was death. Still, the thought drilled in: that truck wasn't just his. It was an engine. Tires. Fuel. And the keys—still in his pocket.

It was a way out.

If it still ran.

If they could reach it.

If they didn't die trying to take it back.

Chunk slid backward, mud clinging to his elbows, rain filling the prints he left behind. Every inch away from those lights felt like pulling his skin back onto his bones.

When he finally turned toward the ridge, he looked

once more over his shoulder. A figure had stepped into the trailer doorway, framed by the yellow light. He wasn't looking in Chunk's direction—not yet. But he would.

Chunk moved faster, heart pounding, forcing his mind to keep strategizing instead of spiraling. Options spun with every step:

If the truck ran, they had wheels.

If it didn't, it was bait.

Either way, it was leverage.

And by the time the night swallowed the last of the glow, he already knew exactly what he would tell the others:

The truck wasn't at the trailhead.

It was here.

And it might be the only card they had left to play.

83

Our Coffin

We waited in the dark where the pines thickened, breath shallow, eyes working at nothing. The rain had slackened to a mist, but it still clung to us, dripping from brows, soaking everything we were wearing. Nobody spoke. Not until Chunk came back.

I saw his outline first, sliding low through the brush. His rifle was cradled close, his steps deliberate. When he dropped beside us, mud flaking from his elbows, we all leaned in, waiting.

"Trailers," he whispered. "Just two of them like we thought. Lights on. Somebody's home."

That much we expected. But his expression stayed tight, like he had more he wanted to say.

John cut him a look. "What else?"

Chunk's breath hitched before he let it out. "I saw something I didn't expect. My truck."

The silence after that was heavier than the rain. Even the woods seemed to stall.

Zombie gave a low laugh, not from humor but disbelief. "You're seeing things in the dark."

Chunk shook his head, voice flat. "I know what I saw. Passenger fender's still dented. And the wheels, I know the wheels. It's mine. They stole it. Brought it up here to cover their tracks if someone reported it abandoned."

I felt my throat go dry. "You sure?"

"I'm sure." His words were a stone dropped in still water. "It's sitting on the far side of those trailers like they park it there regularly. They've been driving it. Using it. Hell, they might've hot-wired it that second night after we didn't leave when are food bags were cut down."

John leaned forward, eyes sharp, voice low. "If it's there, it changes things. Vehicle means a way out."

His gaze flicked to Chunk. "You still got the keys?"

Chunk nodded once and tapped his pocket. "Never left me."

Zombie's laugh cut short, bitter. "Or it's a trap. You walk into that lot, and you don't walk out. Simple as that."

Chunk didn't flinch. "I'm telling you, if it's running, it's our best shot. You don't get an escape like that handed to you twice. But to get it, we'd have to move closer. And trailers aren't thick, any sound will carry through those thin walls. Whoever's inside will hear us before we hear them the second the engine cranks over, if it does at all."

Thomas shifted against me, pale and worn, whispering through cracked lips: "Wheels... means home."

His voice was fragile, almost breaking. But it cut sharper than anything else said that night.

John finally broke the silence. "We get one chance. Either we ghost it right and drive out, or we burn here trying. Decide quick."

Chunk dug into his pocket and pulled out a key, smeared with dirt, edges dulled from years of wear.

"Ignition's still mine. If they hot-wired it, maybe the lines were cut. Maybe it's trashed. Maybe it doesn't even run anymore. But if that engine still turns over, it's clean. We're invisible in the rearview before they even know we touched it."

Zombie shook his head, rain dripping off his chin. "That's a lot of maybes. You roll dice like that, you don't always like what comes up."

I leaned closer, my voice low. "What ifs might be all we have left. That truck's the first actual play we've seen in days. The question is, are we willing to gamble everything on it?"

Chunk's eyes were steady, but there was a fire in them too. "We don't win by crawling forever. We win by moving. By risking. You boys want to limp through another day hoping the road spits us out safe? Or you want to take what's sitting right in front of us and fight to make it ours?"

John nodded, slow. "We get as close as we can without being seen. Scout the yard. Watch their patterns. If it's possible, we take it. If not, we melt back into the trees and try and find where the road leads out. But one way or another, that truck's a pivot. Could be our last one."

Nobody argued. Not out loud.

Chunk turned the key over in his palm, the little piece of metal catching what little light leaked through the trees. It looked almost laughably small, like it didn't belong to anything important. But in the silence, it felt heavier than a rifle.

"That's the play," he said. "Truck's either our way out... or our coffin."

Nobody answered. We didn't need to.

The rain thickened again, pattering through the canopy, each drop sharp as a tick of a clock. I felt the shivers return, crawling up my back, and I wasn't sure if it was the cold or the thought of walking toward those lit trailers.

For the first time in days, we weren't crawling away from death—we were walking straight toward it.

And the forest seemed to know.

But the question hung in every chest the same way: was it salvation... or suicide?

84

Chosen Brothers

We sat folded into the lee of the pines, mud working at our sleeves, the trailers out there a dull promise of light and sound. The rain had blunted into a constant thread, nothing dramatic—just enough to keep the world soft and make every noise slide without a clean edge. The truck sat between two squares of grim light. Fifty or so yards. Closer than it felt in any honest way.

Complete darkness was creeping in, not all at once but in layers—the trees breaking the light and dragging it out.

John rubbed the back of his neck. "We don't have the margin for a long play. Thomas bleeds minutes. A truck bought now buys miles. But a truck taken wrong doesn't buy anything." His eyes stayed hard on Chunk. "You said you saw your rig. How sure are you?"

Chunk didn't hesitate. "A hundred percent."
John waited.

"Fender ding I never fixed. Sticker I peeled off crooked. Wheels I replaced myself—every scratch earned." He shrugged, almost bored. "I'd bet my life on it."

I shook my head, a breath slipping out despite myself. It was a bad joke in a bad place—but the split second of levity mattered.

The tiny notes of possibility threaded through our bones, but they didn't make the math simpler. We traded ideas, each one a brittle coin.

"What if we slip straight in?" I asked. "Slow crawl, hit the passenger door, shove Thomas in the back, and gun it?"

Chunk scoffed, not unkindly. "Straight push is a prayer. They'll see the motion and light the place up."

John folded his arms tight. "Diversion. Something that throws the patrols off post. Not an all-out firefight. A noise they can't ignore fifty or so yards away. A pair of men will peel off to check it. That thins the lot."

"Gunshots?" Zombie said the word like a challenge and a warning at once. He knew how loud hope could be. "That's a gamble. Dogs. Triangulation. They'll know if it's close."

Chunk rubbed his forehead, thinking in bullet-quick measures. "I can give them an angle. There's a bowl north of the clearing. Fire into it and the echo will throw direction away from the trailers. North ridge will sing louder than the truck. They'll go toward the sound."

I cleared my throat. "We need a Plan B."

Zombie and Chunk answered at the same time.

"There is no Plan B."

Chunk nodded once. "Plan B is we die."

Silence settled over it—heavy, final. No one argued. John didn't soften it. He just accepted it and moved on.

"So we make Plan A clean," he said. "Tight. No wasted motion."

Chunk crouched with us in the rain, his voice low and steady.

"One shot first. That'll pull them. You don't move on that one. You wait. When you hear the next two—back-to-back—that's your cue. You get to the truck, hunker down, and wait for me to loop back."

Chunk would peel off into the north bowl and get set. John and I would take Thomas straight to the truck, one on each side, moving him fast and quiet. Zombie stayed with us, rear guard tight, John's rifle in his hands and ready. No backup. No second chance.

Just execution.

The plan felt ugly and honest in equal measure. It was the plan men stitched together when the alternative was to do nothing.

He looked at each of us, making sure it took.

Then something passed between the three of us—quiet, heavy, earned. Zombie stepped in first and pulled Chunk into a hard hug that ended in a sharp slap between the shoulder blades. When they broke, I stepped forward and wrapped Chunk up too. No jokes. No smart ass comments. He squeezed hard, slapped my back once, and let go.

Zombie pulled us both in after that, knocking shoulders like he was trying to shake loose whatever doubt was left. We'd been doing life together for more than twenty years—marriages, kids, failures, miles on trails across the country. And now this week. This stretch of hell.

There was a real chance one of us wasn't walking out of these woods.

None of us said it.

We didn't have to.

Chunk nodded once. "We weren't born family," he said. "But we damn sure ended up that way."

Zombie's voice was barely above a breath. "Ain't a thing stronger than chosen brothers."

I tightened my grip. "You come back. That's the only rule."

Chunk's expression hardened. "I will. Or I'll make damn sure you two make it out."

He reached into his pocket and pulled out the keys, holding them toward Zombie.

"In case I don't—"

Zombie pushed his hand away. "No. We all get out, or none of us do."Chunk didn't argue. He just pocketed the key again, gave one last look, and slipped into the dark without another sound—just gone, absorbed by the black.

Seconds seemed like hours. Thomas breathed in shallow, pained bursts. John kept a hand on his shoulder. Zombie watched the black where Chunk had vanished, fingers flexing on the grip of his pistol.

Then—

A single shot.

Sharp. Close.

We didn't move. Not yet.

The trailers erupted—curses, commands, boots hitting wet earth. A dog barked, then another. Flashlights jittered through the treeline. The whole camp tilted toward the noise Chunk had thrown at them.

Time stretched into slow torture.

Then we heard it—two shots, fast, back-to-back. Our cue.

"Move," I whispered—once to Thomas, once to myself.

John hooked Thomas under one arm, I took the other, and Zombie fell behind us, dark and silent. We flanked wide around the trailers, slipping in the opposite direction from the chaos Chunk had carved open. Each shout, each bark, each beam of light bought us another step.

Branches scraped our jackets. Roots and pits rose up under our feet like traps, but we moved like things meant to crawl under them—low, fast, unseen. Thomas hissed once when his bad leg clipped a stump but kept upright by pure spite.

We rounded the last trailer and saw it: a truck slumped under loose blue tarps. In this darkness, it could've been anything to anyone else.

But the silhouette—long extended cab, the camper shell's familiar hump—was unmistakable. I'd felt that shape across a hundred trailheads and parking lots. Even buried in shadow, it was Chunk's truck.

And God willing, it had one more run left in it.

We crawled the last few feet and dropped behind the back bumper, the cold metal beading rain onto our sleeves. The tarps overhead slapped in the wind, a hollow, nervous sound. We crouched low, pressed in tight, the three of us breathing like we were hiding from a wild animal instead of men.

The camp behind us was still alive—men shouting directions, dogs baying, boots splashing through mud. Every sound felt too close, too loud, too wrong.

Then it happened.

Five, maybe six—hell, maybe seven shots—cracked in the trees.

Fast. Hard. Not part of the plan.

My stomach flipped so hard I thought I might throw up.

Not nerves.

Not fear.

Something heavier—a sickness born out of the idea of Chunk on the other end of those shots.

Zombie looked over at me.

I looked back.

We didn't need words. It was already written on my face.

"Do we go to him?" I whispered, barely a breath.

Zombie shook his head, his expression going rigid, eyes locked on the darkness where Chunk had disappeared. "Chunk's got this," he said. "We wait right here."

I wanted to argue. To bolt. To do something. But Zombie's voice—calm, certain, loyal—held me in place.

We waited.

Time pulled at me like a stone being hauled uphill.

The dogs barked again. A voice shouted something about "the ridge." A flashlight glanced across the tarps, too close, then swung away.

Then a shape broke loose from the treeline—low, fast, moving like it belonged to the dark.

Chunk.

He slid in beside us, mud up to his knees, breath sharp but controlled. He didn't look hurt. Didn't look rattled. Just drenched and alive.

"They're chasing ghosts," he murmured. "Window's still open."

Zombie exhaled in one long, quiet release.

I only realized I'd been holding my breath when my

chest burned.

Chunk leaned in, eyes flicking from Zombie to me, then to the mound of blue plastic hiding the truck.

"Ready," he said.

We moved as one.

Zombie grabbed the passenger side, I took the driver's, and Chunk got the center. The tarps were slick with rain but loose—just waiting for a hand with enough anger or hope to take them.

"One—two—now."

We ripped.

The whole mess came off in one violent swoop, like peeling skin from an orange. The tarps tore free, slapped the mud, and the truck finally stood exposed in the dark—dented, filthy, but real. Ours.

A cold gust hit the bare metal, and for a split second everything felt too loud—like unveiling it had alerted the whole damn forest.

Chunk hissed, "Low, low—move," and we ducked down again, using the open bed and bumper as cover. Rain drummed on the truck roof. Voices still carried from the camp, but none were pointed our way yet.

The escape was about to start.

Chunk flicked the key free of his fingers and pushed it into his palm.

His mouth was a thin line. "Go."

The rain answered with a hard note, and we rose.

We slid around to the shadow side, keeping low. No hesitation this time—Chunk's hand wrapped the driver's handle and pulled. The latch gave with a soft click. Unlocked.

Of course, it was. They didn't have keys. Why would they bother locking it?

John and I lifted Thomas together, one under his shoulders, one under his knees, and pushed him carefully into the back seat. His breath rattled shallow, his head knocking against the glass before I steadied it. Zombie swung into the passenger side, rifle angled across his chest, eyes scanning the trailers.

I slid in next, heart hammering in my ears, rain still dripping from my face. John followed, shutting the back door with a low, final thud.

Chunk closed last, the cab filling with the smell of wet earth and old grease. For a second he just held the key, eyes locked on the dash like he was about to put his entire life into that slot.

The truck was ours again. Or maybe it wasn't.

Chunk thumbed the key to life, not yet turning it. He let the metal rest between his thumb and index finger as if weighing what it might cost. Rain hammered on the roof, steady and patient. Somewhere out past the trailers, a shout cut loose and then sank. The world narrowed to the key and the small hiss of our breathing.

"On three," Chunk said, voice low.

I nodded, because there was nothing else to do.

"One—" He paused so long it felt like the number had already landed.

"Two—" John whispered.

"Three."

Chunk turned the key.

85

Coffin Fit for Five

The key turned.

The truck coughed. Once. Twice. A dying thing in the dark. The engine wheezed as if it had lungs full of mud—the starter grinding teeth. For a moment it didn't feel like a truck at all—it felt like a coffin fit for five, sealed shut with nothing but rain ticking on the roof. Nobody breathed. Nobody dared.

A low, ugly rumble shuddered through the frame, weak sparks clawing into life. The whole truck shook like it hated waking. Then, with a final growl, it came alive—loud, raw, wrong.

Frankenstein's monster in steel and grease. Alive when it shouldn't be.

The cab closed in fast, all trapped breath and rising panic. Then Chunk barked—too loud, too urgent: "Lights or no lights?"

He didn't have to explain. Old truck—no auto sensors, no mercy. The choice was ours. Lights meant vision but painted us on a stage. No lights meant blind and crooked on a road that didn't forgive.

Zombie snapped before anyone else could speak. "No lights now. Get us out of the hot spot. Then we burn 'em."

Chunk's hand dropped off the switch. He jammed

the gearshift, clutch grinding, and the truck lurched forward into the dim.

Shapes existed but refused to commit. The road was a suggestion more than a thing, mud and memory braided together. The tires spun, caught, spun again. Chunk hunched over the wheel, eyes wide, trying to pull edges out of the gloom. His lips moved without sound, counting ruts and bends he knew by feel.

Every bump threw Thomas against John's arm in the back. John held him steady, murmuring rough reassurance even though Thomas drifted in and out. I braced a hand on the seat in front of me, not helping—just keeping myself from rattling apart.

Branches scraped the sides like fingernails. The truck bucked, coughed, and surged. Somewhere behind us, a dog barked—too far to be sure, too close to ignore.

"Hold it steady," Zombie muttered, white-knuckled on the dash. "Stay centered. This trail'll eat you if you drift."

Chunk didn't answer. He leaned closer to the glass, breath tight.

We rolled half-blind for what felt like forever. Tires kissed the edge of the ditch once, close enough to tilt us, and all of us inhaled together. Chunk corrected, hard and fast, and the truck straightened.

Then the light thinned ahead—just a shade brighter, the canopy loosening its grip. Not warmth. Not safety. Just space.

"Now?" Chunk asked, voice frayed.

John looked at Zombie. Zombie looked at me. No one wanted the call.

I nodded once. "Now."

Chunk flicked the switch.

Light exploded into the wet gray. Twin beams cut through rain and trees, stark and alien after the blind. The forest looked caught in the act, shadows thrown long and sharp. For a fleeting moment everything was still—no dogs, no engines, no men—just us and the monster we'd woken.

The truck rolled on.

Then, in the rear view, a glow broke through the trees.

Chunk's knuckles locked on the wheel. "We've got company," he said, voice flat.

The cab went quiet, all of us craning toward that mirror. The lights bounced, lifted, vanished, then cut back again. Whoever it was, they were pushing hard. The rain made them blur and smear, but not enough to pretend they weren't real.

"ATV's?" Zombie asked.

Chunk shook his head once. "Too high. Truck. They're coming."

The engine growled under us, still shaky from its Frankenstein birth. The road pitched left, then right, and every rut tried to throw us. I braced a hand in the door handle, heartbeat slamming in my throat.

We weren't alone in the dark anymore.

86

World Tilting

The glow behind us had been steady for the last hundred yards—one set of headlights, high and hard, the kind only a truck throws. Chunk kept glancing at it in the mirror, his expression sharpening, knowing exactly what was tailing us.

Then something else cut through the dark.

Four smaller lights snapped alive beneath the truck's glare—lower to the ground, jittering, bouncing with every rut they hit.

"There," I said. "ATV's."

Chunk's eyes flicked to the mirror again. The newcomers darted under the bigger beams like wolves running with a larger animal.

"More company," he growled.

He punched the accelerator. The truck kicked forward, mud snapping out from under the tires. Rain sheeted across the windshield, the wipers fighting a losing battle.

In the rearview, the single truck-light glow widened, the ATV's weaving in and out of it like they were trying to find angles.

Zombie twisted in his seat, squinting past the headrests.

"They're splitting!" he barked. "One peeling left,

one right. They're trying to squeeze us."

Chunk spat a curse and leaned harder on the wheel.

"Hold on!"

Thomas groaned in the back, his head sliding against John's arm. I pressed him steady, feeling the warmth of blood seeping fresh through his bandage with every jolt. John's jaw was tight, his rifle balanced across his knees, eyes on the glass like he could will bullets to bounce.

"Hold him!" Chunk shouted. "I can't drive if he slides!"

"I've got him," John snapped back. "Just don't flip us."

The road pitched into a washout, and the truck slammed down so hard my teeth clacked. For a second the headlights vanished, swallowed by the dip—then they flared again, closer.

Gunfire cracked behind us, sharp and vicious. A round punched into the bed metal with a clang that rang through the cab like someone hitting a steel drum. Another skipped off the tailgate, showering sparks.

Zombie slammed his hand against the window switch, dropped the glass, and leaned out into the rain-soaked wind. He braced his rifle on the window frame, elbows locked.

He fired three fast shots.

Each muzzle flash lit his face in a harsh, stuttering strobe—teeth clenched, eyes locked, every bit of him carved into the moment. Brass rattled against the door panel and spilled into the footwell.

"Hit something?" I shouted.

"Made 'em duck. That's all we need."

One ATV howled up the embankment, cutting a wide flank. Its light swung through the trees like a swinging blade, searching for an angle to dive back onto the track. The other ATV pressed tight behind the truck, rooster-tailing mud, so close I thought the rider could grab the bumper if he leaned.

Chunk wrenched the wheel. The truck fishtailed, almost sideways, the world tilting with it. I slammed into the door, Thomas slammed into me, and John barely kept us from crushing him.

"Stay on it!" Zombie barked. "Don't let 'em herd us!"

"Trying not to!" Chunk's voice was ragged, but his hands were iron.

The trees closed in, trunks flashing inches from the mirrors. A branch snapped off the passenger side mirror with a crack like gunfire. Rain smeared every inch of glass. The track forked—one rut climbing hard, the other dropping into black.

"Uphill or down?" I yelled over the engine.

Chunk didn't answer. He picked the drop, tires catching mud like claws, the truck slamming into another skid. The ATV behind us didn't flinch—it followed, engine screaming, light drilling our backs.

Then the other one reappeared from the ridge, cutting across our nose. Its light exploded against the windshield, a blinding flare.

Chunk cursed and jerked the wheel hard. The truck bounced off a rut, and for a breathless instant we were weightless, leaning way too far. I thought we were done. The roof was about to plow into the mud.

But the tires bit. We slammed back down hard. Thomas gasped. John swore. Zombie fired blindly into the flare.

The ATV swerved, clipping a stump. Its rider screamed once before the machine cartwheeled into the ditch, lights snapping out.

"One down!" Zombie's voice was a ragged snarl.

The victory didn't last. In the mirror, more beams cut through the rain. Higher, heavier. A second truck.

The cab went dead silent for a beat, all of us watching the glow swell behind us. The forest wasn't empty anymore—it was filling up with engines and fury.

Chunk's knuckles went white on the wheel. "Hold on," he said. "This road's about to get tight."

87

This is Mine—Sheriff

Rain wrote its own law across the windshield. Thin, slanted strokes breaking faster than the wipers could slap them away. The county truck wandered in the mud like it had old injuries, the front end drifting unless the sheriff kept two hands locked on the wheel.

Deke's call still hummed in his ear.

"Sheriff, they're moving. Get to the road. Don't let 'em slip out."

That was all Deke ever gave him.

Just enough to make the sheriff responsible and to keep Deke clean.

The radio buzzed with half-broken voices:

"…south spur…still heading that direction…"

"…one ATV down…"

"…storm's killing the radios—sheriff, you out there…?"

He let the mic hang.

They could talk themselves hoarse.

The truck climbed the old logging grade, tires dropping into ruts like they remembered more than he did. The storm ate most of the sound. The engine grumbling and rain hammering the roof like it wanted in.

He lived close to this cut road. Too close.

Deke knew that.

It made it easy for him to call when things got sloppy—when he needed someone to stand between himself and whatever mistake he'd let off the leash.

The sheriff kept heading north, steady, letting the woods close around him, letting the storm give him a minute to think. White beams slicing the rain in front of him. Just the long, wet stretch of road and the weight of whatever was coming toward him.

That's the thing about paths, if you wear them long enough they wear you back.

Another burst on the radio:

"...they're headed right at you..."

"...I've got the tail..."

"...Sheriff, confirm you're inbound..."

"Inbound," he said finally, surprised by how his own voice sounded tired and young at the same time, like both men had shown up tonight and neither wanted the passenger seat.

Water sheeted across the glass. The heater rattled. Something in the dash buzzed in sympathy every time he hit a washboard strip. He could've fixed it last week. He didn't.

Let a machine complain long enough and it gives you a map of everything you've ignored.

The road curved, and the pines tilted in, towering like a jury that already knew the verdict. He eased off the gas as the mud slid into a low spot and the truck rose weightless before the tires grabbed again. Down in the hollow, light flickered the way lightning does when it's not sure if it wants to be seen. Lights rose—more than one. A procession without a priest.

"This has gone on too long," he said quietly, and the cab absorbed the words the way it absorbed everything else.

He tried on a few endings in his head—the kind men try when they know there aren't many left that fit. Paperwork and tape. Calls at two in the morning. A dog shot behind a shed because somebody didn't aim where they meant. Dealing with bodies. Young faces getting older in dusty picture frames, nobody asking questions because nobody wants the answers.

The sheriff had grown onto this road step by step, and each step had cost something he never wrote down.

He knew these woods in the dark.

The creek undercut the bank and lied about solid ground.

A rock ledge looked like a shoulder from above and a grave from below.

And the pines trapped the stink of sweat, cordite, and the slick fear soaked into unwashed gear.

The storm couldn't wash that out. Nothing could.

The radio hissed again, the voice he expected.

"Sheriff, we got 'em on the ridge road. We need you at the fork."

"Copy." His thumb stayed on the mic a breath longer than needed. Then he let go.

It should've ended a while ago. Should've cut this tumor out before it spread.

Now it was infection deep in the bone.

Maybe tonight it ended.

Lightning stitched the slope, white-blue. In the darkness ahead he saw three sets of beams slicing through the timber—one ahead, one behind. The headlights hunted their way down a bad trail in worse weather.

He thought about turning on the siren.

There's a rule about noise out here—some nights it saves you.

Most nights, it only makes your intentions public.

He left the siren dead.

The badge on his chest caught a brief glow from the dash and winked like it knew a joke he didn't.

"You're late," he told the mirror, and the man in it didn't argue.

The grade rose, the engine lugging until he feathered it back. Trees thinned enough for the storm to land a full swing. The road split past the next bend—left into the low flats, right toward the shoulder where the land remembered how to drop. He'd watched plenty of folks choose wrong when it came to easy and quick. Watched what that cost.

A memory pushed up like a root: his father, boots damp from ditch water, telling him the job isn't the law, the job is carrying it.

The difference was the weight.

He had carried it a long time.

Carried it when it felt like something strapped across his shoulders, and when it felt like a second spine.

Headlights blinked through the trunks on his left— closer now, jittering, fighting a road that didn't want them. Another set behind, steady and patient in the way a man gets when he believes the ending already belongs to him. A third pair of smaller lights brought up the rear.

He could hear the cadence. Sloppy bravado of the hungry and the metronome of the men who file reports afterward. He knew both songs.

He rolled down the window two inches. Rain touched his sleeve and cool air slapped the heat out of the cab. Beneath the storm, there was another sound. Not engines. Not wind. The quiet that comes right before something decides what it's going to be.

The shotgun lay beside him in its rack, oiled and utilitarian. He could remember every nick in its stock and where they came from. He could name most of the men who'd ridden these miles beside him—and where they ended up.

Drive a place long enough and it puts a ledger in your glove box, whether you open it or not.

The radio crackled again, urgent.

"Sheriff…Sheriff, they're almost to the county road. We got 'em pinched. Say again, we got 'em pinched at the fork."

"Ten-four," he said. Habit.

The rest wasn't.

He eased the truck through a stand of poplar and saw it again—the bouncing of white lights skittering over mud, fishtailing, correcting, climbing hope like it had a time limit. Shapes moved in the glow behind them, faster and meaner.

The chase that ends loud.

His hands settled on the wheel at ten and two. It felt like a steering wheel and a verdict both. Rain hammered hard enough to blur the world. The tires hummed their low hymn.

"Tonight it ends," he said, and this time he meant it the way a man means a thing he can't walk back.

He dropped the truck a gear. The engine rose under him. The fork waited just beyond the next curtain of trees—so did the kind of choice people tell stories about later, the kind that never survives the retelling because the details won't fit in a warm bar.

The radio spit one more shard:

"…we see the truck lights—Sheriff, that you?—"

He clicked the radio off.

The road ahead laid itself out like a sentence finally reaching its period.

He breathed once, slow.

He didn't blink.

The lights ahead burned like judgment.

He pressed the throttle.

One way or another, this ended now.

Lights slid across it—red smears, white knives, all of them wanting to live long enough to blame somebody else in the morning. Somewhere under the badge and the rain and the ribs, something quieted. Not peace. Not that. Just quiet.

"This is mine," he told the wheel.

He pushed the pedal down and felt the truck gather itself, heavy and sure. The bend opened. The fork showed.

The world picked its teams.

Blue lights flicked on.

88

We're Fucked

The cab went tight when the fresh glow hit us—not white like the ATV's, not yellow like work trucks, but cold blue and red strobes cutting through rain. They pulsed against the trunks, turning every wet pine into a flashing spine.

"Shit," Zombie breathed. Not loud. Not surprised. Just the sound a man makes when the last card flips over.

"Sheriff."

No siren.

Just the flashers—steady, merciless—coming straight down the narrow track like judgment on rails.

Chunk's teeth clinched so hard I heard the grind over the engine. His knuckles went bone-white around the wheel. "No room to pass," he said. "It's trees or him."

John let out a hopeless little noise. "Then we're fucked either way."

Chunk shook his head once. Not fear—not even anger—just decision.

"No. Then it's a game of chicken. For our lives."

The truck shuddered as he pressed deeper into it, engine screaming high and thin. The road funneled in, the trees leaning tight on both sides, the blue strobes painting the rain in violent beats.

That's when the sickness hit.

Not fear. Fear lives in the mind. This was lower—deep—a nausea that rolled up through my ribs and into my throat. The kind of sickness that tells your body it recognizes death the way it recognizes cold. My hands went numb around Thomas's shoulders. I braced myself against the door, trying to breathe, trying to believe we had more than seconds left.

The blue lights ballooned in the windshield, swelling until they were all I could see—no road, no sky, no separation between us and whatever was coming.

The sheriff wasn't slowing. Chunk wasn't either.

The world pulled tight like a bowstring.

The rain hammered the glass.

The engine wailed.

My pulse stumbled.

Thomas mumbled something slurred by pain.

Zombie's hand found the door handle, not to bail out, but just to hold onto something that wasn't shaking.

And just as the lights blew wide open—blue flooding his vision—the world tore itself loose.

"Buckle up and hold on!"

89

His Decision—Sheriff

The blue strobes washed the pines in pulses and crawled across his hands, turning the scars on his knuckles into old confessions. Cuts from fences. Splinters from doors kicked in. One bone that never set right. Marks from a job that had always taken more than it gave back.

He'd told Deke he was fed up.

That part hadn't been a lie.

But being fed up didn't mean you got to walk away. Not from what you'd taken. Not from what you'd helped bury. There were debts that didn't come with paperwork—only looks held a second too long and favors that never stopped being due.

It wasn't the hikers in the truck ahead that wore him down.

It was the years.

The years of saying just this once, until just this once became habit. The campaign money slid under tables. The quiet envelopes that never needed explanation.

The accidents that didn't quite read right when you slowed down enough to really look.

Bodies hauled out of hollows and logged as falls.

Men who "ran off" when no one wanted to keep

asking questions.

Spring thaws that always smelled wrong, like the mountain was coughing something back.

He'd learned not to look too closely at certain reports. Learned which deputies would hold the line and which ones needed distance. Learned to recognize the moment when a man decided it was easier to live crooked than to stop.

Sometimes he saw it in his own reflection in the cruiser window—those nights when he leaned forward and gagged, hands braced on glass, wondering when exactly the badge had stopped feeling like something earned and started feeling like something used.

The truth sat heavy and unmovable:

He'd carried Deke's sins so long they'd started to fit him.

And still—this was his road.

His county.

The only stretch of the world he could still point to and say mine without lying outright.

And tonight someone was running it.

Deke wanted them stopped.

Wanted it done clean. Quiet. Final.

And part of him—the part ground down by years of compromise—knew exactly how this ended. He'd do what he'd always done. Close the loop. Keep the ridge fed. Keep the mess contained.

But there was another part, too.

An older part. A younger one. The version of himself that had once believed lines mattered. The man who'd sworn an oath before the debts piled high enough to block the view.

That part stirred now, thin but stubborn.

No more.

Not like this.

Not tonight.

The strobes flared again, blue light syncing with his pulse. He tightened his grip on the wheel until the leather creaked.

He didn't have a clean choice.

Didn't have a good one.

Every road out ran through something broken—him, the ridge, or the people caught between.

But he still had a decision to make.

And it was coming fast.

He glanced at the narrow stretch ahead where the road bent and the trees closed in—a choke point where a man could drive straight through, lights on, guns out, and end it the way it always ended. Another problem solved. Another lie signed clean.

Or he could swing wide and put his cruiser where it mattered—between Deke's men and the truck running out of the ridge for safety. Take the hit if it came. Buy them distance he'd never be able to explain later. If he chose that line, he wasn't fixing anything. He was just choosing who got out alive.

The thought hit him like a fist in the chest.

His boot went down on the clutch.

His hand found the gear.

The engine rose, eager, impatient.

Blue light flashed once more across his eyes.

And the cruiser surged forward—toward the bend, or away from it.

The ridge waited for his decision.

90

We Go Through

The track narrowed into a coffin. Rain hammered the windshield, wipers smearing it into streaks.

"Nowhere to go," John muttered.

Chunk didn't blink. "Then we go through."

The sheriff's truck bore down, steady, straight, no siren. The blue glow swallowed us until it was nothing but light and panic.

Thomas groaned, Zombie cursed, and I dug my nails into the door waiting for the hit.

Chunk gave the accelerator one last punch.

The engine howled. The truck leapt.

In front of us the sheriff's cruiser burst out of the gray, blue strobes tearing the dawn into pieces. Too fast. Too close. The distance collapsed until there was nothing left but motion.

Chunk saw it and eased the wheel—just a breath, not a swerve. Enough to shift our line without breaking it.

At the same instant, the cruiser drifted a hair off center. Not a dodge. Not a commit. Just a fraction of give.

Two men reading the same bad math and refusing to own the result alone.

The space between us cracked open.

The sheriff's tires ripped free of the mud track and bit into pine duff. He cut an ugly angle—one that would've put him straight into us if either of them had held steady. The cruiser slid past us, scraping the side of the truck and bounced off the ground, and his front bumper clipped the lead pickup.

Steel screamed. Sparks burst. The pickup snapped sideways like it'd been yanked by a cable, fishtailing before slamming into the ATV. The rider disappeared under his own machine, headlights blowing out in a spray of mud and rain.

The cruiser bucked back onto the track behind us, straddled the ruts for a single breath— lights stuttering as they faded away in the distance behind us.

Chunk let out a sound that might've been a laugh or might've been disbelief.

John stared after the disappearing cruiser, jaw set. "That could've gone either way."

The gray light thickened as the bend swallowed the taillights.

Whatever happened in that blur of rain and steel, the result was the same—we were still moving.

91

Pavement

The truck rattled as if its bones were about to shake loose, but it kept going. Every jolt threatened to throw Thomas into the dark, but John and I kept him pinned steady, whispering to keep him awake, blood visibly running down his leg into the floorboard. Zombie sat pale in the passenger seat, one hand clamped to his ankle, the other gripping his rifle like it was all that tethered him to life.

Chunk muttered under his breath, the same words again and again. "Embrace the suck. Embrace the suck." A prayer, a curse, a promise.

Then the trees peeled back. The trailhead. And waiting for us—another fucking ATV parked with its headlights burning white fire into the cab. A man stood braced on it, rifle up, steady as stone.

The first rounds hit the windshield, webbing the glass, holes popping in the dash. We ducked, heads down, the cab full of fear. Thomas moaned, John dragging him lower.

Chunk's knuckles tight on the wheel. "Hold on," he growled. "I'm getting us out of these fucking woods."

He dropped his boot. The truck howled forward. Bullets spidered more glass, but the old rig didn't flinch. The ATV filled the windshield, the shooter's face flashing once in the beams.

At the last second, the man dove. His rifle barked, fire chasing us, rounds punching the tailgate as the truck plowed through the ATV, crushing plastic and steel into a scream.

We burst onto the pavement, the truck fishtailing, but alive. Behind us the wreck shrieked, headlights twisting skyward. The road stretched ahead—black, wet, empty. Both of our headlights reduced to darkness.

For the first time, the woods weren't closing in from both sides. They were behind us.

And we were still alive.

<h1 style="text-align:center">92</h1>

Stay With Me

The truck rode like shit. Bullet holes spidered the windshield, the wipers dragging across cracked glass so Chunk turned them off but they stuck half way. The front end was mangled from the ATV collision, the hood rattling like it wanted to rip free. Every bump in the road was a new groan, but the beast still carried us. One more run. It had one more fight left in it.

Chunk had both hands welded to the wheel, his expression carved into focus. His eyes never left the road.

He didn't dare blink.

Zombie leaned against the passenger glass, pale, sweat dripping off his nose, rifle braced across his lap.

John sat braced in the back, Thomas's head cradled against his thigh, whispering steady, low words every time Thomas's chest hitched.

My phone flickered back to life.

One bar.

I hit 911.

"911, what's the address of your emergency?"

"I—I don't know. We're on a county road, heading west. One of us is badly hurt. We need a hospital."

Her voice came calm, controlled "Okay. Stay with

me. "Are they breathing?"

"Yes."

"Good. Keep them as still as you can. If they stop breathing or lose consciousness, tell me immediately."

"Do you see any signs? Crossroads? Mile markers?"

"No. Just woods. We're trying to get out."

"I'm getting a weak GPS ping from your phone. It looks like you're near an old service spur.

Radio chatter bled faintly through her headset.

"I'm directing EMS toward the nearest paved intersection west of you. Stay on that road. Keep heading west. If this call drops, leave your hazards on and do not turn off. Units will move to you."

Static surged.

The line cut.

But it was enough.

John pressed harder on Thomas's chest, voice low and fierce. "Stay with me. Just a little longer."

I hit 911 again.

"911, what's the address of your emergency?"

"It's me again. We just passed a sign, Highway 113."

"Copy. Do not turn off. Keep heading west."

A pause. More distant voices.

"County General is your closest hospital. When you reach County Road 143, turn right—northbound. You'll see a blue hospital sign. Follow it."

"How far?"

"About ten minutes at safe speed. EMS is trying to intercept, but the storm is slowing them."

Thomas groaned and sagged. John caught him.

"He's fading, I'm applying pressure as hard as I can" John said.

"Keep him talking," she said. "Ask him questions. Make him answer. If he loses consciousness, tell me. And don't stop."

Static swelled again.

The storm pressed harder.

"Hello? Are you still—"

The call died.

Just the engine.

Just rain.

Just the road dragging us toward whatever came next.

Thomas moaned, eyes rolling, then slipped under again. John never took his hand away.

And then, somewhere ahead, a sound rose thin through the rain.

A siren.

Not chasing.

Coming for us.

The mirrors stayed dark.

No headlights.

Just us, the open road, five men and a truck that refused to die.

We weren't safe.

But we were out.

And help was finally moving toward us.

Hike Ninjas

Fluorescent lights buzzed like hornets. White walls, plastic chairs, coffee that tasted like rust. After days of dirt, blood and rain, the hospital was too clean. Too bright. It felt wrong to even sit here.

Thomas was somewhere behind double doors, lost to machines and hands in gloves. John had followed the gurney until the nurses shoved him back. Now he sat in the corner, elbows on his knees, staring at the tile like it might tell him the odds.

Zombie's ankle was too swollen to walk, so they'd wheeled him off for X-rays.

When they brought him back his leg was in a soft boot, hospital sock loose around his foot.

"Bones look clean," he said, settling into the wheelchair with a grimace. "They're waiting on an MRI order—see if I tore something in there."

Not broken.

Just a wreck of soft tissue that would scream at him for months.

I let out a breath I didn't know I was holding. "So it's not broken?" I said. "Jesus, Zombie. All that limping for nothing? You're a damn pussy."

Chunk barked out a laugh first.

Then Zombie cracked one.

Then me.

The first real laugh any of us had managed in days—thin, tired, crooked, but real.

It didn't last long.

But for a second, it felt like we'd made it out.

While waiting Chunk and I had scrubbed off in the bathroom sinks, the water running brown, then red, then clear. It didn't make us clean—just less haunted by the forest still stuck to our skin. The cafeteria gave us food that wasn't dehydrated meals or mud-smeared protein bars. Salt. Grease. Real calories. For the first time in days, I chewed without thinking about who was listening.

Then two deputies stepped through the automatic doors. Uniforms clean. Faces not.

Gunshot wounds brought law enforcement. Always. Hospitals didn't ask. They called.

Still, nothing about this week felt like procedure anymore.

I looked at Chunk. He gave the faintest nod, the same one he'd given on the trail when it was time to move. Zombie leaned back in the wheelchair, boot elevated, ankle wrapped, grin thin but real because he was breathing. John sat silent near the wall. Thomas was back there fighting.

We were wrecked.

But we were still here.

The taller deputy stopped a few feet away.

"We need statements," he said. "Individually."

Chunk didn't move.

"Not without lawyers."

The deputy didn't argue. Didn't sigh.

"You're being detained," he said.

Not loud.

Not angry.

Just fact.

My stomach tightened.

The second deputy opened a small notebook.

"The hospital reported a suspected gunshot wound. That alone requires a full investigation."

He glanced up.

"Your vehicle has multiple bullet impacts. Possible felony assault. Until we establish what happened, none of you are free to leave."

I started to speak.

He shook his head once. Professional.

"This isn't questioning. This is custody."

They walked us down a short hall to a small empty family consult room—bare tables, chairs around the perimeter, no windows or cameras.

"Have a seat gentlemen."

We went in.

Before it shut all the way, he said:

"The sheriff is on his way."

Then the door sealed.

And every instinct I had left told me the man coming wasn't here to save anyone.

Chunk eased down slowly.

I sat beside him.

John rolled Zombie in last, ankle elevated, gaze steady.

We were bruised, bandaged, swollen, exhausted down to the bone.

But alive.

Still here.

Still together.

Chunk. Zombie. U-Haul.

Not bound by blood.

Not by birth.

By choice.

Whatever waited on the other side of that locked door, we'd face it the only way we ever had.

Brothers.

Side by side.

HIKE NINJAS

THE MEN BEHIND THE MILES.

THE BROTHERHOOD BEHIND THE STORY.

HIKE NINJAS — CHUNK · U-HAUL · ZOMBIE